BURYING REGGIE

Alan Parkinson

Copyright © 2021 Alan Parkinson

All rights reserved.

ISBN: 1-9997402-8-3

ISBN-13: 978-1-9997402-8-3

Dedicated to those who have kept me alive, and those who wish me dead.

Chapter One

"Daddy?" Molly stood on her tiptoes and retrieved the Cheerios box from the cupboard. "Will you drive me to school today?"

"Your Daddy doesn't have time," said Andrea. "Watch out you're spilling the milk." She grabbed a cloth and mopped up the mess with one hand whilst snatching an Action Man figure from her daughter's grasp. "Can you not put this thing down for one minute?"

Jack Ferris sat at the kitchen table, wrapping both hands around his 'Super Dad' mug as he braced for impact.

"You're going away again?" said Andrea.

"It's my job."

"Get somebody else to do it, that's the whole point of you being the boss."

"We don't have any drivers free. If I get someone in from outside it costs money, money we don't have."

"But you promised Molly."

"This contract could be a game changer. I have to make sure it is done right."

"It's driving a lorry, not open-heart surgery."

"You wouldn't understand." He poured the remains of his coffee down the sink. "I'll go one better than me taking you to school," said Jack, winking at Molly, "I'm driving the bus today."

"I give up," said Andrea, grabbing a bag full of schoolbooks and storming out of the kitchen.

Jack smiled in the rear-view mirror as he eased the coach out of the junction. He enjoyed spending time with Molly, even if it was only driving her school bus.

Molly giggled, her copper curls bouncing as Jack negotiated his way over the hundreds of speed bumps. He knew they were essential to protect the youngsters, but feared they'd end up with brittle bones from the battering they were taking.

The drivers ahead of him didn't appear to share his concerns, nor did they notice the traffic control measures as a young mother in her Fiesta left the ground and sailed over one. Any other day, a barrage of abuse would have spouted from Jack's lips. But he wasn't in his lorry cab on a long-haul drive to Southern Europe; he was in a coach transporting forty primary aged schoolchildren, and despite the kids of Sunderland being well used to industrial language; he thought it wise not to introduce them to more.

Even if they were singing that bloody song again.

"Charlie had a pigeon, a pigeon, a pigeon…" they sung as he gripped the steering wheel tighter. "Charlie had a pigeon, a pigeon he had…"

After chanting it on bus trips himself as a child, he hoped the tune may have died out by now, but if there's one thing he knew about kids, it was that when they found something that annoyed adults, they'd continue to do it until the grown-ups cracked.

"He flew it all morning, he flew it all night…"

Jack looked in the mirror. His daughter joined in with the singalong, and he couldn't help but smile again. This was the

Molly he loved. A cheeky grin on her face, knowing she added to her dad's irritation, but realising he secretly enjoyed it.

"And when it came home, it was covered in…"

It contrasted with how Andrea described his daughter to him. Quiet, withdrawn, missing her dad. Long stints away from home weren't his fault. The haulage business wasn't getting any easier, and he had to make sacrifices to provide a future for his family.

"Charlie had a pigeon, a pigeon, a pigeon…"

Children swayed along to the tune as Molly held on tight to her Action Man doll.

Jack couldn't even recall where the toy came from, convinced he never bought it for her but, then again, Andrea did most of the present buying. It wasn't as if she didn't enjoy traditional dolls; she had plenty at home and loved playing with them, inventing long elaborate conversations between them, but when she walked out of the house, Arthur joined her.

"Charlie had a pigeon, a pigeon he had…"

Jack knew Andrea's theory; she'd never been shy about sharing her opinion with him. He didn't accept it; the doll wasn't a substitute, and Molly would grow out of it. At ten years of age, she may be a tad old to be carrying a toy everywhere, yet the teachers indulged her, perhaps because of her mother's influence in the staff room.

"He flew it all morning, he flew it all night…"

Jack took the bend around to the right and descended the steep bank towards the docks and Molly's school. Driving the coach was a rare treat, he should have been catching up on paperwork. He rarely found time for admin, but he'd given the usual driver the morning off, so he could grab more precious minutes with Molly. They approached the crossing where Reggie, the Lollipop Man, stepped out in front of the bus. A mate of Jack's from the Queen's Head, only doing it to annoy him.

"And when it came home, it was covered in…"

"Shite!" Jack had stamped on the brake pedal, but the coach didn't slow.

His sudden outburst halted the singing, the confused silence only interrupted by the odd scream. He tried the handbrake to no avail.

The realisation hit Reggie seconds after it struck the children; his feet cemented to the spot. A fluorescent lollipop stick powerless against ten tons of metal hurtling towards him.

Jack had to decide. And fast.

"Hold on kids," he shouted, swerving the bus hard left.

Reggie's fifty-year-old legs caught up with his brain, and he sprung to his own left. He smacked the tarmac just as he heard the crash. The screeching, scraping metal. The thud. The terrifying sound of shattering windows. And then the screams. Those God-awful screams.

He daren't look, but he had no choice.

Reggie propped himself on his pole. Scenes of devastation greeted him, with shattered glass strewn everywhere. On the road, on the pavement, in the hair of bewildered onlookers. The bus radiator grill had wedged itself into a bin wagon. The bin man sat unharmed, yet his fingers grasped the wheel as if letting go would let slip any sense of normality he had. Then there was the body sized hole in the bus windscreen.

"Jack." Reggie hobbled across the road and lifted his friend's bloodied head, hoping, praying for signs of life.

Then Jack spoke, "Molly, Molly's on the bus."

"I'll get her, don't worry," said Reggie. "Stay still and I'll get you an ambulance."

"I don't need a fucking ambulance, I need Molly. Give me a hand."

Reggie put his arms under Jack's armpits and hauled him to his feet, supporting him as they returned to the bus. Jack dragged his shaking legs back up the steps, terrified of what he might find.

As he crawled in via the emergency exit, Jack didn't anticipate the stench. The acidic tang of vomit singed his nostrils, and a couple may have soiled themselves. They were sobbing, screaming, yelling and making various other moans and groans, but if they made a noise, at least they'd survived. It was the quiet ones that worried him.

"Mr Ferris," called out a tiny voice. The trembling desperation stopping Jack in his tracks.

"I'll be back in a second."

"But Mr Ferris…"

Jack didn't look in the direction of the voice. He didn't know what he might see and to do so might force him to act. He couldn't be distracted. Only one child occupied his mind.

"Hold tight, everything will be fine."

Entering the coach from the rear meant he had to readjust his bearings, but he knew Molly should be halfway along on his right. Jack always told the children to fasten their seatbelts, but knew that half probably unfastened them as soon as he turned his back. Not Molly, she'd buckle herself in tight. But maybe Andrea was correct. What if Jack didn't know his daughter as well as he thought he did? Confronted by a vacant seat where he expected

Molly to be, he saw it. The shock of rusty hair. Rusty hair surrounded by a thick, red pool.

"Molly," Jack flung himself to the ground, dragging her from under the seat. "Molly, are you okay? Where are you bleeding?"

"Daddy…?"

He did a quick inventory, every limb still in place, and he couldn't locate any obvious source of blood.

"Where are you injured, love? Tell Daddy where you're hurt?"

"Daddy…?"

"I'm so sorry, pet. The brakes, my brakes—"

"Daddy, I've spilt my juice."

"What?" Jack knelt in the dense, sticky stream, dipped his finger in and tasted it. Blackcurrant. Not knowing whether to laugh or cry, he did both.

He stood, steadying himself on the backrest of a seat whilst hoisting Molly up with his spare arm and leading her to safety. Bewilderment, confusion and horror filled the children's faces, but above all, they looked to Jack, the authority figure, for direction.

"I'll be back. Stay calm, and we'll have you off here faster than you can sing 'Charlie had a pigeon'."

As Jack guided Molly to the security of the wall by the side of the road, Reggie was organising passers-by and implementing crowd control, utilising his lollipop stick.

Then the shouting started from the crowd. "What the fuck were you doing? There're bairns on that bus."

"I'm aware of that," said Jack. He turned to Molly, "Just stand here for two minutes, pet. I'm getting your mates to safety."

None of the crowd offered to help, but all seemed to want

a closer look, to grab a better picture on their smartphones.

"Daddy…?" Molly's bottom lip trembled as she spoke, tears imminent.

"Two minutes." He gave her a brief hug and jumped back aboard the bus.

"Right, is anybody injured?" He looked around the bus as dozens of young heads shook in the negative. Every pair of eyes focused on him.

He knew these moments were crucial, not that the children were in any immediate danger, but the shock was about to hit them, and how he acted would have a major impact on how they recovered from the trauma.

"Good news and bad news, kids. Good news is I think you might get the morning off school." Silence. "Bad news, I'm not sure I'm going to get that job as stunt driver on the next James Bond film."

It raised a couple of giggles, but not much more. They were a tough audience, understandably.

"We're sure nobody is hurt?" said Jack. "Check around you, check your friends. Let me know if anybody is injured."

Silence, then a single voice from near the front. "I think Jamie's broken his bum," he said, "it's sprung a leak."

Sniggers broke out around the bus. They were alright. It didn't take long for kids to rebound from serious trauma, at least in the short term. He wasn't so confident about himself.

"Okay, one row at a time, starting at the back, I want you to unfasten your seatbelts and leave by the emergency exit. Once you're off the bus, line up against the wall next to Molly."

As the last boy exited, the blue flashing lights arrived. It was inevitable, and now that the youngsters were out of immediate danger, Jack's thoughts shifted to the paperwork and loss of money with his coach off the road.

He addressed the policeman who was exiting the car. "Jack Ferris, I'm the driver. No idea what happened, the brakes, they—"

"No problem, Mr Ferris," said the officer, "we don't need a statement yet. Is everyone okay? Is anybody hurt?"

"Only bumps and scrapes as far as I can see. Little buggers listened when told to wear their seatbelts." He pointed to the kids, reliving the tale to each other, gesticulating and exaggerating with every word.

"And the other driver?"

"I never thought, I haven't—"

"No worries, he's contending with other issues." The constable jogged over to where the bin crew were dealing with a baying mob.

"What about me bins?" said a dressing gown clad woman. "First you change to fortnightly collections and now you're using this as an excuse not to empty them."

"Excuse?" The driver looked shell-shocked.

"Bloody disgrace, if you ask me. Typical council worker trying to get out of doing his job."

The police ushered the crowd away, leaving the bin man even more convinced that he should have stayed in bed that morning.

"Are you the bus driver?" A slim lady with her hair scraped in a ponytail approached Jack and flashed a warrant card at him. "Detective Sergeant Sidra Ramsay, I was passing."

"Yes, it was the brakes…"

She'd moved on to berate the young policeman managing the crowd. "Why isn't this scene cordoned off? Have you breathalysed this man yet?"

"I've just got here."

"Priorities, constable, priorities," she said, pointing at Jack. "Detain him and make sure he doesn't tamper with any evidence."

Molly was beside Jack, tugging at his sleeve. "Daddy…?"

"I'll be with you in a second, pet."

He was watching the drama unfold before him and realised his day had become considerably worse with the detective's arrival. Molly tugged his coat with greater force than before, and he bent to hear her. She whispered in his ear. He looked at her, then the bus, and sprinted across the road.

"Stop that man," shouted DS Ramsay as the youthful constable made a grab for him.

Jack swerved him and leapt aboard, covering the aisle in a few steps and diving between the seats. "Got you," he said in unison with the PC, who grasped the back of his jacket and hauled him to his feet.

As the policeman led him from away, Jack winked at Molly and handed her the Action Man.

Chapter Two

"They'll not recognise you," said Reggie.

"It hasn't been that long," said Jack, cradling a pigeon in his bony hands and stroking its head with his fingertip.

"Hasn't it? You cover so many miles on the roads in Europe, I'm surprised you aren't talking to them in French."

"You sound like Andrea."

"Is that a negative, sounding like your wife?"

"I see her point and that," said Jack, "I just wish she'd see mine and understand that I'm trying to grow the business. There will be sacrifices."

"Sacrifices? Is that what I was when you tried to mow me down?"

"Don't start that shite again." He caught the smirk on Reggie's face and checked himself. "Makes no odds now. My wings have been well and truly clipped."

"That copper woman?" said Reggie. "She's got a hard on for you."

"That's one way of putting it. Has me down as some sort

of maniac. Thinks I'd endanger a coach full of kids to flatten my best mate on a school crossing, then change my mind on the vinegar strokes to make a political statement regarding bin collections."

"She hasn't rubbed it off her whiteboard." Reggie lit the Calor Gas stove and rested the kettle on it.

"With the bus off the road, paperwork up to my knackers and the investigations into the crash, there's no way I'm going on another European road trip."

"And Andrea killing you might hamper your driving skills?"

"Aye, there is that." He placed the pigeon back in the cree.

Reggie handed Jack a cuppa. "At least you get to spend time with your birds."

"Cheers for looking after them." Jack surveyed the pigeon lofts, located up the river bank from his haulage depot, overlooking the docks.

"It's no bother, you have a canny view from up here."

They both sat in silence for a few minutes, taking in the vista. The peace only broken by the odd flutter of wings and a gentle cooing. In the distance, lorries beeped as they reversed and dockers went about their daily business, oblivious to the two pigeon fanciers basking in the tranquillity.

Jack noticed a couple of lofts had a fresh coat of paint. Red and white to match most of the others, but they were a mishmash of colours. The redecorating schedule dictated by half a tin of emulsion becoming available from a completed DIY project or workplace makeover. "You've done a cracking job, Reggie. You didn't have to, I only needed you to feed the birds."

"Might as well make myself useful whilst I'm up here." He drained his cup and sprinkled the remaining dregs on the grass.

"Come on, time you got those delicate office worker's hands dirty." He stood and stretched, then passed Jack a small shovel.

"One of my favourite jobs," said Jack. "What've you been feeding them? They don't half produce a shitload of crap."

"The seagulls contribute and leave a donation when they can."

"I hate those bastards. I swear they will overrun the country in the next few years. Newspapers and politicians bleating on about immigrants, they want to bother about the bloody gulls."

"I'm having a nightmare with them at home," said Reggie, picking up the stepladders, "Been on the roof fighting the buggers with a broomstick."

"On the roof?"

"Aye, the neighbours don't think I'm wired up right."

"You're not wired up right. What the hell are you doing up there amongst the tiles? That's their territory, not yours."

"Until they pay council tax, it's my territory, and I want them nowhere near it." Reggie handed the stepladders to Jack.

He paused, reluctant to take them. "Can you not—"

"What? I've been caring for these birds for weeks, even giving the place a lick of paint, and you won't clean a few pigeon droppings?"

"It's not that, you know I don't like—"

"Get yourself up there." Reggie plonked the ladders beside the loft.

Jack tested the stability of the steps, then checked again and looked for a way of carrying his shovel whilst still being able to hold the ladders with both hands. He threw it onto the roof and confirmed the stability again. Jack planted his right foot on the lowest rung, not convinced. Would he offend Reggie if he asked to carry out a Health and Safety assessment? He lifted his left foot, and the steps shook. He put his left foot on the first step as well and forced his weight forward to steady the ladder. Reggie looked on with ill-disguised mirth. Jack attempted to move his right foot again. It felt as if he was wearing diving boots welded to the bottom rung. He was convinced the top of the ladder moved.

"What's the matter with you?" said Reggie. "It's barely six-foot off the deck."

"It's not the six-foot, it's the rest." Then he did what his brain, body and every bit of his being knew he shouldn't. He looked down.

The familiar symptoms returned, the crushing pain behind his eyes blinding him. Blind was preferable. If he was unsighted, he wouldn't catch sight of dozens of little people working away on the docks hundreds of feet below him. His brain rattled around his skull like an out-of-control satellite. Legs, previously lead weights, turned to feathers that could drift away on the breeze. He was nauseous.

"Here, you daft shite," said Reggie as he took his elbow and led him to safe ground. "I'll do it."

Jack wobbled back to his chair, relieved his terrifying ordeal had ended.

Reggie descended from the roof with a shovel in one hand and a bucket full of pigeon droppings in the other. Despite being bulkier than Jack and a good ten years older, he skipped down the ladders as if they weren't there. Jack couldn't watch without feeling sick again.

"If I had any doubt before," said Reggie, "that you were attempting to bump me off, there's none now. First you try to plough into me with a bus full of kids and now you've sent me six-foot off the deck without a safety harness."

"Don't take the piss, you know I hate heights." At a little over five-foot six tall, everything had seemed huge to Jack, yet he hadn't a clue where his dread of heights had come from. He remembered jumping off walls and fearless climbing of trees as a kid. Maybe it was since Molly came along that he'd seen danger in every situation.

"Is pigeon fancying not an odd choice of hobby, then? It must have crossed your mind you would need to be up a height at some point?" said Reggie.

"I was hoping they'd take care of most of the flying, not me," said Jack, who had regained his sea legs. "I took the lofts over from my dad, wasn't a conscious decision."

"You don't always need to follow your father."

"You're sounding like Andrea again. I don't run the haulage company because it was the family business. I enjoy it and if she lets me put the hours in, it could provide a canny future for us and Molly."

"Wasn't having a go, mate, just an observation."

"Aye, well. She's been twisting my ear non-stop about it. Especially after the accident."

The kettle boiled again; the whistling rousing the odd dozing pigeon from their slumber. Reggie handed over another cuppa and squeezed into the tattered leather armchair he'd dragged from the shed. "If you're ever successful in your quest to kill me—"

"Don't start that shit again."

"No, there's a serious point here. I'm in my fifties, twenty clem with soaring blood pressure. There's a decent chance I'll pop off before you."

"This is a lovely discussion. You'll upset the pigeons."

"If the worst happens, I need you to do me a favour."

"A favour?"

"Aye, nothing big, but something that's bugged me for a while."

"No problem, what is it?" said Jack.

"I own a collection." Reggie leaned in towards Jack and lowered his voice despite only the birds being within earshot.

"A collection?"

"Lad's material, you know?"

"Lad's material?" said Jack.

"Do I have to get my crayons out and draw a picture for you?"

"I'm not following."

"I'm a single lad who lives on his own. I have interests. Interests you wouldn't want your sister or aunty stumbling across whilst mourning your untimely death."

"Oh, I see. You own a collection."

"You understand now?"

"People still have collections? Do you not have access to the internet?"

"This is special interest, something I've built up over decades," said Reggie.

"Nowt dodgy, is it?" said Jack. "You're not into scarecrow porn or something?"

"Scarecrow porn?"

"First thing that came into my head, you know what I mean. Nothing suspect, you're a lollipop man, for Christ's sake."

"Of course there's nothing suspect, I just don't want my family finding it."

"You've never mentioned family."

"Aye, we don't speak." Reggie moved the discussion on and handed a keyring to Jack. "Here, take this."

"What's this?"

"Keys to my house. If I die, get rid of my stash before the family gets there."

"Get rid of it?"

"The lot. It's all in a wardrobe in the spare room. DVDs, magazines, laptop and anything else you might find."

"Anything else I might find?"

"The lot. Promise me you'll shift everything."

"This has all turned serious. You'll be around for years yet."

"The close shave the other day got me thinking, do you swear?"

"Aye, man."

"There're bits and pieces that might interest you."

"Bits and pieces that might interest me? I'm not raking through your old jazz mags. The lot's going straight down the tip."

"Not the tip. Anywhere but there."

"Not the tip? That's the best facility to dispose of your grumble mags."

"Never go near the tip. Not with my stuff, not with your stuff, not with anybody's. Trust me on this."

"Now you're being weird."

"Believe me, Jack, you don't want to be anywhere near that place."

"If you say so. This sister of yours, what's she called?"

"Mary Poppins."

"Your sister's called Mary Poppins?"

"No, the interesting items I mentioned, keep your blinkers open for Mary Poppins."

"You're beginning to disturb me. Someone's made a mucky movie based on Mary Poppins?"

"I can't explain. Just search for Mary Poppins and Dick Van Dyke."

"That sounds disgusting."

Reggie stood, the conversation over. "You'll thank me when I'm gone."

Lottie Caldwell sipped on her first gin and tonic of the day as she surveyed the garden. The brunch G&T, as she and her friends in the Women's Institute liked to call it. The edging of the lawn was crooked again, and it was time for yet another stern talking to for the gardener. His standards were slipping as he aged, but Noel wouldn't hear of Lottie replacing him with the Polish gardener all of her friends raved about. His constituents wouldn't approve. She fingered the tassels on the curtains, wondering if they were something else that needed replacing, when the phone rang. She kept the glass in her hand as she picked up the phone.

"Hello?"

"Mummy?"

"Andrea? Why are you ringing me now? What if your father had picked up?"

"Is he there?" said Andrea.

"No, he rarely is, but that's not the point. We need to stick to the agreed times."

"There's been an accident, and I thought it better you heard it from me than on the grapevine from the gossips in W.I."

"Accident? Are you and Molly okay?"

"We're fine. So is Jack. Thanks for asking. He was driving Molly's school bus when it crashed into a bin lorry."

"Oh, Andrea. We tried to warn you."

"Warn me about what?"

"That he was nothing but trouble and it could only end one

way."

"He was doing his job and there was an accident."

"Yes, but it wouldn't have happened if you'd married someone who worked in the city. He'd have nothing more than a paper cut and my granddaughter wouldn't be anywhere near it."

"You're pretending to care about your granddaughter now?"

"That's cruel, Andrea. Of course I care."

"Not a card or a phone call on her birthdays or Christmas. You've never been to visit. She only knows who Daddy is because he's always on the news."

"You know how difficult it is with your father. He's stubborn."

"And you have to do everything he says?"

"It's the secret to a happy marriage."

"I haven't got time for this. I'll email you some more photos of Molly. She's growing up fast. And there's still an open invitation for you to visit."

"You know I'd love to see Molly, but it's not that easy."

"Goodbye, Mummy." The phone line went dead.

Lottie replaced the handset, rattled the ice cubes in her glass and decided it was time for a top up.

Chapter Three

"It's like herding cats," said Andrea Ferris as she attempted to shepherd several schoolchildren onto the stage in the main hall.

Whilst the children got over the minor bumps from the bus crash, none had recovered from the excitement, and it was still the number one topic of conversation. It was tempting to make a play about the accident, because at least then they would show an interest.

"Mr Ferris," shouted a child to Jack, who was loitering at the double doors.

He wasn't sure whether they viewed him as the hero or the villain from the smash, but his arrival guaranteed the excitement levels and volume ratcheted up another notch.

Leader of the commotion was Molly, who rushed over and grasped onto his leg, attempting to squeeze the life out of it. "Hi, Daddy."

"Hi, love. You okay?"

"Jack, what are you doing here?" Andrea wasn't happy to see her husband, she rarely was these days.

Her family never approved of Jack. They'd met in Majorca. Jack on a lads' holiday, Andrea on a break in Palma in the gap between leaving boarding school and going to uni. Their paths crossed when Andrea and her pals found themselves fathoms out of their depth in Magaluf. They'd ventured into the party resort for the night to experience what the fuss was about. Life in a private school and the leafy villages of North Yorkshire hadn't prepared her for the unwanted attention of pissed up Brits. When Jack stepped in to protect her, she rewarded him with an unexpected kiss.

They hit it off and kept in touch, even when Andrea moved to London for university. At the turn of the century, a destined to fail long distance romance became permanent when she relocated to Sunderland to marry Jack. The wedding ostracised her family and friends, who insisted it would never work. That was a long time ago.

"I just wanted a chat," said Jack.

"You want to talk? Maybe you should have bought a parrot instead of those pigeons." She swept her arm around the hall to show the hoard of children causing chaos. "Can you not tell I'm busy?"

"We never get the chance. You're busy with school stuff, or I'm away with work, or I've got meetings with the pigeon club. We're never home together."

"There's an easy way to solve that."

"We're not selling the business."

"We're not, are we not? Since when did I get a say? I thought it was you deciding everything."

"Don't be like that. I'm building a future for the three of us." He nodded over in Molly's direction. After acknowledging his arrival, she'd wandered off and was talking to Arthur.

"What's the point of building a future for Molly if you never see her? She needs her father to be here."

"I'm here now. To watch her rehearse for the play."

"She's not in the show."

"What do you mean, she's not in it? Last night she said you'd given her a leading role."

"I've reconsidered."

"Reconsidered? She's excited. How can you change your mind?"

"Parents have been complaining, suggesting I'm showing favouritism because she's my girl."

"That's ridiculous," said Jack.

"Is it? Look at her, she's withdrawn, sat on her own talking to that bloody Action Man. Not the outgoing drama queen we need in the lead role."

"That's nonsense, she'd be brilliant."

"I've heard teachers sniping about it behind my back."

"Bollocks to the other teachers." Whilst the noise levels from the kids were seismic, nothing beats a swear word from an adult to focus them, and the room became silent.

"I don't have time for this discussion, Jack."

The children returned to creating havoc. A piece of curtain had appeared from nowhere and three kids were being dragged across the stage on it. Until one fell off the platform, proving what great acoustics a parquet floor can offer when a child cracks his head off it.

"Will you please stop messing around and do as you're told?" Andrea ran to the fallen boy, discovering little more than a bumped forehead and a wish to try it again.

She moved on to the next crisis, rescuing Jamie from a stage prop that had become his crucifixion, using the sleeves of his parka to keep him upright.

Jack watched on in awe at her firefighting skills, and Molly had come back to give him another hug. "Are you stopping for the play?"

"That's your mam's decision, her hands are full at the moment. Are you children always this naughty?"

"I'm not naughty." She laughed at the suggestion and dashed off to join the others on the stage.

Andrea had returned. "Not now, Jack."

"You can't let the staff room dictate how you raise your own child."

"This role might not matter to you, but it matters to me. I don't just need to do a good job, I need to be seen to be doing a good job. That's difficult when you teach your own daughter, and your husband is trying to wipe the entire class out in one of his defective buses."

"Whoah, that's not fair."

"It's not, is it? But I fend it off every bloody day. Everyone having their snide little remarks, parents, teachers, governors." She pointed to Reggie, who was heading to the office where he kept his lollipop. "The only person not complaining is him, and he's the one who came closest to dying."

The hall was normally empty when he arrived, and he had tried to sneak in unnoticed when he realised it was busy. But it was hard to be discreet when dressed head to toe in hi-viz.

"Reggie!" The kids were hyper again.

"Jack, I can't handle this now. When you're away on your little jaunts, I run the house, look after Molly and hold down a full-time job and the crap that throws my way." Andrea picked up a discarded cardigan. "Your fault picking with how I juggle those priorities is as welcome as your bus tyres on Reggie's toes."

"But you'll think again about the show?"

"My decision is final, Molly will not be in any play."

Neither of them had realised that Molly had returned and was staring at them. They couldn't tell if there were tears in her eyes, but she spun on her heels and looked at her Action Man. "Mummy says we're not in the play, Arthur."

Maurice Groom leaned back on the desk and let out a hearty laugh at the school receptionist's joke. She prepared his coffee just as he liked it and retrieved the tin of special biscuits from the filing cabinet, reserved for VIP guests only. The rest of the office staff had stopped working and swivelled in their chairs to chat to him. They enjoyed his visits.

A self-made millionaire whose smart suit and immaculate silver hair betrayed the fact he'd earned his fortune from refuse collection. Already successful when the council privatised their operations, Maurice had both the experience and influence to win the contract and double the size of his business. A fleet of new trucks came in, and his rubbish tip on the outskirts of town became both the home of his private enterprise and the official city site. Once his financial future was secured, he rebranded himself as an altruistic benefactor, giving to charities, funding many local schemes and being the face of a multitude of worthy projects. The school sign even carried his company logo after a generous donation.

He was here to see the headmaster, but insisted on arriving early to catch up with the reception staff. The office was where the salacious gossip was and as head of the board of governors, getting a handle on what was happening in the classroom and staffroom gave him an edge over anybody who may wish to unseat him from his position of power. The big talking point of the day was still the bus crash, and as Reggie squeezed past, he couldn't help but reference it.

"Jack could have flattened our friend here." He ruffled Reggie's hair. "But he took out my bin wagon instead, one of the new ones. But as long as nobody was hurt."

Reggie shrugged him off and left without speaking.

"He's still in shock, poor thing," said the receptionist as she offered the biscuit tin to Maurice once more.

Mr Shakespeare, the headmaster, wandered into the office and the staff made themselves look busy again.

"Shaky, how's tricks?" said Maurice as he hoisted his six-foot-five frame from the desk, wrapping his arm around the headmaster's shoulders. "Couple things to run past you." He led Mr Shakespeare out of reception and into his office, where he slammed the door behind him.

"What is it, Maurice? We've a governors' meeting next week. Could it not have waited until then?"

"I thought it needed the personal touch." Maurice had placed himself in the headmaster's plush leather chair, leaving Shakespeare to sit on the small couch as if he was a visitor in his own office. He picked up a copy of Othello. "I wanted to ensure we're reading the same play regarding the upcoming proposals."

"The decision making is the responsibility of the governors. As chair of the board, I'm sure you have the influence and votes you need."

"Always nice for the optics if you support us. We want no tears in the playground."

"Nobody has informed me of the plans. I'm oblivious to what proposal you want me to back."

"All in good time, Shaky, all in good time. I need reassurance you're planning on backing the people who employ you."

"There's not just the governors. I need to please the council and the local education authority, and depending on what we're talking about, the unions and parents on top. I'm answerable to many people."

"As we all are, even me. The people I'm accountable to want me to remind you of your obligations, that's all this is, a courtesy visit." He stood, repositioning a picture frame and pile of papers on the desk before he left.

"Let me know as soon as you have those details," said Shakespeare. He offered his hand.

Maurice ignored it and ruffled the headmaster's hair. Hair that lacked adequate glue and led to frantic readjusting.

Maurice shut the office door, not giving the headmaster the opportunity to follow him, and as he was about to pop in to say goodbye to the receptionists, he spotted Jack and Andrea in the hall.

"Jack, Andrea, lovely to see you," he shook Jack's hand.

"You know Maurice, don't you?" said Jack.

"I think we've met," said Andrea. She never remembered meeting him in person, but his face was everywhere, so it seemed like she had.

"Returning to the scene of the crime?" said Maurice.

"The crime?"

"You vandalising my shiny new bin wagons."

"Sorry, yeah, still not sure what happened there, and I had to decide in the blink of an eye. It's a shame one of your trucks got hit, but it was that or take a life."

"Don't worry about it, Jack, I'm sure it was an accident and we're all insured, so no harm done. Hazards of the trade, I guess."

"Jack doesn't care about the hazards of the business, only the money," said Andrea.

Jack shot her a glance, not wanting to air their grievances in public.

"Should listen to Andrea, Jack. Far more important commodities in life than money. What price can you put on family?"

"Daddy…" Molly had wandered back over to join her parents.

"And this must be the lovely Molly," Maurice said whilst rubbing the top of her head.

Molly looked at the man towering above her, then to her Action Man figure, putting it to her ear as if it was speaking. She looked the doll in the face, "No, Arthur, I don't like him either."

Chapter Four

DS Sidra Ramsay arrived unannounced. This wasn't her case. Road Traffic Accidents weren't her domain, but she'd asked for updates after Jack's less than helpful behaviour after the accident. The instant dislike she'd taken to him was reciprocal. His flippant disregard to her authority, in front of impressionable children, irked her. She didn't care why; it's not as if she hadn't encountered it every day. Not least from her fellow officers.

    A rugby playing, female Muslim, albeit non-practising, and fast tracked into her role. Married with no interest in the lad lifestyle and bed hopping workmates, she'd done little to fit in and make friends. And this made her colleagues suspicious. Nothing like a clean cop to get the tongues wagging. Rumours were rife around the station, who they believed she worked for, the secret behind her real motives, but they didn't concern her. She had a job to do.

    With this in mind, it was tricky extracting a favour from the Traffic Police when Sidra wanted first dibs on Jack when the results of the investigation came back. But old-fashioned bribery with cakes, a mutual passion for rugby and a pulling of rank got her what she required. A multiple car pile-up on the A19 occupying their time this morning gave her a small window of opportunity. A frustrating minor calf injury cutting short her 10k run first thing had put her in the perfect mood to tackle Jack Ferris.

Whilst locking her BMW, she scanned the yard. One wagon in the garage with two mechanics hitting something with a hammer. They'd noted her arrival but pretended not to. She doubted they would give most women arriving on site the same courtesy. But her business suit, athletic build and scraped back hair with minimal make-up screamed copper to them, and they knew when to keep quiet.

Sidra estimated the lot would hold six good sized wagons at its busiest, maybe one or two buses, but most would be out earning an income for Jack. A couple of forklifts lay idle alongside a diesel pump and a pile of empty pallets. Nothing amiss she could see, but that didn't mean she couldn't make life difficult with Health & Safety if Mr Ferris refused to change his manner.

Her flat-heeled shoes clanged as she jogged up the flights of metal stairs to the Portakabin, home of Jack's office. A slight tweak in her calf reminded her to slow down, and she muttered under her breath. She didn't plan on knocking, but the door swinging open as she reached the top of the staircase surprised her.

"DS Ramsay, isn't it?" said Jack, holding out his hand and wearing a welcoming smile.

"It is," said Sidra, wary of his change in character.

"I saw you drive into the yard, so I've put the kettle on."

"Nice view you have here." Sidra stood at the window beside Jack's desk. Not only a full vista of the business and the entrance, but of the docks, the harbour and the North Sea beyond that.

"Perks of the job, I guess. I'd prefer to be out on the road, but if I'm desk bound, there're worse places. Brown or black?"

"What?"

"Your tea?" The kettle clicked off and Jack picked out the closest he had to clean mugs.

"Coffee, black." She didn't intend to have a drink, but Jack's pleasant manner had knocked her off balance.

Jack had a slight panic as nobody at Ferris Haulage drank coffee, it was tea all the way, but he discovered an ancient jar of Nescafé at the back of the cupboard. Way past its use-by date, he had to separate the granules with a couple good whacks of the teaspoon, but he didn't want to let the DS down. "Take a seat, please." Jack pointed to a well-worn swivel chair next to his desk.

Sidra found she unsettled suspects by wandering around a room whilst they sat and sitting to deliver a punchline added a touch of drama to the proceedings. She wasn't getting that freedom here, and anyhow, her leg was hurting. She tried not to grimace as Jack handed her a cup of weak instant coffee before sitting opposite her.

"Sorry if I was offhand the other day," said Jack, "all overwhelming with Molly being on the bus, and me almost hitting Reggie."

"What is your relationship with Reggie Higgins?"

"He's a mate, known him a few years now. Gets down the Queens Head and helps with my pigeons."

"Pigeons?"

"Yeah, I race them. At least I do when I get the chance. I'm away a lot. That's when Reggie steps in for me. He's the ideal guardian for the potential champs I've got up the lofts."

Sidra had to take a moment to check if Jack was having her on, or whether she was starring in a gritty black and white drama set in the sixties. "People still race pigeons?"

"Yeah, not as big as it was, but it still has a significant following in the traditional mining communities. If they ever have to wring the neck of one that has gone lame, they change its name to Maggie, makes things a lot easier."

She was sure he was joking now, although for the briefest moment she wondered whether he'd noticed her limp and suggested she was lame. A veiled threat, perhaps? Overthinking again.

"You would have no reason to harm Reggie?"

"He's a great bloke. That's why the accident shook me up so much, I could have killed the chap."

"The accident?"

Jack paused for a second. "Yes, the accident, the bus crash. That's why you're here, aren't you?"

"I'm here about the coach crash, Mr Ferris, but that was no accident, no accident at all."

Jack asked Sidra to repeat her explanation, as it was failing to register.

"It's simple, Mr Ferris. A detached brake pipe caused your accident. A brake pipe that didn't detach itself."

"That's, that's not possible."

"I'm afraid it is possible," said Sidra, "and I need to establish why."

"You're not the only one."

"There are several theories I'm running through at the moment." Sidra had no concrete suspicions yet, other than her hunch that something wasn't right. She intended casting things out there to see what reaction she got. "Theory number one is that someone has it in for you."

Jack scored rock bottom on the popularity stakes with Andrea at the minute, but she was more likely to hide the remote than cut his brake pipes. He struggled to think of anybody else who he'd annoyed. "I'm not having that."

"Theory two, somebody wanted to harm the kids, but I dread to even consider that as an option."

"Me, too."

"Theory three," the interesting one, "is that you knew precisely when the brakes would fail and take out Reggie Higgins. The fact you changed your mind at the sight of his hi-viz doesn't alter the theory."

"No, no, no. I'm not taking this shite." Jack was out of his chair. "I was in an accident that nearly killed me, my daughter and my best mate, and you come swanning in here hoying accusations."

Sidra got her reaction. Not that it proved anything. Yet.

"Just theories at this stage, Mr Ferris. We must cover every possibility, or I'd not be doing my job."

"Yeah, well, while you're sat here drinking my finest coffee and spouting your rubbish, I'm not doing my job. So unless you have anything sensible to say, I need you to leave."

"There's no reason to upset yourself, Jack."

"Only my friends call me Jack, and there's every reason to be upset. Goodbye, DS Ramsay."

Sidra left without offering to shake hands, but stopped at the top of the stairs. "One other theory, Mr Ferris," she said whilst looking towards the garage. "How long have you known your mechanics?"

"Long enough, DS Ramsay, long enough." He closed the door behind her.

Jack watched as Sidra crossed the yard and spoke to the

lads. The temptation to chase her was strong, but the conversation was brief and one sided. There were several reasons not to speak to her. Top of that list was the single fact nagging away at him; she could be right.

Derek Pearson hadn't been with the company long and had proven himself to be both unpopular and incompetent, a toxic pairing. Jack had given him multiple warnings because of his shoddy workmanship, but they'd fallen on deaf ears. The hapless mechanic had come with glowing references and a personal recommendation from a lad in the pigeon club, which made it even more unusual.

"What did she want? Nosy cow." said Derek as he wiped the sweat from his fat bald head with a dirty rag.

"She was asking for recommendations on where to get her brakes done. Hardly the Spanish Inquisition," said Ted.

"I don't talk to coppers." Derek stepped out of the garage into the spring sunshine, the bright light changing the tone of his Reactolite glasses, hiding his eyes that followed Sidra as she left.

"An innocent enough question, Spacey." said Ted, invoking his colleague's unwanted nickname. A nickname Ted discovered from lads down the Ship Inn who'd given it to the five-foot one and sixteen-stone Derek after an unfortunate incident with a spray tan. Added to his sticky out ears, his resemblance to a space hopper became legendary and the name stuck.

Derek hated it.

"She wasn't wearing a poppy," said Derek.

"Why would she be wearing a poppy? It's the middle of bloody March."

"They never wear one, her sort."

"What do you mean by her sort?"

"You know what I mean."

"Another word of that racist crap in here and I'll bounce this wrench off your head."

"How can I be racist? Muslim isn't a—"

"Don't say it, do not fucking say it." Ted went back to working on the lorry, wondering why Jack paired him with this idiot.

Jack watched Sidra leave and considered what she'd told him. Accident or not, a detached brake hose was a major worry, signifying either criminal tampering or incompetence, neither of which reflected well on the people he employed. Recent events suggested the latter, but they could also point towards the former. Jack needed to find out for himself before DS Sidra Ramsay came sniffing around again.

He'd call Ted in first, so it didn't look like he was making any assumptions. Ted had worked at the firm for twenty years, going way back to when Jack's dad owned the company. Jack trusted him with his life, the endangering of which they were about to discuss. On top of everything else, Jack couldn't be arsed dealing with this right now.

His phone rang. It was Andrea. "This is all I need."

He answered.

"Jack?"

"Sorry, Andrea, I'm right in the middle of something. Can I call you back?"

"This is important."

"It's always important with you. I'm dealing with serious stuff of my own right now."

"I've had a thought about a job for you."

"Didn't you notice I have a job?"

"I could have a word with Mummy, see if she'll speak to my father."

"Never mention that despicable Tory bigot in my presence again." With that, he hung up, throwing his phone on the desk.

Chapter Five

Reggie placed his cuppa and two custard creams on the side table, eased himself into the armchair, and raised his slippered feet. He'd eaten lunch and settled down to watch the news, part of his daily routine. Reggie liked to keep abreast of world events. In between lollipop shifts, he had a lot occupying him, but this was his time when he sat back and relaxed.

Apart from today.

Reggie had just reclined in the chair when the racket from the roof began, enough to require him to turn the volume up. "Bloody seagulls," he said as he slammed the remote on the table, causing his cuppa to jump and spill over the sides. "Oh, for fuck's sake."

He went to the kitchen to grab a cloth, cursing the gulls with every step. He hated the buggers. After wiping up the mess he'd created, he returned the tea towel to the sink, but the commotion was louder than usual. Reggie swore the birds had worn hob-nailed boots to annoy him. He also suspected they had taken ownership of a loudhailer, judging by the pitch and loudness of their screeching.

It was once believed that you could tell there was a storm at sea when the gulls ventured inland. Now you monitored student-loan day and the buy one get one free offers at the local takeaway by the amount of seabirds congregating in urban areas. The pests evolved from hunting for mackerel to scavenging for margarita pizzas. They were a constant nuisance and found Reggie's rooftop a popular playground, much to his annoyance.

He put up with the noise and inconvenience, but he didn't want them anywhere near his roof, and not solely for the destruction of his tiles. Reggie had to do something. He grabbed the broom on his way outside to identify the source of the racket. A flock of seagulls swooped and dive bombed each other. The excitement so frantic they evacuated their bowels, missing Reggie's head by inches, and providing a Jackson Pollock masterpiece in his backyard. Half a dozen birds vied for space on the chimney stack, the heftiest, most aggressive ones asserting their authority over this prime bit of high rise real estate.

"Shift your arse from there," shouted Reggie as he snatched the ladders.

For someone so big, he was nimble getting up them and wasted no time taking a swipe at the birds. He struck lucky with his first swing, catching a large male right on the beak, sending it hurtling backwards, feathers fluttering to the deck. Far from scaring the others, it made them more determined, gave them a challenge. And a target.

He swung the broom above his head in a circular motion until he became dizzy and had to grab onto the steps to regain his balance. With his next swing, he connected well, sending a gull hurtling into the roof, cracking a slate. Reggie considered it collateral damage. He deterred some younger birds who swirled above him, dropping the odd load but not getting close enough to receive a brush in the beak. The larger, more senior members of the clan looked on from the chimney with indifference.

Even at the top rung of the ladders, they remained out of his reach, so he had to inch closer. With his one free hand, he grasped the roofer's ladders secured against the ridge and lay flat against the slates. He dragged himself up and carried the broom by his side whilst making his ascent. The raucous seabirds continued to swoop and bomb but kept their distance, as bothering him would leave no room for manoeuvre and see them crashing into the building. Reggie gripped the ridge tile with his left hand and hoisted his weight up, swinging his leg over, so he sat astride the roof, facing the chimney.

This was when he was at his most vulnerable, and he spotted a gull making a renewed assault from his right. He caught it square with the brush head and sent it sailing into next door's yard. He made a mental note to collect it and apologise later, and entertained brief thoughts about reigniting his amateur cricketing career. The flying birds had got the message, keeping their distance, but the ones on the chimney pot sat in defiance, taunting him. But he wouldn't allow it. They couldn't be there. Not now.

Reggie edged along the roof, maintaining eye contact with the biggest and baddest of the lot. He reckoned if he took out the chief aggressor, the rest would flee. Calculations done. Guessing he was near enough, he steadied himself. Raising the broom but hiding it away from view until the last moment, Reggie launched one huge swipe. Whilst he had success in eliminating the leader, the handle slipping from his grip and lodging itself in the windscreen of next door's Volvo was less of a victory.

The blaring alarm not only scared off the remaining seagulls, but brought out the neighbours who weren't at work. As the gulls fled the scene, why he'd scaled his house to hurl a broom through his neighbour's car window would take some explaining. Reggie would worry about that later. Now he needed to check on the flue. He clutched the top of the chimney and hauled himself up, inspecting the pot.

Relief at his masonry surviving intact turned to regret at his choice of footwear. The crowd that gathered to investigate where the noise was coming from witnessed twenty-stone of slipper-wearing, soon to be ex Lollipop Man, hurtling to his death.

A neighbour who previously smirked at the broom through the windscreen of next-door's Volvo shed tears at the Reggie shaped dent in his Volkswagen Golf. Reggie now lay nose down on the tarmac after bouncing off the car. A single tartan slipper remained on his right foot, the left delivering a posthumous slap in the face to the yappy Yorkshire Terrier he'd wanted to slipper for months. The dog scampered off and took refuge under the dressing gown tails of his chain smoking owner. In shock at what she'd witnessed, she considered phoning an ambulance. After a glance at Reggie, she lit another cigarette.

Then the screaming started.

Screeching seagulls, blaring car alarms, yappy Yorkies and hysterical housewives. This was far from a quiet street. The sirens of the police cars soon joined the cacophony, at least one neighbour having the sense to alert the authorities. The noise died down as the colours intensified, blue flashing lights and a plethora of hi-viz jackets. Red and white tape to keep the crowds back and the hundred smartphone screens videoing the chaos to post on social media.

This was the scene that greeted Jack as he arrived. He'd received another call from Andrea as he questioned Derek about the faulty brake pipes. He'd been reluctant to answer at first, but the moment he heard her voice, he knew something was wrong. It had taken minutes for the story to travel to the school via social media and concerned mothers desperate to be first to break the news. Andrea phoned Jack as soon as she heard.

Jack reached the throng at the police cordon, realising he didn't understand why he was there. Saving Reggie was out of his hands. Being here dashed any lingering hopes that Andrea's call was nothing more than a sick prank.

"Buried in crap."

"What?" Jack turned to the scruffy bloke beside him.

"Drenched in guano, poor lad, that's no way to go," said a man aged between forty and seventy. He sported a beige fleece under a body warmer, navy jogging bottoms tucked into thick socks and a sturdy pair of walking boots. A woolly hat perched atop his head covering his unkempt greasy hair. His jacket displayed an abundance of badges, ranging from Blue Peter and Greenpeace to UKIP and Jim'll Fix It.

Jack didn't ask about the badges. He recognised the man as the local hoarder and eccentric, Harold Beeston. He wasn't sure anybody had heard him speak before, and now he had, Harold's accent eluded him. Anywhere from Scotland to the Home Counties and everything in between were possibilities.

"Did you see it happen?" said Jack.

"The aftermath. I was in the neighbourhood," said Harold. "I put the blanket over him, don't want people gawping at his shit stained body."

"We've heard enough about the shit, thanks very much." Jack edged away, looking for whoever was in charge. Then he spotted her. "Oh, for fuck's—"

"See you later, son." Harold patted Jack on the back and

disappeared into the crowd.

"Mr Ferris, what a pleasant surprise seeing you again so soon," said DS Ramsay.

"Pleasant? In what way can this scenario be pleasant? My mate's dead, he's covered in shit, and your reaction is pleasant?"

"Covered in shit? You've seen the body?"

"Somebody mentioned it."

"Somebody, who is the somebody, Jack?"

Jack looked behind him, but Harold had gone. He contemplated giving up the name, but identifying the local oddball wasn't worth the hassle. "Just someone in the crowd."

"How were you and Mr Higgins acquainted?"

"Thought I explained our relationship this morning."

"Tell me again."

"He's a mate. We have a pint together sometimes. He looks after my pigeons when I'm away."

"Are you aware of anyone who wished to harm him?"

"Harm him? He fell off the bloody roof whilst fighting seagulls."

"Did he?"

"Of course he... wait up, are you suggesting he didn't?"

"I'm not suggesting anything, merely keeping an open mind." DS Ramsay checked a message on her phone. "What about relations?"

"What about them?"

"How well do you know them?"

"I don't."

"You've never met them?"

"Never realised he had a family, to be honest."

They stepped aside as the coroner lifted Reggie's corpse onto a gurney and wheeled it towards the euphemistically named

Private Ambulance. His feet stuck out from under the blanket Harold had placed over him, one slipper on, one slipper off. A clinical white sheet covered the rest of his body. Jack struggled to equate this scene with him enjoying a cuppa and a chat with Reggie at the pigeon lofts.

"Do you not consider it strange," said DS Ramsay, "that you know nothing about your best friend's family? His parents' names, or where they lived, for instance."

"Not something we talked about, we were engrossed in the pigeons."

"Interesting." Sidra was unsure why she considered it unusual, but saying it aloud put a squirt of WD40 on the cogs in her brain.

"Hold on, he's got a sister," said Jack with a mix of triumph and relief, "and an aunty, he told me the other day."

"Did you get names of the mysterious sister and aunty?"

"I didn't, sorry."

"Why did Mr Higgins share this information with you this week? You've known him for years. Why hasn't he mentioned it before now?"

"It's when we were discussing what to do… oh, shit."

"What is it, Mr Ferris?"

"Nothing, just remembered something important I should be doing."

"The porn collection," he thought, *"I have to get rid of Reggie's porn collection."*

Chapter Six

Jack wasn't sure what he expected to see, but Reggie's street reverted to normal a couple of days after his death. The remnants of police tape flapping from a tree and a few bunches of flowers from well meaning or attention seeking neighbours were the only evidence that a tragedy had occurred. A replacement windscreen adorned the Volvo, and the Golf was gone. Jack assumed it beyond repair, but being the penultimate resting place of a flying Lollipop Man didn't make it an enticing drive. People pottered along with their daily business, the news crews packed up and left, and the Yorkshire Terrier was yapping its lungs out again.

      The legality of Jack's impending actions remained unclear. He'd agreed to a pact with Reggie, but a verbal contract only. Reggie giving him a key didn't entitle him to rifle through his belongings and take them from the house. But a promise was a promise, and a wish made so near Reggie's death became a dying wish. He took one last look up the street to check for any police still lurking and he ventured inside, shutting the door behind him, praying he'd arrived unnoticed.

Despite being friends, Jack had never been to Reggie's home. It was more of a social friendship. A couple of pints at the Queen's, a cuppa at the pigeon lofts, they never invited each other around for dinner. Too late now. As Jack entered the sitting room, he noticed two custard creams on the side table and an abandoned mug of tea with a skin developed on the top. The police had been in for a good poke around, and whilst he wasn't certain where their responsibilities began and ended, they could have washed the mug. Jack took the cup into the kitchen and rinsed it, throwing the biscuits in the pedal bin. He was partial to a custard cream, but it didn't seem right scoffing a dead man's biscuits.

The home was clean, yet unremarkable. A TV and DVD player sat opposite a well-worn armchair. The shape of Reggie's frame moulded into the leather. Jack ran his fingers over the dent that formed his head. The settee remained pristine, suggesting he received few visitors.

This backed up what Jack discovered over the past couple of days. Everybody recognised Reggie, yet nobody knew who Reggie was. He was the cheery face on crossing duty; the kids loved him. The parents spoke to him each day, and the school receptionists had nothing but positive words to say, a rarity for them. People chatted to him in the Queen's Head, but two pints was his limit before heading home. He helped with Jack's pigeons but never bothered buying any of his own, as he always dropped hints he might not be around forever to care for them.

Knowledge of his family was non-existent, where he grew up, or life before his Lollipop Man career remained a mystery. Ingrained in everybody's routine, yet he gave nothing away. Window dressing in people's lives. Reggie had been someone everybody expected to be there, and they noticed once he'd gone, but nobody bothered to stop and have a proper look.

Jack had a job to do, and maudlin in his dead friend's lounge wasn't getting it done. He climbed the stairs with trepidation. The borderline illegality of his task worried him, and what if his findings fell on the wrong side of the law? He may stumble across content he didn't wish to see. The police searched the property earlier so there couldn't have been much amiss. But he doubted they made time to sit and watch hundreds of porn DVDs, or they at least waited until they got back to the station.

The first door to his left led to the bathroom. Jack sneaked a quick nose inside Reggie's throne room. Same as the rest of the house, tidy and unexceptional. Towel on the radiator, electric toothbrush, old-school razor and shaving brush and a half-finished Stephen King novel beside the toilet. Next was Reggie's bedroom. Nothing of note, a bed not slept in, a jumper lying over the back of a chair and cheap but modern furniture. He moved into the spare room and unlike the others; it contained a modicum of chaos and mess. A basic office chair sat in the corner alongside a desk strewn with papers, but little of great interest at first glance. It was possible the police raked through Reggie's things to find details of his next of kin and never tidied after themselves. The lack of a bed suggested a study where Jack suspected Reggie spent most of his time. Another TV and DVD player occupied the opposite corner and Jack tried to blank out images that screen had seen.

He returned to the task at hand and the Victorian style wardrobe against the wall. Its ornate feet and detailing at odds with the simple furniture in the other rooms. He rotated the small brass key in the lock and swung the door open with a loud creak. It could have done with a squirt of WD40. Now he understood what Reggie meant by a collection. No wonder he didn't want his family discovering it. Boxes and boxes of magazines and DVDs stacked to head height, along with a laptop and a small Tupperware box full of USB sticks. Pride of place atop the porn mountain sat a black rubber zipped horse's mask, its dark dead eyes hiding a multitude of secrets.

Jack wasn't expecting this. He wished he'd brought a wagon instead of the Toyota Yaris, but he'd still squash everything into the hatchback. Before risking a hernia with the heavy lifting, he had a quick rifle through the magazines and DVDs to make sure no mucky surprises lurked in the boxes. The horse's mask shocked him and he imagined being caught possessing a carload of donkey porn endangered his reputation somewhat. Everything looked normal, or as normal as any other six-foot pile of pornography in an antique wardrobe.

He opened the laptop, but password protection came as something of a relief. Jack wasn't ready for what he might find on the hard drive, he would access the files later. At least Reggie had the decency to box everything up, making it easier to transport.

The ultimate destination of the collection remained a trickier proposition. Straight to the tip was his preferred choice, but Reggie had been adamant, don't go near the tip under any circumstances. God knows why, but a dying wish was a dying wish. Next option was to take the jazz mags to the yard, dumping the lot in the skips, but that was problematic. The lads would be like a dog with two cocks if they found Jack disposing of a ton of filth. He wouldn't get a scrap of work from them for weeks once they got their mitts on free porn. Taking it home was his only choice.

He'd told Andrea he had to pick stuff up from Reggie's, but he hadn't gone into detail. Better to seek forgiveness than permission. Jack couldn't hide a raffle ticket in the house without her finding it. They didn't live in a country mansion, but he didn't want Molly stumbling across Reggie's collection. He'd worry about that when he got home. First, he had to get the boxes out of Reggie's.

Jack took the first box to the car and struggled to open the boot whilst resting the carton on his knee. He realised what a challenge he faced, and didn't intend to make multiple trips. He folded the rear seats, wrestling with Molly's booster seat and cursing himself for not thinking ahead and removing it at home. Jack removed the parcel shelf and placed it behind the driver's seat, giving himself room to manoeuvre. The Yaris was a spacious hatchback, given its size.

He then realised his next problem. The pornographic publications were on show to anybody walking past the car. The street wasn't busy, but it only took one person to take an interest and the whole neighbourhood would be out. Jack owed it to Reggie to keep his secret just that, a secret. He grabbed a handful of Sainsbury's carrier bags from the boot and stuffed them in the box. He'd grab a blanket from upstairs to hide everything from view.

After a lifetime working in haulage, Jack prided himself on his skill in both shifting boxes and finding space where others struggled, and in less than half an hour, he'd almost finished. The load made seeing the back window impossible on the drive home, but that risk became a necessity. Jack collected the last crate from the wardrobe, noticing an open DVD box lying on top of the TV. He'd missed one.

He looked for a remote but it remained hidden, so he pressed the eject button, the cogs whirring and clunking inside, waking from a deep slumber. Except the machine didn't spit the disc out as he expected and the TV came to life. The volume cranked up, bellowing out moans and groans he wouldn't be able to blame on the creaky wardrobe. And Jack saw spitting out he hoped he'd never see. He bashed the buttons on the DVD player, stopping the film, and the disc slid out of the machine as if nothing had happened.

Jack rested by the chair for a moment to gain his composure and get his heart rate to something resembling normal. That's when the unmistakable sound of a key turning in the lock shattered his plans. Frozen to the spot, he hoped he'd misheard, but the murmur of voices entered the hallway. Women. The sister? The aunty? Without an explanation, Jack had to park his arse until they left. He crouched for five minutes, listening for clues on how long they planned to stay. Male voices joined the party. An uncle? Brother in law?

The tap ran in the kitchen, and a kettle filled. Then cupboard doors opened and shut. They were making cups of tea; fuel of those dedicated to not shifting in a hurry. He had to escape. Jack placed the final DVD in the crate and plonked the horse's head on top, wishing he'd taken that downstairs first. Once they'd settled with their cuppas, he sneaked out for a brief check from the landing. The sitting-room door was closed, and the television played providing a distraction. He prayed Reggie left no DVDs in the player.

If he remained quiet, he should get downstairs and out of the house unnoticed.

And then the door opened.

He snapped his head back and crawled into the spare room, nudging the door shut. Heavy footsteps came up the stairs. They'd caught him and bullshitting a grieving family was a bar he was unprepared to limbo. His only chance was to dash past them as they found him. Even if he got out of the front door and away, they'll have seen him, which added an extra level of awkwardness to Reggie's funeral.

Unless he hid his face.

Jack snatched the mask and dragged it over his head, squeezing it past his ears. Reggie's head was much bigger than his, but it was still a tight fit. He yanked the zip until he morphed into Black Beauty. His view impaired, he could only see straight ahead. The mask amplified his breathing because of the confined space his nose was in and his increased heart rate. Sweat leaked from his brow. He stood by the door, package in hand, and prepared to run. But the handle didn't turn, nobody came in the room to confront him. He heard the bathroom door open and close.

This was his one and only opportunity. He stepped onto the landing. There could be people either side of him and he had no way of knowing. He had to move. Once he cleared the stairs, he craned his neck to sneak one last look and nobody seemed to follow him. He eased the door closed behind him and ran to the Yaris, launching the last box towards the passenger seat.

He wasted no time speeding from the scene, not even waiting to remove the equine headwear. Which came as a baffling surprise to the chain smoking lady in her dressing gown as a horse raced an overloaded Toyota Yaris down the street at full pelt.

Chapter Seven

Jack dreaded Andrea returning home from work. Not that he didn't want to see her, he didn't want her to see what he'd stashed in their bedroom. Wall to wall filth. He hadn't worked out where to dump the collection yet, and he couldn't leave it in the car. With the garage full to overflowing with junk, the bedroom became the only space with a chance of preventing Molly from finding the stash before he disposed of it. The boxes dominated the room, blocking him from getting down one side of the bed.

The one thing he'd discovered in his dealing with Reggie's belongings was his eclectic tastes. Whilst he planned to ditch the DVDs and magazines, it seemed a shame to dispose of the brand new laptop, a high spec one at that. If he formatted it and cleared any muck Reggie may have on the hard drive, he might give the computer to Molly and make a peace offering to Andrea.

The laptop fired up and in seconds a password screen appeared. Thwarted at the first hurdle. Jack tried a few ideas, **REGGIE, LOLLIPOP, PIGEON**, but nothing worked. The idea was a good one while it lasted. He threw the laptop back onto the top of the pile and knocked a few DVD cases to the carpet. The titles raised a smile, and whilst shocking him wasn't easy, several covers left little to the imagination. The Hair Bear Bunch couldn't be unseen, and he needed to shift the lot before Molly stumbled across it.

Jack had a moment where he considered selling them to raise money to put behind the bar at Reggie's wake, but realised that was wrong on so many levels. He remembered Reggie advised him to look for one film in particular, Mary Poppins with Dick Van Dyke. The porno conjured up visions he never wanted to see, but if it was exciting, as Reggie had hinted, he'd give it to the lads in the pigeon club. Something to remember Reggie. Jack searched the boxes one by one. They were in no order, but he guessed it took a special brand of pervert to alphabetise their porn collection.

Apart from the generic collections, most titles were puns loosely based on existing films or TV shows. The Queen Vic in Rearenders resembled no Angie Watts he'd ever seen, and Holby Shitty defied description. He lay on the duvet chuckling, inspecting each DVD and slinging them into a box by the bed when they didn't match his search criteria. He was enjoying himself.

Until Andrea walked into the room.

"What the hell are you doing, Jack?"

He'd been so engrossed in the task he hadn't noticed her.

"I was looking for a Mary Poppins DVD."

As soon as the words spilled through his lips he realised a lie, any lie, would be more convincing than the truth at that stage.

"Mary Poppins?" said Andrea.

"Mary Poppins?" said a third voice neither expected, "I want to watch Mary Poppins."

Molly had wandered upstairs unnoticed and was joining her parents in the bedroom until a skilled parental arm scooped her up and ushered her away.

"Play downstairs, love, I need a word with your daddy."

"About Mary Poppins?"

"Something like that. I'll be down soon."

Molly left, unaware of the tension between her mother and father. "You can be the chimney sweep, Arthur," she said as she made her Action Man do a tap dance on the bannister.

"Jack," said Andrea, "why does my bedroom resemble the red-light district of Amsterdam?"

"I promised Reggie."

"That you'd buy enough porn to satisfy a ship full of sailors?"

"I didn't buy them, Reggie did." Jack pulled himself up off the bed. "He didn't want it in the house."

"And I want a shed load of mucky movies in mine?"

"He didn't want the family to find it."

"Can you hear what you're saying or do you have a disconnect between your mouth and your brain? You didn't want a dead man's family to discover his porn stash, so you brought it home for your ten-year-old daughter to enjoy?"

"It can't go to the tip."

"Why not?"

"Reggie said."

"Reggie said? I get better excuses from the ten-year-olds I teach," said Andrea, slamming the door. "And that includes the one who said he'd dropped his PE kit on the way to school when an escaped tiger chased him."

"But it's true." Jack realised he sounded more pathetic each time he opened his mouth, and that silence offered the safest approach.

Andrea picked up a DVD case. "Holmes under the

Hammer. Really?" She chucked it aside and inspected another, The One Show, that featured a very realistic, though inventive, Alex Jones lookalike with several dildos. "Ridiculous." The third one she flung at Jack. "That's a bit basic."

He had to agree that the producers of Bargain Cunt hadn't put a huge chunk of imagination to the title.

"I'm sorry, I had nowhere else to take them."

"I want them gone, Jack. Right away. Before Molly stumbles in here and finds a copy of Cuntryfile on the bedside table."

"I'll have finished searching in a—"

"You're finished searching now."

"What if—"

"Get rid of them, every last one of them, now." Andrea slammed the door behind her, sending a pile of DVDs crashing to the floor.

And lying right at Jack's feet, as if it were fate, wasn't a porno, but the original Disney DVD of Mary Poppins.

Jack snatched the DVD case from the floor and chased after Andrea. "I told you I was looking for Mary Poppins," he shouted down the stairs, brandishing the Disney classic in his hand as if Julie Andrews had the power to erase Through the Peehole from her mind.

"Not interested, Jack, I want them gone."

He closed the bedroom door behind him, wondering how to ditch so much pornography without being noticed. Did charity shops still take DVDs? Youth clubs? By law, they might be too young to watch them, but Jack was yet to meet a man who'd waited to turn eighteen before stealing a glimpse at a pair of breasts. He could resort to the seventies technique for porn disposal and chuck the magazines in a bush. Whatever he dreamt up, Andrea was in no mood to change her decision and it had to go.

Jack looked at Mary Poppins and wondered why Reggie had singled the film out. Why put one children's DVD in amongst the smut? Maybe that was the joke Reggie played from beyond the grave. Get him searching for the ultimate porno to find it was a Disney film from the start.

Well, he'd had his laugh. At least Jack could give the DVD to Molly to keep her happy. Jack thought he best check it was the original DVD and not a porno disguised in a standard case. The mind boggled over a dirty Dick Van Dyke, and he didn't want Molly to be the one to discover what that entailed. He snapped open the case, but it lacked a DVD. Only a small USB drive sat in the plastic folder.

"What the—" Jack double checked, but there was nothing else. No clues on the USB drive to suggest what it might contain. He'd found a Tupperware box full of memory cards and USB sticks, but Jack hadn't bothered checking them. He assumed they contained more mucky pictures.

Why did Reggie hide this one? Why had he pointed him toward it in the result of his death?

Jack ran downstairs to fire up his PC. As he waited for the computer to whir into life and download the multitude of Windows updates, Andrea followed him into the office.

"Have you disposed of those boxes yet?"

"I need to check—"

"You're not even checking your watch until that filth is out of my house."

"But it might be important."

"I don't care," said Andrea. Her hands-on-hips stance

suggesting this wasn't up for debate.

"It's Mary Poppins."

"Not that nonsense again."

"It's not nonsense, I found the box. This was inside."

The Windows home screen now showed the familiar icons, and Jack plugged in the USB drive. Just as Andrea snatched it from his hand.

"You must have had a bigger bump on the noggin in that crash than I realised."

"What?"

"Have you no notion of online security?"

"Online security?"

"You planned to plug a USB drive from persons unknown into our PC? Our PC that has our bank details, your business bank details, our logins and passwords, photos of Molly. Our whole world is on this computer."

The reality of his plight registered with Jack, but he still sought to fight his corner. "It wasn't from persons unknown, it was from Reggie."

"And you knew Reggie well?"

"He's my mate."

"You had an intimate knowledge of his personal viewing habits, I take it?" She raised her eyebrows.

"I admit that was a shock."

"And you studied his family tree, his history? His aunty and sister? Where he grew up, went to school?"

"Not as in depth as that." It was dawning on him.

"You know sweet Fanny Adams about him, Jack, and there's not a chance in Holy Hell I'm letting you corrupt us by plugging his wank sticks into our PC."

"What if it has crucial information?" Jack realised the

battle was over, but his mouth kept going like a chicken attempting to reacquaint itself with its severed head.

"Did you miss the bit where I said I don't care?"

Jack sloped off upstairs. Admitting defeat, he slumped on the bed, sending a copy of Loose Women flying across the room, desperate to unearth the secrets that USB stick held. He gazed at Reggie's collection one final time, admitting defeat and knowing he had to dispose of it. Then inspiration struck.

Jack grabbed Reggie's laptop, restarting it from hibernation mode. He typed in the password **MARYPOPPINS** and pressed enter. **INVALID PASSWORD.** "Shite off, man." Jack realised starting a new career as a hacker was a tad optimistic. He boxed up the DVDs, moving the rubber horse's mask to one side. "Hold on." **BLACKBEAUTY**, then enter. No invalid password this time. The Windows logo appeared. The email application opened. Only one email in the Inbox, dated last week from a name he didn't recognise.

RE: Progress Update

Did you delete your copies of these files after sending as instructed?

**

Jack scrolled down the email to read the original from Reggie, but it didn't give much away.

Plans as agreed.
Reggie
<File Docks Plans.zip deleted>

**

Jack wouldn't call himself a computer whizz, but he understood that replying to emails removed the original documents to save on server space on continual back and forth of emails He clicked on the Sent Items folder, but it was empty. Who deletes their Sent

Items folder? Jack inserted the USB drive; it was password protected.

He typed **BLACKBEAUTY,** but the laptop thwarted his attempt. "Bollocks." He tried again with **MARYPOPPINS.** Success, he wasn't so daft.

Only one zip file on the drive, Docks Plans, the same as in the email. He unzipped the folder and opened the first document. Jack didn't like what he read; he didn't like it at all.

Chapter Eight

People considered Reggie a man with few close friends or family, yet the crematorium bulged with mourners for his funeral. Standing room only. Several parents attended, as Reggie had always been popular in his role. A handful of children, along with Andrea and the headmaster, Mr Shakespeare, represented the school. The two women Jack had avoided at Reggie's house sat at the front, escorted, Jack assumed, by their partners. Maurice Groom towered over everyone in his pew, including local journalists and several policemen, most of them detectives. Jack glared at Maurice, wanting, needing to say something, but knowing this was neither the time nor the place.

Andrea noticed his discomfort and took his hand. "Are you okay?"

"It's him, sitting there as if his turds don't reek."

"Language, we're in church."

"It's not a church."

"Same difference," said Andrea, "keep it down before someone hears you."

DS Sidra Ramsay joined Andrea in taking a keen interest in Jack's uneasiness. She stood at the back, keeping a close eye on proceedings. Most of the lads from the pigeon club formed part of the congregation, along with regulars from the Queen's Head. Even Harold the Hoarder was present, yet faces Jack didn't recognise packed the building. Faces accompanied with shaven heads, ill-fitting suits and tattoos they struggled to conceal. An Eastern European contingent was in attendance, none of whom appeared relaxed in each other's company. In the back row, hoping to blend in but standing out even more for doing so, sat the expensive tailoring and polished brogues. The air of privilege and menace oozing from them. Reggie's mourners were as eclectic as his tastes in adult entertainment.

The funeral was a humanist service, so nobody had to suffer any prayers or hymns. After a few words by the celebrant, Reggie's sister got up to do a brief speech. In her late forties, Jack thought, made her Reggie's younger sibling. Petite, with bobbed blonde hair and understated make-up, she sported a smart suit and simple yet pricy looking high-heeled shoes. Whilst her face showed a hint of hardness, she looked comfortable in the clothes. On the wall behind her hung a TV screen showing photos of Reggie on rotation. A familiar sight at funerals nowadays and apart from one in his road crossing uniform, most reflected his younger days, the days of which Jack knew nothing. Many of the group shots, in pubs and restaurants, in places he didn't know. Several faces in the pictures Jack could match to people in the congregation and others remained unfamiliar. Stranger still were the ones they blurred out.

Reggie's accent had been unremarkable, but his sister had a London twang. If not Bow Bells, at least on the outskirts of the M25. "This is my first time in Sunderland, one of my few forays up North. I don't appreciate the cold." This got a few smiles from the shoddy suit contingent, but little from Reggie's Northern friends. "It's as far away from home as you can get without leaving the country. They say that's why Reggie relocated to this northern outpost. And the locals made him welcome, I'm glad somebody did."

"We've spoken little over the last couple of decades, after… you know, but that doesn't mean I didn't love him. Reggie was my big brother."

"His choice of occupation up here surprised us somewhat, considering his history. Amazed he passed the checks."
This gained a few heartier laughs.

Jack and Andrea exchanged glances. "His history?" she whispered.

The giant porn collection, criminal record checks, a Lollipop Man with easy access to children, to Molly. "Oh, God," said Jack as he bowed his head.

Reggie's sister continued, "He was a hard man, but fair. He hurt no one who didn't ask for it."

Jack climbed out of his seat to shout his objections, but Andrea dragged him back.

"He was only ever protecting his family. I don't care what anybody says, I'm not having that word associated with him."
The crematorium echoed with murmurs of recognition, and heads nodded.

"A lot of you wouldn't be here today if you still thought the rumour surrounding my brother to be true. It's a shame he had to go into hiding in this wilderness, and it's taken his death for everybody to accept what we knew all along. Our Reggie was no grass."

People applauded. Jack had no clue what was happening

now, and even less of a clue who his friend was than when he walked in thirty-minutes ago.

"I'd like us all to stand and raise a toast."

"Raise a toast?" said Andrea. "In a crematorium?"

Reggie's sister produced a hip flask from her inside pocket, as did fifty per cent of the congregation. The others looked on in bewilderment.

"Reggie!" She took a big swig and put the flask back where it came from, right arms bent in unison as half the crowd followed.

Jack wondered if he'd dreamt it when Shut Up by Madness played through the speakers and everyone filed out.

Jack waited his turn and as he stepped out of the pew, he caught a overpowering whiff of Kouros, something he hadn't smelled since the eighties. He nodded in the general direction of where the stench of aftershave came from, but didn't make eye contact. He kept a tight grip on Andrea's hand, tighter than the grip he had on today's events. A twenty-minute service had been a rollercoaster ride, and it wasn't over yet. He had hundreds of questions when he arrived this morning; he had thousands more now, and he wasn't missing the opportunity to get answers.

Jack stepped out into the spring sunshine. To his right, he saw the next funeral scheduled to join the crematorium conveyor belt. A small queue had formed to pass condolences to the sister and aunty. He'd introduce himself, but he wanted to catch up with them at the wake.

"Sorry for your loss, Reggie was a good mate."

"You knew him well?" said the sister.

Jack doubted that now. "We got on, he took care of my pigeons."

She appeared surprised. "Didn't catch your name."

"Jack, Jack Ferris."

"You're Jack? Nice to meet you."

She acknowledged Andrea, but more a way of moving Jack along the queue than a warm greeting.

Jack took up a position at the entrance to the garden of remembrance and studied the diverse groups huddled, talking, conspiring. He may have been paranoid, but he was sure a few sent glances his way.

The expensive suits didn't hang around and two chauffeur-driven cars led them away. The cheap suits gathered in their various factions, with only the briefest nods to other groups. They were building themselves up for a big session later, and that worked in Jack's favour. The drunker they were, the more likely they let the odd secret slip out. Jack had been on edge since his discovery in the Mary Poppins case, and he hadn't mentioned it to anyone. He needed convincing that what he had in his possession was what it suggested.

Reggie, it appeared, was nothing like the person he'd presented to the people of Sunderland, and this gathering backed that up. What Jack didn't understand was why or how Reggie got this material and why he hadn't told Jack sooner. Because what Jack had discovered were plans, plans that threatened to change his life forever.

One man in the congregation could answer his questions, but he'd wait for now.

This may be his only chance to speak to Reggie's family and former associates. And discover why a hardened criminal, from one of the south of England's largest crime families, found employment as a Lollipop Man in Sunderland.

Andrea chatted to the children and their parents, so Jack

approached one group of undesirables.

They were the shaven-headed, musclebound types, although not the Eastern Bloc contingent who smoked by the floral tributes.

"Jack Ferris." Jack offered his hand to the biggest and most senior looking of the crowd. He took it without offering a name. "You knew Reggie?" said Jack.

"I'm at his funeral." A gruff Cockney accent, straight from central casting.

"Friend of his?"

"Acquaintance."

"Get you, work colleagues?"

Jack's presence irritated the group, and they had no wish for a conversation. He doubted that was because they were grieving, and he vowed to get the information from them.

"Who did you say you were?" said the gruff Cockney.

"Jack, I'm a mate of Reggie's."

"Are you the bloke who cleaned his lollipop?" This gained a laugh from the crowd and reinforced their feelings toward him.

"He used to look after my pigeons." As soon as he uttered the words, he wondered why he'd allowed them to escape his mouth.

"Is that a yoof, a yoofa thingy. You know, that word that means when words mean something else. Like dropping the kids off at the pool when you're having a dump."

"A euphemism?"

"Aye, that. Is looking after your pigeons one of them?" He looked to his mates to recognise his long, drawn out joke.

"No," said Jack. Realising he was wasting his time.

"Reggie looked after your pigeons?"

"He did, aye. Had a way with the birds."

"Bet he did, eh?" He sought recognition again. "Real life

pigeons like they have in Trafalgar Square. You own them?"

"Got fifty odd," said Jack.

"Do they not fly away?"

"They're homing pigeons, they always return."

"Strange bunch, you northerners." He turned his back on Jack, the conversation finished.

Jack surveyed the grounds, looking for another group that may be more receptive. People drifted away. Getting in their cars and heading to the wake, ensuring they reserved the best seats, and got to the bar before the crowds arrived. Seasoned funeral professionals bought two rounds on arrival as mourners rammed the bar for the first hour. He spotted one faction of Eastern Europeans who hadn't left, although Andrea motioned for them to leave. If he introduced himself now, it made it easier to pick their brains later once they'd had a drink to loosen their tongues.

Just then, a big hand ruffled his hair. "Jack," said Maurice, "a sad day."

Jack forced himself to acknowledge him. "It is, Reggie was a decent man."

"Can I give you some advice, Jack, from one friend to another?"

Jack bristled at the word friend. Maurice was very far from being a friend. "Go on."

"I think it's best you don't show up at the wake. Family and close friends only."

"I am his close friend."

"It's for the best on an emotional day." Maurice leaned in, towering above Jack. "The family has heard rumours about the bus wreck and how you almost killed Reggie. A few drinks in and they'll bang two heads together and come up with five."

"That's nonsense. The crash was an accident." Jack also

recognised the nonsense in his statement.

"Was it? Trust me, Jack. You don't want to be in their orbit when they get to five." He ruffled Jack's hair again and joined the two detectives in the car.

Jack took Andrea's hand. "Let's go home."

Chapter Nine

Six hours after being bumped from Reggie's funeral, Jack's blood still simmered. He was angry with Maurice for his faux friendliness, annoyed at Andrea for agreeing to leave when he offered, but top of his rage list was himself for allowing Maurice to intimidate him. Jack had nothing to do with Reggie's accident, and the family had no reason to believe he was involved. Unless Maurice planted that seed. Maurice didn't want Jack speaking to Reggie's family or associates, and whatever the reason, it related to the files he found on the USB drive.

His phone rang, a number he didn't recognise, and he wasn't in the mood to talk to strangers, but it could be work. He took a couple deep breaths, not that they calmed his anger, and pressed the answer button. "Jack Ferris."

"Hi, Jack," said a young female with a breezy air of familiarity. "Nancy Whitworth."

"Who?" Jack recognised neither the name nor voice and had no time for guessing games.

"From the Post."

Still none the wiser. "Okay."

"I'm covering the Reggie Higgins story."

"It's a story?"

"A man falls to his death in suspicious circumstances days after narrowly avoiding the same fate at the hands of his best friend. I'd consider it a story."

Jack bristled at the implied accusation, but tried not to react. "If you say so."

"I was wondering if you had a quote."

"On what?"

"Reggie's death."

"No."

This surprised Nancy. In the social media era, everyone always wanted to share their views. "It's your chance to get your side of the story across to the public."

"There is no my side of the story to get across to the public."

"You have no thoughts on your friend's demise?"

"I have plenty of thoughts."

"Care to share them?"

"No," said Jack with his thumb edging to the end call button.

"Do me a solid please, Mr Ferris. This is my first big article and Maur… someone suggested you might know why Mr Higgins climbed onto the roof and what drove him to commit suicide."

"Do you a solid? Suicide? Who said he committed suicide?"

"Nobody, yet. Are you saying you've evidence to the contrary?"

"Who did you say gave you my name?"

"As a journalist, I never reveal my sources."

"A journalist? You sound like you're doing a school project." A little harsh, but she irritated him.

"I'll have you know I was highly commended for my end-of-year project at university."

"Well done, you. I'm assuming it wasn't on compassion for people grieving the loss of their friends?"

"It was on make-up aiding mental health," she said, oblivious to Jack's point. "Do you wish to give me a quote or not?"

"I don't."

"You realise how poor this will look if you go no comment?"

"How it looks to the half a dozen readers of your church newsletter is of no concern to me." Jack suspected she wasn't phoning on behalf of the newspaper she purported to work for. "Run back to your masters and inform them I have nothing to say."

"Are you calling my journalistic integrity into question?"

"Nancy, I'm not sure you could discover what integrity meant if you sat in a library full of dictionaries." Jack hung up.

"Are you going to tell me what's wrong?" Andrea was getting sick of Jack pacing the floor, mumbling to himself.

His face bright red, blood pressure rocketing, he could spontaneously combust if he didn't calm himself. "Nothing."

"If it's nothing, will you plonk your backside, please? I'm not sure we can afford to replace the carpet if you keep on tramping all over the sitting room."

"We'll not be able to afford to eat if they take my business off me."

"Who's taking the business off you?"

"Maurice and his pals. They have plans. Plans that don't include me."

"What on God's green earth are you babbling on about? Plans, what plans? What's Maurice got to do with the price of kippers?"

Jack hadn't shared his discovery with Andrea, he didn't want to worry her, he'd hinted something was up, but kept it to himself. "Maurice, the man of the people. Face of the city, altruistic businessman with his finger in every fucking pie. He wants to ruin me, ruin us."

"Why would Maurice Groom want to ruin us?"

"Because of what we own."

"A three-bed semi in Fulwell and a Toyota Yaris. I can see why he's jealous of us."

"The haulage firm, Andrea, he wants Ferris Haulage."

"Maurice made you an offer for the business?" Andrea was alert to the possibilities. Get a good price and they could invest it, pay off the mortgage, and if Jack got a job closer to home, he'd have quality time with Molly. "Why didn't you tell me?"

"He hasn't made an offer."

"Then how do you—"

Jack was out of the door and racing up the stairs, two steps at a time. On the return trip, he glimpsed Molly playing in her room. This should have calmed him, but triggered his anger. He launched himself down the stairs and plonked Reggie's laptop on the coffee table.

"I thought you'd got rid of that," said Andrea. "Don't even dream of sticking that filth on here. Molly could walk in any minute."

Jack had disposed of Reggie's porn collection, as agreed.

He'd waited until the lads had gone home and filled a skip at work, knowing the waste disposal people emptied it first thing the next morning. He'd held on to the laptop and memory stick.

"Molly's fine, she's playing upstairs. It's not what you think. It's much, much worse."

He fired up the computer and plugged in the USB stick. Jack ignored the single email for now. He didn't know who Reggie was corresponding with; the name wasn't familiar, and it wasn't his priority. He opened the file that had caused him so much angst. The file that contained detailed technical maps of the port area of Sunderland. Maps that included his yard and his pigeon lofts.

"What are we looking at?" said Andrea.

"Mr Groom's Masterplan. He wants to take over the docks and expand them."

"This might help us. If he needs the real estate, he must be willing to pay top whack for it."

"Maurice has money, but he's not rich enough for this. He's in with someone else or he'll expect the land for pennies. Or both."

"How does he pick up the land for pennies?"

"Discredit the firm, discredit me. It's happening, can't you see?"

"Now you're being paranoid," said Andrea.

"You think everything that's happened over the past couple of weeks has been an unfortunate coincidence?"

"Maurice can't have had any involvement with Reggie. Why would he?"

"Because Reggie knew about these proposals; even better if Maurice can implicate me. Two birds with one stone," said Jack, slumping back in his armchair.

"If he is as dangerous as you say, and I'm struggling to

believe he's a threat, is it not wise to take what we can and get out now?"

Andrea's wish was Jack spending more time with Molly. She now wondered if it was changing to him spending more time alive.

"He's not stopping at grabbing my yard."

"Hold up, are you saying the bits in red are where he plans to develop?"

"Yes."

"But that includes the school, he can't do that."

"He's head of the board of governors, nobody will question him."

"That's not legal."

"He'll get around it. Maurice has the police in his pocket and journalists onside. He'll no doubt have politicians tucked up in preparation."

"The Queen's Head, the lofts, the public won't allow it."

"They won't have a say. More expansion and more jobs equals compulsory purchase at rock-bottom prices. We're out, Andrea, all of us."

"Why not sell the yard and move elsewhere? Why's it so important to base yourself on the docks?"

"It's the perfect location for a haulage business, right in the centre of the action. He doesn't just need the land, he wants the business. Maurice Groom is moving into the haulage industry."

Andrea had a moment of clarity. She left the room, rummaging in the cupboard under the stairs before returning with a lump hammer. "I need you to destroy it, Jack."

"Destroy what?"

"The laptop, the memory stick, the evidence. I don't want it in the house, I don't want it near Molly. If there's even the slightest chance they harmed Reggie for owning this, I want no trace of it."

"You're being ridiculous."

"Am I?" she offered him the hammer.

Jack looked at the laptop and the plans one last time, knowing Andrea was right. "It's not right, letting him get away with this. Taking everything we treasure, everything we own. My business, your job, Molly's school."

"We'll still have each other, we'll still have Molly. We can start again."

"He can't get away with it," said Jack.

"What will stop him?"

Jack snatched up the hammer and headed for the door, determination etched in his face.

"It's not what will stop him, it's who."

Chapter Ten

Jack jumped out of the cab after handing over a tenner. "Keep the change." The first words he'd spoken since giving the address. Gravel flew and gears crunched as the taxi left. The driver couldn't pull away quick enough, relieved the madman with the hammer was off to bother somebody else. He considered calling the police but didn't want his night taken up by making statements and losing crucial fares.

    Jack rang the doorbell and brayed on the thick oak door. Lights were on in the gaudy mock Tudor mansion, so somebody was home. If someone didn't answer soon, he contemplated taking his demolitions skills to the statues on the lawn until he grabbed their attention. The door opened with the imposing figure of Maurice Groom standing behind it, a glass of red in his hand. Aside from his top button being open, he wore the funeral clothes from earlier.

    "Jack?"

    Now he was here, Jack was unsure of what he wanted to say. It wasn't as if he'd planned his speech. "We need to talk."

"It's been an emotional day, Jack. Can't this wait until morning?"

"It can't." Jack adjusted his grip on the handle, checking over his shoulder for whoever might be watching.

"I've friends visiting, Jack. Arrange an appointment and come and meet me in the office as any civilised person does."

"Civilised, who are you to lecture me about civilised?"

"Jack," said Maurice, eyeing the hammer, "you've attracted police attention with the Reggie business. How do you suppose they'll react when they hear you've turned up on the doorstep of a respected businessman brandishing a lethal weapon?"

"Respected businessman? The only reason I've attracted the law is because of you."

Maurice gave a dismissive laugh. "Keep telling yourself that if you need someone to blame, but it was your own doing."

"I've seen the plans," said Jack.

Maurice hesitated for a moment, enough for Jack to realise this development surprised him.
"What plans?"

"The proposals for the port, for my yard, the school, everything."

"You've lost me."

"You even want to take over the fucking pigeon lofts."

Maurice moved outside, drawing the door around behind him and using his full height to tower above Jack. "I'm not sure which plans you think you've seen, but you're mistaken."

"There's no mistake, I know what you're planning."

"Where did a piss poor bus driver see these so-called plans?" Maurice considered who in his organisation knew the drawings existed, and who was foolish enough to share with Jack.

"Doesn't matter where I saw them, it only matters you understand I have."

"You're not making any sense, Jack. Have you been drinking?" Maurice placed his arm against the concrete pillar, one of two supporting the giant canopy adorning the front of the house.

"I'm here to give you fair warning it's not happening, not for any price."

"You're giving me fair warning? You? Jack Ferris, coming to my home and making threats?"

"No threats, merely advising you of the position."

"You don't have a clue, do you?" Maurice leaned in. The stench of booze and cigar smoke was strong. "You've got as much chance of blocking these proposals as you had of stopping that bus. It's out of your control."

"You believe I'll sell up just because you say so?"

"You have no choice, Jack. In anything. Whether running your business, driving your lorry or flying those rats in the sky, it's only because we allow you to do so."

"Rats in the sky? You're showing your ignorance. Pigeons are majestic creatures. They're more intelligent than you realise."

"If only you could borrow a touch of that intelligence, Jack. You've had your say, got your little whinge off your chest, and now I'd appreciate you leaving my property, so I can get back to my friends." Maurice stepped onto the front step and opened the door.

"You might assume I'm daft, Maurice, but I know you can't afford such a development. Yeah, you've got an expensive, if tasteless, house and you park a Bentley on the drive to impress whatever associates are hiding inside. But an expansion of this size takes big money, money you don't possess."

"Don't you worry on my behalf, I'll have the funds."

"You have the funds, or you will have the funds? You don't sound confident."

"Come back to me in a month and ask me if I have the capital. Come back in thirty days and you'll be begging me to buy your shitty little business."

"What's happening in a month?"

"Never mind what's happening, you concentrate on keeping your family safe, focus on what's important."

"Is that a threat?" said Jack, gripping the hammer he'd forgotten he was holding.

"Do you think I need to make threats to you? You're a nobody, irrelevant. Now run along and let me return to my party. I've wasted enough time with you."

"I'm sure they're missing you."

"And tell whoever is filling your head with these stupid ideas of plans and expansions to keep their nose out."

Maurice had no inclination that Reggie had been the one with the documents, and he wasn't aware Jack held them now. He still had an advantage. "And you tell whoever is financing your transaction, that I'm not selling."

"Bye, Jack." Maurice walked back inside, slamming the door, the conversation over.

Jack peered through the window and could see Maurice heading back into the dining room to greet his guests. A few he recognised from the funeral and one face from elsewhere. A face from his past that could spell trouble for Jack if involved in the scheme.

Maurice closed the dining-room door behind him.
"Sorry for the interruption, gentlemen."

"Trouble?" said one of his impeccably dressed guests.

"A neighbour, bit excitable as their dog's gone missing. We had a look along the drive it's but not here, so they've taken their lead elsewhere. Back to business. Where were we?"

Maurice laid the plans out across the dining table, each corner pinned with a crystal whisky tumbler.

"You're confident you have this under control, Maurice? You can acquire the property with no fuss?"

"Yes, quite confident."

"And the haulage company? It is imperative we don't just buy the land it stands on, we need the entire operation."

"It's under control."

"From where I'm standing, it's very far from under control. The business owner was in a crash that could have wiped out half a primary school. His best friend tumbled from the roof whilst fighting seagulls. His pal had more connections to the criminal underworld than most of this gathering put together. Does that sound under control?"

"He won't be an issue." Maurice took a swig of his Bordeaux.

"This should have been under the radar. Secure investment, buy the land, get the planning permission and start building before anyone questions what we're doing."

"Everything will be in place."

"The capital, you've got your financing secured?"

Maurice couldn't help a glance to the other side of the polished mahogany table where the cheaper suits were. "It's in hand."

"Are you sure? You don't sound confident. We must be ready to act in six weeks and once we leap, there's no returning to the cliff top."

"I'm sure." Maurice took another gulp.

"Noel," the guest turned his back on Maurice, finished with him for now, "you're positive the application will go through with no objections."

"As you know, expanding the docks is fundamental to the growth of not only the city, but the whole region," said Noel Cardwell. "It will see a boost to jobs and the economy, unprecedented in modern times." He exuded an air of polished smugness only senior politicians own.

"Enough of the bullshit you present to the TV cameras. Will this get planning permission?"

"The local stuff is Maurice's domain, and there'll always be a handful of grievances. But if Maurice is incapable of handling that and they refer it to the Secretary of State, I have people waiting for my call."

"Maurice assures us he has it covered, so the Secretary of State shouldn't be necessary. What we can't allow is for local objectors to get organised. We need to keep this under wraps, announce at the exact point to give them the least opportunity to object before planning approval."

"Agreed. I've briefed those in the highest level of government on a need-to-know basis. The pigeon botherers of Sunderland won't hear it from me," said Noel.

"Even those with whom you have a close personal relationship?"

"Believe me, no such relationship exists."

"That leaves you then, Maurice. Everything tight at your end?"

"Watertight, no leaks, no chance of a leak." He raised his glass to gulp his wine, but it was empty.

"This is the last time I'll say this, but it's crucial nobody discovers these proposals before we present them. Besides the financial and reputational cost, anybody who lets slip our little secret faces significant penalties. Am I understood?"

Maurice nodded, his mouth too dry to speak.

The party was over and everyone, especially Maurice, had their responsibilities, and the graphic punishments for non-compliance, reiterated. A tad unfortunate, considering the man gracing his doorstep not ten minutes before, had an intimate understanding of the scheme and vowed to stop it. As they filed out, none offered their hand to Maurice. He reached to ruffle the hair of the main man but realised the error of his ways and ran his fingers through his own locks instead.

He needed a way of dealing with Jack, uncovering the leak and finding how to distance himself from it if it ever came out. Jack was the easy part, but as Noel Cardwell's car exited the gate, Maurice had an idea that might just save him.

Chapter Eleven

Jack loitered in the car park of Southwick Police Station, wondering whether he'd be safer with an anonymous tip-off. But he was unsure what he was tipping the police off about and whether anyone cared. He knew Maurice's plans but as yet, that's all they amounted to, plans. Even if he executed them, secured the land and expanded the docks, it wasn't illegal. Knowing the last location of the documents, who had owned them and how he died, would prick up the ears of the law and call for further investigation. If he was going through with this, Jack had to admit the evidence came from Reggie's house and he had removed it after his death.

It was a tough choice, but Jack saw no other way forward. He had no firm evidence of the criminal status of the people in Maurice's home last night. But there was a better chance of a Grizzly declaring he didn't defecate in the woods than there was of them not being crooks. Whilst not duty bound to provide the evidence; he needed to guide the police in the right direction and let them get on with it.

Jack gripped the USB stick in his left hand and entered the station via the sliding doors into the busy reception. A lad in his early twenties sat with his dirty Nike trainers on the chair, the former white socks he tucked his tracksuit bottoms into accessorised with his electronic tag. Spitting on the floor with a power and accuracy that suggested he undertook extensive practice. A young mother stood with a double buggy and another toddler grabbing onto her visible G-string as a safety harness in case she thought of running off and leaving him. Her verbal tirade left the officers in no doubt why she was there. "You've gotta let owa Gary gan, man, he's done nowt wrong. The stuff you found in the flat wasn't even his."

"We're well aware it wasn't his," said the disgruntled sergeant behind the desk, "that's why we arrested him."

"Ahh man, you can't dee that. The nash have just lashed his dole, and he was taking me and the bairns to McDonald's."

Her protests fell on deaf ears as the officers, used to her outbursts, let her blow off steam until she stomped out, without 'owa Gary'.

A sweet old lady ahead of Jack in the queue explained the tale of her missing cat. The sergeant once again explaining it wasn't missing. A squad car flattened it three years ago on its way to handle a domestic disturbance involving 'owa Gary'. The elderly lady had been every Wednesday since then to report it missing, and the officer appeared unsure if she was a befuddled pensioner or one inflicting a cruel revenge.

As she left, he appeared relieved to see Jack, someone who, on first impressions, appeared semi-normal. "Morning sir, what can I do for you?"

"I want to report a crime," said Jack.

"You've come to the right place."

"I'm not sure it's a crime. Well, I am sure, I just haven't collected the evidence yet."

"What category of crime are we talking, it's not a wayward cat, is it?"

"No. It's a murder."

The sergeant made himself taller, his interested piqued. "Go on."

"Not a murder, manslaughter maybe. A suspicious death at least."

The sarge slumped back into his seat, wondering if they were still discussing the cat. "Do we have a name for the victim of this suspicious death?"

Once Jack hinted there was something questionable surrounding Reggie's death, there was no scope for retraction. He had to give them everything he held on Maurice, what he suspected had happened with the bus crash. And how he had seen half of London's criminal underworld partying with Maurice Groom and a prominent Tory MP, Noel Cardwell. Andrea's father.

"Give me a second."

Jack slipped the USB drive into his pocket and took out his phone as if he was searching for a number, giving himself room to think.

"Stoker, the ideal gentleman for the job. Over here son," said the sergeant to a detective walking past, "I might have something for you."

Jack glanced up from his screen and at DC Stoker, who was staring at him. The detective who had flanked Maurice Groom at Reggie's funeral. "I'm sorry. I've made a mistake. I'll get back to you." He shuffled outside, his head pointing at the floor, but there was no doubting the coppers got a good look at him. He'd screwed himself before he'd even started.

"What did he want?" said DS Sidra Ramsay, nodding towards the departing Jack.

"How should I know?" said Stoker.

"Is it not your responsibility to investigate?"

"Have you not got more important things to worry yourself, love?"

Stoker barged past Sidra, making snide comments relating to both her religion and perceived sexuality. Either of which could land him in serious trouble if she could prove it, but getting anybody in this nick to corroborate her story was nigh on impossible. Sidra considered pulling rank, but as Stoker had said, she had more important things to worry her.

Jack punched the dashboard, fuming at his stupidity. How did he ever think Maurice didn't have the law in his blazer pocket? There was a knock on the window, the last thing he needed, DS Ramsay.

"Good morning, Mr Ferris. How lovely to meet you again. What brings you to Southwick Police Station this morning?"

"I was reporting a missing cat." He wound the window up before she responded.

Jack had one last throw of the dice. He looked up a number and dialled. "I'd like to speak to the senior crime correspondent, please."

"That's me." The voice sounded familiar.

"You're the senior crime reporter? I phoned main reception."

"I was passing and answered the phone."

"What did you say your name was?"

"Nancy, Nancy Whitworth."

Jack bounced his head off the steering wheel, sounding the horn. "How can you be a senior crime reporter? You've just left uni."

"Technically, I'm the only crime correspondent, the only paid reporter at the paper. We use interns to trawl Twitter for our stories now. Sorry, who is this and how can I help?"

"I don't think you can help me, I don't think you can help me at all."

Chapter Twelve

Jack tried to make himself comfortable in his chair, but whilst he wasn't a tall man, squatting on a seat designed for an eight-year-old proved problematic. Unsure whether to rest on his left or right cheek, or centre himself and bring pain to both cheeks; he shuffled around, hoping constant movement would help keep the discomfort at bay. Andrea could have found him an adult's chair or explained where they were, but she was making him suffer. Storming off grasping a hammer on Tuesday night hadn't been his greatest moment, and his follow-up aborted trip to the police station cemented his position on her naughty boys list. It wasn't so much that she was giving him the silent treatment; it was as if someone had pressed the mute button on their relationship. On the chessboard of their marriage, turning up at a rehearsal of the school play was another suicide move. At least Molly was still speaking to him. Relegated to the most minor of bit parts, she missed the main rehearsal and sat beside Jack, more relaxed in her seat.

"Were you ever in a school play, Daddy?"

"Only once." He could have starred in more and blocked the memory. "Ali Baba and the Forty Thieves." Jack wondered for a moment if they allowed it today, in more enlightened times. Probably not.

"That sounds exciting." Molly took full advantage of having her dad to herself for a change. "Who were you in the play?"

"I was one of the forty thieves," said Jack, "although there were only four of us. It was a small school."

If Molly was disappointed, she hid it well. "What did you steal?"

"Steal?" Jack panicked. It was dangerous enough he'd got himself into the mess with Maurice, but he didn't want Molly knowing he had the stolen laptop and USB stick. He couldn't understand why Andrea had told her.

"As one of the forty thieves, you must have stolen loads of stuff."

"I expect so. I can't remember. I think we had to pretend to steal from market stalls."

"Like the ones in Jackie White's Market?" Molly had a good recollection. It was years since Jack had taken her to Sunderland's market, hidden away off The Bridges shopping centre. The sights and smells and the noise enthralled her. The whiff of pork, fish and body odour could fascinate only a child.

"They may have been more exotic in Ali Baba's day," he said, wishing to transport himself back a few years to when he and Molly explored the stalls.

"Can you remember your lines?" The thought of her dad as a child-actor intrigued Molly.

"I had none, I was thief number four, only the first three had speaking roles." This wasn't one hundred per cent true. Jack had lines but delivered them so poorly, even by primary school standards, that the teacher removed them and gave them to one of the other junior thieves. "It was a silent role."

"Like the one I have?"

"Yes." Maybe this was how he placated Molly after her mother demoted her.

"Like the one Mummy has with you?"

"What?"

"A silent role where she doesn't speak, she's great at it."

"An expert." Jack changed the subject. "What's the name of this show?"

"MaXbeth."

"MaXbeth? Sounds heavy for a class of ten-year-olds. Doesn't look like Macbeth from where I'm sitting."

"That's because it's the new version, silly."

"The new version?"

"Like Macbeth, but also like the X Factor," said Molly in all seriousness, "and like Coronation Street."

Jack wondered if his daughter had developed a glue sniffing habit. "How does that work?"

"The three witches are the judges, but Macbeth is also a judge, the boss. I guess he's Simon Cowell because of the high pantaloons. I'm not sure who the rest of them are."

"Your Mam came up with this?" Jack was worried Andrea's sanity had gone for a wander.

"It was Mr Fitzpatrick."

"Mr Fitzpatrick, I've never heard of him."

"He's new. Well, not a new teacher, he's here for the play. He goes to the university, so he must be really clever."

"Sounds it."

"That's him wearing the enormous glasses playing the part

of Deidre, whoever Deidre is." Molly pointed to a man on stage. In his early twenties, he sported an oversized scarf, skinny jeans, Crocs, an immaculately manicured beard and a giant pair of jam jar bottom spectacles. Jack was unsure if that was his costume, what fashionable ironic students wore these days, or whether Mr Fitzpatrick was more crackers than a packet of Jacobs. Possibly all three.

"He has a role in the school play?"

"He said it couldn't work without him, and I don't think Mummy wanted him involved, but he cried, so she let him stay. I never cried when she told me I wasn't in the show."

"I'm not convinced you're missing out, if I'm honest." Jack had another look at Mr Fitzpatrick and thought if he'd been spotted anywhere near the school fence in that get-up, it warranted a quick call to the police. The fashion police, at the very least.

"I want to act, Daddy, I really do. But if Mummy says I'm not good enough—"

"She didn't say you weren't good enough."

"I don't mind, I'll make my own play with Arthur." She looked at her Action Man. "Won't we, Arthur?"

"For God's sake, will you let the children perform?" Andrea's voice booming across the hall stunned everyone into silence.

"This isn't a trivial Am-Dram production," said Mr Fitzpatrick.

"It's a school play, with ten-year-olds, not opening night on Broadway."

"With that philosophy, no wonder it's such a shambles."

"They're ten-years-old."

"If you allowed them to call me Fitz, as I requested, they'd be more receptive to my ideas."

"Nobody is calling you Fitz."

"I'm tired, Miss." A short, chubby girl had her hand in the air.

Mr Fitzpatrick turned to her. "You want fame? Well, fame costs. And right here is where you start paying… in sweat." He flounced off stage. "Amateurs."

Andrea stifled a scream. She spotted Jack out of the corner of her eye. She'd forgotten he was there and stormed towards him.

"Whatever this intervention is, Jack, I haven't got time for it."

"We need to talk."

"You do, I don't." She stomped back to the stage. "Right everyone, back in your positions."

"Oh, God, there's going to be singing." Jack slumped in his chair, at least as far as his buttocks allowed.

An eight-year-old girl, resplendent in a flowing velvet gown, was centre stage. He assumed she was Lady Macbeth, but she could be Betty Turpin. He remained unsure. What he was certain of was that emulating Beyoncé was a reach she'd never make. Whatever she lacked in talent, she made up in enthusiasm, leaping around in what could optimistically be labelled interpretive dance. What she was interpreting was anybody's guess.

Fitz, who had recovered from his earlier tantrum, was attempting to choreograph from the sidelines. He'd memorised every move and delivered them with gusto. Whether this was to inspire the young girl or to audition for another role himself was unclear. Her voice was somewhere between a shout and a screech and had a pitch destined to bring the neighbourhood dogs racing across the schoolyard. He hoped the assembly hall had toughened glass. Jack wondered how awful Molly must be to not land a leading role in this show.

He endured six more renditions of various tunes delivered with varying levels of inability, confirming his fear that Andrea was punishing him. When the torture was over and parents arrived in the yard to collect their talentless children, Andrea approached him. "I'm serious, Jack, I need you to stop."

"Stop what?"

"Putting me and Molly in danger."

"You don't mind putting her eardrums in danger."

"It's a joke now, is it?" Andrea folded costumes and put them in a basket. She shook her head as she picked up a discarded script.

"Not a joke, but nowhere near as serious as you're making out."

"Molly and you nearly perished. Reggie died. You claim to have uncovered a conspiracy. One that is not only framing you for both the bus crash and Reggie's death, but involves contenders for the top ten most ruthless criminals in the UK and Europe. Tell me, Jack, at what point does it become serious?" She walked off, not waiting for an answer, stacking the baskets in the store cupboard.

Jack followed. "I can solve it. The evidence is there. They suspect somebody has told me something, but they have no clue the laptop or the USB stick are in our possession."

"How long before they learn the truth, before they come knocking?"

"They won't."

"In our house, Jack, the house where Molly sleeps. You're hiding evidence in our home."

"They don't know that, not that I have it," said Jack, frustrated at Andrea not getting it.

"And what use is that?"

"What use is what?"

"You keeping evidence they don't realise exists. Surely somewhere in this Masterplan of yours, you must reveal you have something on them or what's the point?"

Jack hadn't thought this through to its conclusion. The police and the papers were non-starters, as they were both in Maurice's pocket. "I'll think of something."

"You won't, though. That's just it. You can't stop these people, they do this every day, they're in the intimidation industry."

"We can't let them take our business."

"Sell it, get a good price now whilst you can. The longer this goes on, the harder it will be."

"It's our future."

"Jack, if you don't sell the yard, we don't have a future."

"What are you saying?"

"I'm not sure I can make it any plainer. Lose the company, or me and Molly are leaving."

"You can't."

"You're putting Molly in danger and I'm not having it."

"But my dad built this company from scratch."

"And the law states you follow what your dad did? Your father dictates your path for the rest of your life?" said Andrea.

"But it's fine when it's your dad dictating."

"Why bring my father into it? We don't speak."

"But he's still in there." Jack pointed at Andrea's forehead. "His whiny Tory voice telling you I'm not good enough, that I'm just a lorry driver and beneath your sort."

"My sort?" She swiped his arm aside. "It has nothing to do with it, and if you opened your eyes, you'd see it. You never spend time with Molly, you're always away from home. You never spend time with me."

"I've been here for two excruciating hours, and you've not looked in my direction once."

"I'm at work, Jack."

"It's okay for your job to be a barrier, but not mine?"

"Don't even dream of throwing that one at me."

"Guys, guys!" Fitz came bounding across the hall. "I've had a fabulous idea. You remember the bloke who's a ghost in Macbeth?"

"Banquo?"

"Bonkers name. Nothing we can do to change that. Anyway, back in the olden days there was this man, Michael Jackson."

"I'm aware of Michael Jackson." Andrea did little to hide her displeasure at the interruption.

"You know he was a zombie? Not a real one, obvs, but he did a video where he dressed as one. I've seen it on YouTube, amaze-a-bloody-balls. Anyway, I was thinking, right, we should get that kid who plays Banksy or whatever he's called. That ugly child with the big glasses and sticky out ears? Him? We can dress him like this Michael Jackson fella and the other kids as zombies doing the dance. It will be fan-flipping-flopping-tastic."

"The children are not dressing as zombies, at least no more than they do already."

"But Michael Jackson could be great for the kids, Google him."

"Mr Fitzgerald, it isn't happening. We haven't got long before opening night and as yet, we've found nobody who can sing in a tone that isn't capable of downing passing aircraft. We need to stick with what we've got."

"If you want a sub-standard production, that's your prerogative, but this play is a once in a lifetime opportunity to be part of an extravaganza."

Andrea gave him a glare that provided his answer, and he flounced off again.

She gave the same glare to Jack. "Get rid of the USB drive and sell the business or say goodbye to your wife and daughter."

Chapter Thirteen

Jack brayed on his horn for no other reason than everybody else was doing it. Cars backed up the road and past the roundabout. He dialled Andrea from the hands-free but yet again; she didn't answer. Jack punched the horn repeatedly. Nothing changed. He rang her once more. Voicemail.

Andrea could be anywhere now after she'd snatched the laptop and USB stick and said she was taking them to the tip. She'd timed it as he'd just come out of the shower, and Molly and her were long gone before he'd even removed his towel.

Jack was now in his work van, partaking in a Sunderland Bank Holiday tradition, queueing for the waste and recycling centre. Whether she had headed there was unclear. She could have dumped it in someone's wheelie bin or launched it into a hedge, as most others did with their rubbish. He rang again. Nothing.

This was pointless. Andrea had a good head start on him, and even if she was queuing, she'd be miles ahead. The traffic wasn't moving an inch, so he got out of the van to see if he could spot the Yaris. If he reached the brow of the hill, he'd get a clearer view of the queue. He walked along the grass and soon became the target of the beeping horns himself. Half a dozen cars ahead, someone dragged a mattress out of a Transit and deposited it on the verge.

"You can't dump that there," said Jack.

"Blame the fucking council, they're the ones who changed to fortnightly bin collections."

"What's bin collections got to do with it? You can't fit a bed in your bin."

"Blame our lass then, she's the one who wanted a new Slumberland." He slammed the back doors of the Transit and executed a blind three-point turn into oncoming traffic.

This allowed the traffic to shuffle up one, apart from Jack's van, which was empty. The beeping became constant. More people were abandoning their rubbish by the roadside, and most were turning around and leaving with cars still laden.

As he neared the top of the hill, there was a half mile queue to the tip. As if everyone was receiving free TVs there, instead of throwing stuff away. The Yaris wasn't in the queue; it was too late. Jack had lost the evidence and his fight was over before it had even begun. Then he spotted her. It wasn't in the queue because Andrea had arrived at the site. He climbed onto an abandoned wardrobe for a better look. She'd parked next to the electrical's skip. Jack sprinted back to the van, ignoring the abuse that was being sent his way. He couldn't race to the front. They'd lynch him. But he might get close enough to persuade her to change her mind. Hazard lights blinking and with his left hand planted onto the horn; Jack pulled into the wrong side of the road and raced over the hill. Traffic coming in the opposite direction were people leaving, foul moods simmering, and didn't take to Jack's freestyle interpretation of the Highway Code. If he bothered to look in his rear-view mirror, he'd see many drivers pile out of their cars to gesticulate at him. He didn't have time for that. Drivers at the front tensed as Jack's van approached. Normal, timid husbands were ready to morph into fighting machines at the thought of a queue jumper. Luckily for them, instead of veering left towards the entrance, he drove straight over the pavement and grass and parked by the fence. Andrea was still chatting to a hi viz wearing tip worker. He was flirting with her. Jack jumped onto the bonnet and clambered up to the roof, kneeling when he realised how high he was. "Andrea!"

If she heard him, she pretended she didn't, but with the horns blaring, skip lorries reversing and rubbish crashing into skips, it was unlikely his voice carried.

"Get down, you daft bastard." Another tip worker approached the fence.

"My wife, I need to speak to my wife." Jack pointed at Andrea. "She's chucking out my computer, and it has important work on it. I have to stop her."

"Too late, mate. Once it's crossed that threshold," he nodded to the entrance, "it becomes the property of the council."

"That's nonsense."

"Not nonsense, it's the law. We'd have chaos otherwise."

"And this fiasco isn't chaos?" Jack pointed to the queues and the blatant fly tipping.

"What happens out there's not my problem."

"How can it be the law that stuff over the threshold belongs to the council? My wife and her car are still there. You own them as well?"

The tip worker shrugged his shoulders. "I'm not a lawyer, pal."

At least Jack's protest had the desired effect of drawing

attention, and Andrea spotted him. She shook her head and got in the car. Jack slumped onto the Transit roof.

As Andrea left, she pulled up beside him. "What are you doing, Jack?"

"What am I doing? What are you doing? That laptop and USB were our only hope."

"Our only hope of what?"

"Saving the business, saving the school, saving the pigeons," said Jack.

"You need to give a long hard think about your priorities, Jack." Andrea looked towards Molly, talking to Arthur in the back of the car. "Because getting rid of them is the only way of saving our marriage."

Despite it being a Bank Holiday, Jack didn't return home and stewed in the office at the yard. Andrea had been unreasonable. This yard, and this business, was his dad's legacy, and she'd thrown it away. Without the documents on the USB stick, exposing Maurice was impossible, although he lacked a strategy on how to achieve that. He sat back in his chair, willing a plan to come to him, but his brain froze. His father's company was falling into the hands of a charlatan. One who presented it as a boost for the city to disguise it being little more than another money making exercise. Jack surveyed the yard, taking in what he stood to lose. The docks buzzed with life, and he pictured how the fences separating his yard from the port would soon disappear in the interests of progress.

Then a spark of inspiration ignited. Not one that prevented Maurice from stealing the firm, but at least one that took him on the first step towards it. He snatched an old rucksack, discarded in his office, along with his black woolly hat and a torch, and dashed to the tool shed to complete his inventory. Once he identified what he was after, he waited until dusk descended.

Jack returned to the tip and parked where he'd been before and switched off his headlights and the engine. Whilst unsure of the legal status of what he'd done when clearing Reggie's, he was in no doubt as to the criminality of his current intentions. The tip was vast, with the area open to the public only a tiny part of the enterprise. A huge landfill site spread out into the distance, lit solely by moonlight. Faint lights shone by the office buildings, and it surprised him to see movement at this time of night, but it was the headquarters of Maurice's organisation. Signs on the wall suggested a private security firm guarded the site, but as it consisted of nothing but rubbish, they'd concentrated on activities at the far end, guarding the building. CCTV cameras watched the site, none of which pointed outward, and the darkness hid Jack's van.

He removed his hat, pulling it over his face, recognising his first flawed step, as it had no eyeholes. He checked the glove compartment for something to use but didn't find a suitable implement, so he pulled the bolt cutters from his backpack. Cutting eyeholes into a wooly hat with bolt cutters, illuminated by the moon's glow, proved as difficult as balancing peas on a chopstick. Jack dripped with sweat and wasted fifteen minutes by the time he managed what should have been a simple task. Maybe the criminal lifestyle wasn't for him. The holes weren't the perfect distance apart, but they had to do.

Torch in hand, he walked back along the grass verge, away from the tip until he located what he sought. The Sunderland fly tippers hadn't disappointed, and he dragged the mattress towards the van where he heaved it onto the roof. The added benefit of it being dark was having no perception of height. He wasn't sure if this helped with his vertigo, but he had no choice. He was going over the fence.

With a great deal of struggling and manoeuvring, he lay the mattress across the barbed wire that topped the chain-mail. A tip he'd learned from watching many Mexican drug mule documentaries. Jack blanked out any thoughts of his altitude, clambered atop the bed, and eased himself over the barbed wire. He swung his foot around and got a hand grip on the chain-link fence. Whilst descending, the fear of what he was doing wrestled with the realisation of how high he was and he froze six feet from the ground. His legs shook, his heart raced and sweat flowed out of him like water from a defrosting freezer. He needed to put one foot in front of the other and lower himself, but terror paralysed him.

Jack gripped the fence, his nose pushed right up to it and his fingers aching until the pain became unbearable. His body decided for him as he lost his grip and slid downwards, landing in a heap at the bottom. No injuries apart from a chain-mail pattern on his cheek and scraped shins. No vicious attack dogs came for him, or armed guards as much as he could tell. He got his bearings and set off for the electrical's skip. Three steps in and the security lights blazed.

"Idiot," thought Jack. Motion-sensors. At least his forward thinking with the homemade balaclava hid his face.

The electrical's skip, unlike the others where you threw the rubbish in the top, was enclosed with a door on the side secured by a padlock. Jack didn't have long before the lighting drew attention, so he grabbed his bolt cutters and started work on the lock. Not being a seasoned criminal, it was harder work than he realised, and five long minutes passed before he broke the lock.

Once inside, he encountered his next problem. Wall to wall laptops, PCs and monitors. It may have been easier to concentrate on the laptops if he had the faintest idea what distinguished Reggie's laptop from the others. There was no backtracking. He had to try. It must be near the top, as Andrea only dropped it there a few hours ago. He grabbed the first ten from each pile and inspected them, discarding any too big or too small or the wrong colour. This left him with half a dozen, and he feared having to start them and test the passwords. Then he noticed the sticker, a lollipop, that's the one.

Jack faced the same dilemma with the memory sticks. A child's plastic bucket was full. Not as many as there were laptops, but it contained hundreds. He didn't have time to search every one so tipped them into his backpack along with the laptop and sprinted to the fence.

He spotted a bus outside the offices that wasn't parked up before and several people disembarked. Jack could swear the discussions he heard were foreign, but shouting silenced them and they entered a large warehouse.

A more pressing concern for Jack was the dogs barking in the near distance and the voices of the guards weren't far off. He had to be quick. There was only one problem, the security lights highlighted just how high the obstacle was, and he had little to no chance of climbing it. Panicking, sweating, and holding an assortment of unknown content on the memory sticks in his bag, he had to escape.

In the middle of a tip; the solution surrounded him. He gathered as many items of furniture, suitcases, bed frames and bits of wood he could recover to make a makeshift staircase. Not tall enough, but once he'd added the pair of rusty stepladders he'd found, he should be able to reach the top. That was if he wasn't shitting it in dread of scaling the height.

The two German Shepherds hurtling in his direction

outweighed his fear of heights as he sprinted up the ladders, which fell as he grasped the mattress. He hauled himself up and toppled over the other side, landing on the van roof with a tremendous clang. Winded, he tumbled to the ground, got in the driver's seat and sped away without switching on his headlights. Only then realising that the bolt cutters could have had him through the barricade in seconds. He had the laptop and the USB stick again. He had the plans.

Now he had to plan himself. Plan to expose Maurice and save his business.

Chapter Fourteen

A brown bar in Amsterdam was an odd place for Jack to go public with his plot to topple Maurice Groom and his criminal cohorts. To Jack, the Annual Pigeon Club outing was the ideal time to declare his intentions. He needed to discuss it far from prying eyes and ears, not least Andrea's. It was therefore safer for him to announce it in a foreign country.

The communications breakdown between him and Andrea was absolute. The couple had not spoken a word since she'd dumped the laptop, and he'd not bothered to remind her of his trip. There were no guarantees she'd still be home when he returned. But when she discovered he'd retrieved the laptop and was proceeding with his plans, she'd murder him. Jack knew there was a genuine risk of him coming to harm at the hands of Maurice's associates, but he wasn't standing by to watch them take everything his father had built. He couldn't stop them on his own. And that's where the pigeon club helped.

"I thought we'd agreed on no politics on this trip," said Bill Tindall, a stickler for rules.

"It's not politics, it's our lives, my business, our pigeons," said Jack.

"Sounds like politics to me." Bill rolled a cigarette.

"You're happy with them taking our lofts off us?"

"They're not our lofts."

"Of course they're ours. Who else's would they be?"

"The land belongs to the council, always has done, we just lease it."

"You're chairman of the sodding club, Bill. You're meant to be sticking up for us."

"Sticking up for what? We can't block the council selling the land." Bill shoved the tab behind his ear and gulped his beer. "Still not as good as British lager. Can't beat a good pint of Fosters."

"Tradition, Bill, the club's been on that site for a hundred years. There are lofts still used that passed through the generations. You're going to stand by and let that happen?"

"Nowt we can do, lad."

"That's bollocks and you know it. There's nowt you want to do, there's a big difference."

"Times are changing, Jack. The club's on its arse. The young uns aren't interested in pigeons. Too busy on their phones on Faceache and Twatter and those other social media whatnots. They're only engaged in taking selfies, they don't have the dedication to look after a bird."

"We'll never find out if the club doesn't exist."

"Who said it won't exist? We could move."

"They're homing pigeons, Bill. Where do they live when we shift? We'll need to train them again." The lack of interest shown by the chairman exasperated Jack.

"We'll need to train them, will we? Who's this we? You're

never there. You've had Reggie looking after your flock until he took a tumble from the tiles. How will you manage now when you're on your fancy jaunts abroad?"

"They're not fancy jaunts, it's my job. I'll get one of the lads to step in and help. Like Bazza, he's looking after them whilst we're out here."

"Where is Bazza? How was he not on the bus?"

"Had his passport confiscated."

"By the police, what's he done?"

"Worse than the coppers, his lass. Got her eyes on the photos of last year's jaunt to Hamburg. Not a chance of her letting him loose in Amsterdam."

"Oof ya bugger. Have you seen his wife? Amazed she didn't confiscate his knackers." Bill crossed his legs at the thought. "But that's the point, Jack. We can't even fill our annual trip away. There was a time when we had to draw lots to decide who got a seat. Now we've had to bulk it out with non-bird lads. Where did you dig them up?" Bill nodded to the table of misfits in the corner.

"Wherever I could find them. There's also that fat idiot Derek who works in the garage down the yard. If he hadn't paid up weeks ago, I wouldn't let him anywhere near the trip. Lucky I didn't hoy him over the side of the ferry but least said about that cretin the better. At least we've lost him to a bit of window shopping in the red-light district. The bloke in the duffle coat is Angus, a battle reenactment enthusiast. He approached us, asked if he could come along as there were loads of interesting battle sites he wanted to explore."

"Looks as if he's exploring more than battle sites."

Whilst sat with the others, he had positioned his chair to catch a better view of the naked sixteen-stone black woman in the window across the road. She beckoned him with her index finger.

"Aye, suspect he'll be charging into battle soon. The lad in the bright gear, is Karl, Bazza's cousin. Took his place."

"Why's he wearing cycling gear? Did he bring his bike? Didn't notice it on the bus."

"No, he's obsessed. Wanted us to fly to Paris instead, so he could sample the Tour de France route. Said he's hiring a bike later."

"He's fuelling up for a lengthy ride," said Bill.

Karl swallowed his drink in one, then spread mayonnaise on his third bowl of pommes frites.

"He'll be in a canal before the moon shows its face."

"The club can't survive like this, Jack. Back in the day, we had footy cards, bingo, raffles, all sorts happening on the bus trip, but these kids aren't invested. They have their own interests, their own obsessions. We can't compete."

Bill lifted his cap and scratched his head. He dressed the same way for every away day, identical whenever Jack saw him. Navy blue v-neck with a bare but hairy chest underneath. Supermarket jeans that lost colour and shape by the minute and were hanging off his arse, and a polished pair of black shoes. The outfit topped off with a tweed flat cap.

"You might be willing to let the club die, Bill," said Jack as he stood and downed his lager, "but I'm not. I'm fighting until the last feather falls."

Jack's hopes of persuading his pigeon club colleagues to help in his battle with Maurice were diminishing by the minute. The majority on the excursion hadn't even negotiated their way to the first bar. Half went in search of a recommended coffee shop for their weed, and it was doubtful he would see them again all weekend. It was obvious on the bus that fifty per cent were drinkers and the others were smokers and their paths were unlikely to cross. Of the ones heading out for a drink, the red-light district distracted a sizeable chunk as they disappeared into 'Europe's Largest Erotic Supermarket'. Jack needed to lay off the booze on Sunday, so he was fit to drive the next morning, and he hoped to make the most of Saturday.

He knew the city well and looked for the zany t-shirts, dropping his shoulder in the opposite direction to avoid the bars frequented by the squads of marauding stag parties. He'd chosen a traditional brown bar on the outskirts of the red-light district. Close enough to the action that those exploring alternative pleasures could dip in when they wanted refreshment, but far enough away they didn't have to endure the antics of young men who considered spotting a pair of naked breasts in a shop window to be the cultural equivalent of visiting the Taj Mahal or Iguassu Falls.

Whilst satisfied with his choice of hostelry, the company had its imperfections.

Bill's outright refusal to become part of Jack's campaign disappointed him. Most of the remaining pigeon lads partaking in alternative activities lumbered Jack with the stragglers and the hangers-on. And now Karl had left them. Refreshed with six large Amstels and four bowls of pommes frites, he was ready for his tour and was outside limbering up. Even in a city such as Amsterdam, with its many attractions and distractions, someone in a full Team Sky replica cycling kit, without a bike, raised eyebrows.

He balanced his left leg on the bottom bar of the fence leading from the bridge opposite the bar. Karl aimed for a higher rail but had neither the flexibility nor the soberness to carry out such a manoeuvre. He stretched his bulky hamstring, then repeated the exercise with his other leg. It was when he attempted to touch his toes he attracted the most attention, with a distracted girl swerving her bike into the wall of the bridge. Cycles whizzed past left and right, and for such a cycling fanatic, he was unaware of their existence.

Karl then began his shuttle runs. To the nearest lamppost and back. Then the second and back. And third and so on until he was dripping in sweat and his head resembling the skin colour of an Edam cheese. He steadied himself on the railings, hurling his lunch over the side to the cheers of a hen do passing on the far bank of the canal. The tourists in the barge below had their enthusiasm muted by the sudden arrival of digested Dutch potato in their hair.

Before getting embroiled in an altercation, he boarded his hire bike. Not a carbon fibre racing machine sported by his heroes, but a one-speed, no-brake cycle from the forties with a basket and a bell. He set off on his ride, weaving in and out of pedestrians and other cyclists, or forcing them to weave around him. Jack wasn't confident they'd ever see Karl again, and he realised his plans of announcing his intentions in Amsterdam were over before he'd uttered a word.

His fellow weekend trippers were no more capable of helping him take on Maurice and his criminal syndicate than they were of helping him fly to the moon. He was screwed.

Jack bought another drink. If one thing could rescue this trip, it was the quality of the unfiltered lager. Far superior to the beer he got at home. Maybe four or five more of these would give him the required inspiration. Contrary to Jack's expectations, Angus had not sloped off to meet the dark-skinned prostitute over the road and joined Jack at his table. Angus slid a paperback over to him. "Have you read this?"

Jack didn't read much, so knew the answer before he picked up The Art of War by Sun Tzu. "Can't say I have. Was there a film of it?"

"Read it sixteen times now."

"You surprise me." Jack doubted his life choices at this stage.

"Even own an original Chinese copy."

"You speak Chinese?"

"No."

"What's it about?" Jack had no means of escape, so he might as well accommodate him.

"The art of war."

"Yeah, it hints that on the cover."

"You should study it." Angus took something from his pocket and put it in his mouth, spilling crumbs on the floor. The debris on his duffle coat suggested he'd consumed a significant portion of whatever it was.

"To be honest, mate. I'd come to Amsterdam to relax, have a session and a laugh with the lads. I hadn't planned on brushing up on my literacy skills."

"I overheard you talking to Bill regarding your little problem."

"Little problem?"

"With the businessman and your pigeons. I could help."

"I'm not sure it's something you want to get involved in," said Jack before taking a big gulp of his pint.

"If you're getting into a war, you need an expert in your camp."

"You been in many wars?"

"No, but I've studied every single one, and all the winning tactics," Angus tapped the book, "originate inside here."

Angus discussed battle strategy at great length whilst nibbling on whatever was in his pocket. A qualified archaeologist, he was far from an idiot, but Jack was struggling to follow what he was telling him. His twitchy behaviour, glancing over his shoulder before giggling to himself, and leaping from his chair at the slightest sound, were not the actions of a rational man. Angus advising Jack he could overcome the biggest of foes with the advice from this single publication, whilst at the same time jumping at the sight of his own shadow was contradictory. Jack concluded that not everyone realised how strong European lager could be. Maybe he should buy a copy of the book and read it himself, see if it made better sense than Angus.

The doors crashed open, and Karl bounded into the bar. The shock sending Angus crashing to the floor.

"Fully refreshed now," said Karl.

The unmissable bulge in his lycra shorts hinted he had taken a shine to pedalling the cobbled streets of Amsterdam. Or he'd enjoyed refreshment in one of Amsterdam's better known establishments.

After returning to his seat, Angus called him over to their table. "We're going to war."

"We've only been in Europe a couple hours and you've started a war? Doesn't take much."

"Not here, when we get home." He tapped the paperback. "Jack here is in a spot of bother and requires our assistance." His brain spun, and he grabbed the table top as his eyes rolled up into their lids.

"You're off your tits," said Karl.

"Needs our help. Nasty men, commandeering the docks and his business." His world was spinning. "Pigeon lofts. Need a strategy."

"No, I mean properly off your fucking tits. What have you

been smoking?"

"I haven't tried smoking since that incident in the bus shelter when I was thirteen. Terrible smell. Terrible mess."

"Hold on," said Jack, "never mind what you've been smoking. What have you been eating?"

"Eating?" The question baffled Angus..

"You've been nibbling away on something since we got here. In your pocket."

"This?" He pulled out the last corner of a chocolate brownie. "Passed a delightful cake shop on the way here and couldn't resist. Bloody expensive, but worth it. So Moorish."

"For Christ's sake." Jack put his head in his hands.

"What's this war he's babbling about?" said Karl.

"Someone is planning on expanding the port, taking over my firm and closing the school and pigeon lofts."

"They'll leave the cycle path, though?"

"What cycle path?"

"The one that goes past the lofts and onto the coast?"

Cyclists rode by when Jack was feeding the pigeons, but he took no notice. "I guess that disappears along with the rest."

"Bollocks to that, I'm seconds off beating my personal best on that route. They can take that path from my cold dead cleats."

This was Jack's army. A deviant, Bradley Wiggins wannabe, and a spaced out archaeologist in a duffle coat. No matter how many books he read, it was hardly Genghis Khan and his Mongol hordes.

Chapter Fifteen

Jack walked up the aisle counting heads. Whilst he'd instructed everyone what time the coach was leaving, there were always stragglers. Drink and dope, stronger than people were accustomed to at home, created a few casualties, but Jack was relieved to find he was only one body short. It didn't surprise him to discover it was Derek.
"Fucking idiot."

Jack checked his watch and rang Derek's mobile. No answer.

"Gan without the fat twat," said a croaky voice from the back seats.

Jack wished he could, but he had responsibilities and always built in contingency, giving latecomers an unofficial half an hour leeway before he left without them. Few had seen much of Derek since they arrived. He'd been observed going into various strip clubs and visiting ladies who adorned the many windows of Amsterdam's streets. Yet nobody remembered having a drink with him. Jack tried his number again.

He answered, out of breath. "Sorry, slept in, I'll be two minutes."

Jack stuck his head out of the door and spotted the unmistakable shape of Derek waddling towards them, dragging his suitcase across the gravel. "Boot's open, shut it behind you once you've hoyed your bag on and drag your fat, lazy arse on the bus."

After an abundance of banging and crashing, the luggage compartment slammed shut and Derek clambered aboard, sweating and gasping for air. The rest of the group gave out ironic cheers and applause. He waved and plonked himself in the first seat he found. Everyone accounted for it was departure time, but there was one last check for Jack to complete. He stood in the middle of the aisle, facing the rear of the coach. "We're all adults, so I shouldn't be having this conversation, but I've been on enough of these trips to know the score. Before we set off—"

"Yes, I've been to the toilet," shouted someone at the back to rounds of laughter.

Jack chuckled at the interruption. "As I was saying, before we set off, I want you to check your pockets to make sure you haven't accidentally brought stuff aboard you shouldn't have. Little goodies Amsterdam tolerates might not be so welcome with UK customs officials." He scanned the group and checked faces. There was invariably at least one, and he needed to work out who was attempting to smuggle a treat home with them.
"Angus, you've not been brownie shopping again, have you?" Again, the bus burst into laughter. Angus was still green after his incident with the space cake on Saturday and hadn't escaped his bed on Sunday. "I'm sticking to Greggs from now on."

"Anyone else? Last chance. Remember, it's not just yourself you're putting at risk, it's my business and the club's reputation. Don't forget, they have sniffer dogs."

This had the desired effect, and one of the younger lads

spoke. "Err, yeah, just discovered this, I forgot about it." He held up a small packet of cannabis resin.

"Sling it off the bus, son," said Jack.

"Ahh, man. It's Isolator, you can't get it back at home. Cost me thirty notes."

Jack pointed to the door, and the young lad threw the dope towards the bin.

"Anybody else?" Jack examined the faces one last time. Derek's shifty demeanour was worrying, but not a surprise. "Derek, you sure you've got nothing?"

"Nowt." He shook his head without making eye contact and looked towards the floor.

Jack remained unconvinced but wasn't against the fat knacker getting arrested when they got home, so he took his word for it. The doors closed with a hiss, and they departed for the ferry. It was only a half hour journey to the port, and whilst the first five minutes were boisterous. It soon settled to snoring and farting.

The crossing's infamy for being a riotous affair enhanced itself on the way out. Jack wanted to avoid everyone and bury his face in the pillow for as much of the fifteen-hour crossing as possible. He ordered waffles and a sandwich and retired to his cabin, hoping the seas weren't too rough. He dozed, but his mind churned with thoughts of what he must do to tackle Maurice. And how he had to do it without the help of the folk he'd considered mates in the pigeon club. The only people he could rely upon were Angus and Karl, who he'd just met, and neither of them struck him as the reliable types.

Andrea was right. Maybe he should concede defeat.

Back on the bus, Jack did another head count, surprised to find everyone had survived the crossing intact. A few were groggy from their mammoth drinking session, but they'd at least showed up on time. There'd been checks on boarding the boat, but he offered the group a last chance to dispose of any contraband they shouldn't have on them. There were no takers.

As the bus approached customs, Jack glanced in the rear-view mirror for any signs of worry on his passengers' faces. There was only one, Derek.

"Bloody moron," thought Jack.

He chatted with the customs official whilst keeping one eye on Derek in the mirror. His skin colour was now alternating between red and green. He was sweating, and it was coming out in waves bigger than the ones they'd seen on the North Sea. He held one hand across his face as if it shielded his fat cheeks from view. If he got caught with hash on him, he was on his own. Jack was throwing him to the wolves.

The official walked towards the rear of the bus, checking passports. Derek's drowned in sweat when his shaking hand passed it to him. The border agent eyed him with suspicion. "Pleasant trip?"

Derek wasn't sure his mouth could still work. "Aye."

"Young Derek has over indulged," said Bill, "poor lad doesn't venture out much without his mam."

The bus reverberated in laughter again.

The agent shook his head and handed Derek his passport, continuing his inspection, checking the rest. As he returned, Derek stared straight ahead, his fingers clasping the headrest of the seat in front. He felt a hand grab his shoulder.

"Thanks everyone," said the official, "have a safe journey home and try not to let your mate here be sick on himself." He nodded and left the bus, giving Jack one last wave, showing he was free to go.

Jack was fuming, but now wasn't the time. He'd tackle Derek later.

As soon as they were on the dual carriageway, Derek asked for a comfort break. "I'm busting for a piss."

"It's less than an hour until we're home," said Jack, "I don't care if you soil yourself."

"I could do with one myself," said Bill.

"Fuck's sake," said Jack as he pulled into the first lay-by.

Once one needed the toilet, they all did, and they filed off in single file, forming a line, one big pissing fountain.

As Bill let out a big fart, someone pushed past him and tumbled down the bank, then another, and another. Soon there were half a dozen men and women sprinting through the rivers of piss and into the trees.

"Where the fucking hell did they come from?" said Bill.

Jack jumped from the bus to investigate the commotion. "Who's opened that?" The luggage compartment was wide open. "What's just happened?"

As they explained the tale to him, Jack sat on the bus step shaking. Part rage, part fear. He'd become involved in people smuggling, bringing illegal immigrants into the country. He could lose his business, could even end up in prison. No matter how innocent he thought he was, the onus was on him to check his bus for stowaways. He'd been in the game long enough to understand the rules. Crossing the channel from Calais was a nightmare. In the past he'd had people on the roof, even tied to the axle with their own belts. But the stowaways hid in the baggage hold. How could he fall for that? He'd put the bags on himself and there was no opportunity for people to climb aboard on the half-hour trip to the ferry port. It was impossible.

But he hadn't put every bag on himself. He'd kept the

compartment open for one latecomer. Derek.

Jack lunged at him, "You fucking idiot."

Bill dragged him off.

"What have I done?" Derek's plea wasn't convincing.

"I will have you, I swear to God if it's the last thing I do I'll finish you."

"Can everyone calm their jets, please?" said Bill. "There's no harm done. Six or seven more of the buggers won't make a vast difference to anyone. There's no CCTV cameras around here, so if everyone keeps their gobs shut, who's to know?"

Jack booted a can into the shrubs. "It's my bus. Illegals on my bloody bus. If this gets out, I'm finished."

"It won't get out," said Bill, "will it, lads?"

Everyone shook their heads, but Jack knew the truth would come out given time. An amusing tale from a lad's weekend. What incentive did they have to keep it quiet? He only hoped it got dismissed as folklore, one of those urban legends that do the rounds. The story sounded so ridiculous; it was unbelievable. But it wasn't as ludicrous as it appeared. It had happened.

"Whatever." Jack climbed aboard the bus and the others followed.

Derek was last to board, and Jack closed the doors just before he did. He indicated to pull out.

"Don't be a twat, Jack," said Bill, "if there's one way for this story to go public, it's leaving that dozy fuckwit in the lay-by."

Jack opened the door again, and Derek clambered aboard without making eye contact with Jack or anybody else. Jack eased into the traffic, desperate to jettison his passengers and get home, if he still had one.

The doors hissed as they opened, signalling the last drop off for

Jack. Desperate to drop the bus back at the yard and get home, he still had one last job.

"Just a sec, Derek."

Derek pretended he hadn't heard and filed towards the exit with the other stragglers. Jack placed a firm hand on his shoulder and guided him into one of the front seats. "This won't take long."

"I've got to go. I'm late for my lift," said Derek.

"Should have thought about that before you requested that unscheduled piss stop."

"I need to be away. You can tell me whatever it is at work next week."

"There'll be no work next week."

"What?" Derek was rarely far away from confusion, and he was struggling to understand what he'd been told.

"You're finished. You're lucky I didn't bounce your arse out of the gate after the brakes fiasco, but I gave you the benefit of the doubt. But this stunt—"

"What stunt?"

"You're a shit mechanic. The lads all hate you and you stink. There's your three strikes, you're gone."

"I can't help the smell. It's a sweat disorder. That's discrimination."

"Happy to discuss it in your tribunal, but I hope you have good representation."

"You can't sack me, you don't know who you're dealing with."

"Mr Blobby's illegitimate brother? I think I can handle that."

"You'll regret this."

"I regret not doing it a long time ago. If I ever see you within a hundred yards of one of my vehicles, I'll run you down, then reverse over you just to check my suspension is working. Get out of my sight." Jack grabbed Derek and hurled him down the steps of the bus. Much to the surprise of the shoppers stood at the bus stop.

Derek grabbed his bag from the hold just before the automatic doors shut on him and he aimed a punch at the bus. Jack pulled away, watching in the rear-view mirror as Derek's pathetic body crumpled into a heap after tripping on his own bag.

With one of his foes defeated, Jack knew he had much tougher challenges ahead.

**

Chapter Sixteen

It surprised Jack to discover the doorbell worked. The overgrown garden of Harold Beeston's home had weeds growing so tall they obscured the front window. They'd have blocked Harold's view had the curtains been opened. Various bits of rusting metal merged with the undergrowth, empty pizza boxes and kebab wrappers. Jack thought a rat scurried over his foot, but couldn't be certain.

After he undid a series of bolts and locks, the door creaked open and Harold's eyes adjusted from the gloom indoors to the bright spring sunshine outside. Recognising Jack, he nodded and walked back inside without speaking. Jack hesitated, then followed, closing the door behind him but not bothering to wipe his feet. Boxes, carrier bags, old electronics, newspapers and magazines filled every spare inch. The staircase housed cartons to the top landing, and an old filing cabinet blocked the entrance to the cupboard under the stairs. There wasn't even room for him to negotiate the hall, and he had to edge sideways until he reached the kitchen.

"Tea?" said Harold.

Jack surveyed the room. "No thanks, I've just had one."

Harold shrugged, filled the kettle and placed it on the gas hob. An old radio sat open on the kitchen table with an expensive looking set of tools beside it.

"Stopped working?" said Jack, nodding towards the radio.

"In a manner of speaking." Harold pointed to a battered kitchen chair.

Jack dragged the chair out, contemplated giving it a wipe before sitting, but considered it impolite.

"I got your note." He brandished it in his hand.

"So you did." Harold squeezed the tea bag against the side of the cup. Then, instead of putting it straight in the bin, he dropped it in the back of a small model train carriage that rested on rail tracks on the kitchen bench. He joined Jack at the table.

"Bit mysterious, handwritten notes posted in the middle of the night," said Jack.

"Depends on your definition of mystery."

"Why did—" The train distracted Jack as it rolled along the railways, stopping after the bend at the end of the bench. The carriage tipped to one side, depositing the tea bag into a pedal bin that opened itself. It then circled the bread bin and returned to its starting position. "Did you build that?"

He took a sip of tea, staring at Jack. "It's a hobby of mine."

"I'm sure you haven't brought me here to show me your train set. What's this message about?"

"Did you tell anyone you were coming here?"

"Why would I?" said Jack.

"Did anybody see you arrive, anybody lurking who shouldn't be?"

"There could have been a Japanese sniper hiding in the

garden, but he was difficult to spot."

"Reggie Higgins."

"What about him?"

"He's not what he seemed."

"I gathered he might not be the jovial angel he portrayed," Jack thought back to congregation at the funeral, "few people are."

"Let me show you something." Harold pulled a Weetabix box from the cupboard, spilling the contents onto the table. Wheat biscuits way past their sell by date, and a laptop that wasn't.

In contrast to the other belongings in the house, it looked modern and expensive, far newer than the Weetabix biscuits.

"It's a novel laptop case, I'll give you that."

"Let's go in the living room." Harold grabbed the laptop and entered the room via sliding doors.

He'd dotted mismatched pieces of Seventies furniture throughout the place, a sofa and two chairs, a sideboard and a coffee table. A Sanyo television and what resembled a Betamax video recorder dominated the corner. More boxes and half-fixed electrical appliances littered the room. The only part of the house anywhere near tidy was the top of the sideboard, which housed a photograph in a frame. A couple, in their thirties or forties. The woman petite and graceful, Chinese or possibly Thai, and the man, resplendent in a suit, could, at a push, be Harold. It was hard to reconcile the smiling, healthy gentleman in the photo with the mess stood before Jack now. Similar to everything else in the house, it might be junk Harold had picked up over the years.

Jack didn't ask.

Harold opened the laptop and swung it around so it was facing Jack. "What do you see?"

The screen showed what appeared to be a live stream from a CCTV camera. "Is that your kitchen?"

"Let's see." Harold pressed a couple keys, and the film rewound to a point where Jack was at the kitchen table.

"I didn't notice any cameras."

"Funny that." He clicked more buttons and different camera views flickered onto the screen. Jack standing at the front door viewed from the doorbell. Jack walking along the path viewed from the overgrown thistles.

"I missed every one."

"Were you looking?"

"No, but—"

"That's the beauty. Hide them where people least expect to discover them."

"Another hobby."

"Not a hobby."

"Your job?" Jack struggled to hide his surprise.

"Used to be," Harold closed the laptop, "amongst other things."

"Incredible, I had no idea."

"Few do."

"I assumed you were—" Jack attempted to find the right word.

"Mad?"

"Lonely."

"Aye, well," he made the briefest glance towards the photo on the sideboard, "it keeps me busy."

"Locomotives and video, fascinating stuff," said Jack, "but what's it got to do with me, with Reggie?"

"I shouldn't be talking to you, Jack." Harold glanced over his shoulder. "It goes against my training."

"Training?"

"Reggie worked for a band of deeply unpleasant

individuals."

"The council?"

"He thought he'd escaped the criminal life, he had escaped it, but his North Eastern hideaway became known. Sure as shit follows Sunday, his former colleagues in London needed someone up here."

"I get it. He may not have been the clean-cut lollipop man we got to know. I don't understand where you come into it."

"He asked me to build him a camera, Jack. A camera that will get us in a whole heap of trouble."

"Maybe I will take that cuppa." Jack had plenty to digest.

Harold busied himself in the kitchen. "This stays between the two of us, Jack."

"But I don't get it. What was he filming?"

"The less you know, the better."

"Why tell me anything?"

"Because you're touched by it, Jack. Implicated, even. You need to understand what you're walking into."

"What did you build the camera into? How did you disguise it?"

"Again, you don't need the details. I told you as a courtesy. You seem to be a decent bloke, I don't wish to see you tumbling off a roof."

"Tumbling off a roof? Reggie's death was an accident. Wasn't it?"

"These people, they're not the same as you and I, not you at least. They're ruthless." Harold handed Jack his tea. The train set off again. "Reggie realised who he was dealing with. That's why he got the camera. Insurance."

"Insurance against what?" said Jack.

"What did you find, Jack?"

"Find?"

"You've been making your mouth go with Maurice. It's common knowledge. They know you've found something, but they have no idea what, other than something links it to Reggie. What I need to confirm is whether you discovered the camera." Harold's dismissive tone had become very serious.

Jack placed his cup on the formica. "Who did you say you worked for?"

"I'm freelance, but that's not important. You're in no danger from me as long as I am in no danger from you. It won't take much to link the camera back to me and that could cause major issues."

"I don't have it."

"Rich Tea?" Harold offered the packet to Jack.

"And that's that? I don't have the camera so conversation over?"

"I believe you, so there's nothing more to say. Enjoy your cuppa."

"There's everything to say. Reggie's dead. Me and my daughter escaped death by a fanny's hair. A set of crooks is plotting to ruin my business, and now Hoardy of Hoard Hall reveals himself as this undercover electrical genius. This conversation is far from finished."

"Hoardy of Hoard Hall?" Harold nodded, as if appreciating the nickname. "You're in way over your hairpiece as it is, Jack. Don't make it worse."

"How could it get worse?"

"There are no accidents. Everything happens for a reason. If you keep digging, you'll provoke a load more mishaps."

"Who says I'm digging?"

"Your minor break-in at the tip." Harold dunked the end of his Rich Tea and caught it in his mouth just before it snapped.

"How did you—" Jack didn't bother denying it.

"Look around you." He pointed at the boxes and junk. "Where do you think I spend ninety per cent of my time? I covered for you, pretended I was after bits and pieces. The security guards see me as a novelty, a curiosity. Not worth the paperwork from calling the police, so they sent me off with a stern warning and a gob full of insults."

"Thanks."

"No need to thank me, but avoid the tip. It's nothing but trouble."

"You're not the first person to warn me."

"Time you listened, dealing with security guards is one thing but… just stay away, Jack."

Jack nodded. "How do you know Reggie?"

"Our paths crossed in the past, mutual acquaintances."

"And you stumbled into each other on Sunderland's shores. How did that happen?"

"He was hiding, I was searching."

"You were looking for Reggie?"

"A happy coincidence. He admired my skill set and called upon my help when he realised what he was being dragged into, couldn't handle it alone."

"What were they dragging him into?" said Jack.

"You ask a lot of questions."

"You hide a lot of answers."

"It's stuff you don't want to be involved in, stuff neither of us wants to be involved in. Take the hint and walk away now."

"Do you think Maurice Groom scares me?"

"Nobody is frightened of Maurice Groom." Harold

wandered into the kitchen and rinsed his cup. "He thinks he's in charge, but he's being used, as Reggie was, as we all are."

"How come you're so well informed? You have these skills, your training, yet you live…" Jack gestured to the mess, "amongst this."

Harold shrugged. "I'm comfortable with the way I live. I'm hiding in plain sight. If it wasn't for bumping into Reggie, I'd stay unseen."

"Hiding in plain sight? Blending in isn't your style."

"That's the intention. Everyone sees me, but they take no notice. Ever seen a performance poet? That's me. They laugh at my expense, point and mock my eccentricities, but they keep their distance because, by Christ, nobody wants to get stuck in a conversation with me."

"Have you always lived alone?"

"Finished there?" Harold took Jack's cup from him and picked up the Rich Teas.

Harold closed the door behind Jack and locked up, double checking everything. He sighed, squeezed past the filing cabinet and went back in the sitting room where he glanced once more at the picture on the sideboard.

The back garden matched the one at the front, overgrown but with trees lining the fences blocking out the view from the neighbours. Harold negotiated his way around the decrepit lawn mower and decaying garden furniture, stepping over abandoned tools until he came to the solitary maintained piece of grass. Manicured to perfection, it was six foot by three foot but was invisible from the house, an overhanging rose bush obscuring it from the upstairs window. He snipped off a pink rose, took in the aroma, and laid it on the grave.

Chapter Seventeen

After the shenanigans on the Amsterdam trip, it surprised Jack to find Karl and Angus still wanted to help in derailing the plans. With everything that had gone on since, he was regretting involving them. Was it fair to put them in jeopardy to fight his battles? Jack hoped they'd have second thoughts, but their determination remained undiminished. If only he could use their enthusiasm. They'd been badgering him by phone and text, even turning up at his workplace, eager to help. So he'd assigned them to monitor the tip. There was no genuine reason other than Maurice owned it, and he suspected something more than waste disposal was going on there.

They'd dragged along another recruit, Harriet. Jack had asked them to keep the information to themselves until he figured out what was happening. But Angus had assured him Harriet was a close friend and ally with multiple online campaigns under her belt. He attempted to convince Jack that she'd be invaluable in drumming up local support when the time came. Her jam jar bottomed glasses, unkempt hair and fleece depicting a lone wolf under a full moon left him unconvinced.

Jack had sent them on their way with instructions to stay out of sight and keep out of danger. Instructions they neither understood nor followed.

Discretion was not in Karl's nature. A Lycra outfit even more garish than the one he sported in Amsterdam, matched with a very expensive racing bike and Tron style helmet, was never likely to go unnoticed. Especially as he circuited the perimeter of the site, stopping after each lap to look at his watch and scribble something in his little notepad. After his fourth circuit, they had written him off as a nutter after a personal best time and ignored him.

Harriet was harder to avoid. They knew her well, and her presence was more than unwelcome.
Amongst her multitude of online crusades, the one that garnered the most publicity, and still did, was her crusade against fortnightly bin collections. The entire city whipped into a frenzy when they changed from once a week. When they handed the contract to a private firm, her constant questioning forced Maurice Groom into PR overdrive. They could trace his headlong rush into charitable activities back to Harriet's campaign.

If Maurice Groom disliked Harriet, his employees despised her. Unable to distinguish between decision-makers and those on the frontline, she thought nothing of harassing and berating low-paid workers on bin rounds or working at the tip, brandishing her ever present litter picker whilst her Yorkshire Terrier snapped at their heels.

"Oh, for fuck's sake, here's Worzel Gummidge," said one worker when he saw her determined march up the hill towards the entrance.

"Have you seen that mess?" she said, pointing her picker toward the hedgerows and the fly tipping.

"Can't say I have." He tried his best to ignore her and launched a wayward chair into a skip.

"It's a disgrace, someone should do something about it."

"Do something then."

"It's not my job." Harriet attempted to square up to him, but her significant height deficit meant her thick glasses faced his belly button.

"Nor mine, love." He pointed to the fence. "Behind this, me. Out there, some bugger else." He picked up a sizeable piece of cardboard that had blown from the recycling skip.

"That's not good enough."

"I don't give a toss."

"You can't talk to me in that manner. I'm a council tax payer."

"This may come as a surprise to you, but so am I. If we're playing this game, you're not allowed to speak to me in that tone either."

This flummoxed Harriet but didn't deter her. "I pay your wages."

"I can see why my pay's so crap, then. You've been spending your cash on shampoo and fancy clothes."

Karl whizzed by on his bike, distracting them.

"Are you sorting out that mess?" said Harriet.

"No, are you?"

A small crowd had gathered to enjoy the exchange. Members of the public joined the tip operatives and security guards, united on the side of the workers or at least on the side of entertainment.

"I am a concerned citizen. Worried rubbish is causing a public health hazard, and I insist you fix it."

"And I'm an unconcerned tip worker who's not paid

enough to listen to your shite, so if you don't mind, we have work to do." He turned his back on Harriet to laughter and applause from the crowd.

"I'm not finished with you yet." Harriet poked him in the back with her litter picker.

The mood shifted. "You've had your fun, pet, but that's classed as assault. If you don't fuck off now, I'll snap that stick of yours and snap you while I'm at it."

"That's a threat," she looked to the crowd, "you heard it. This man is threatening my safety. You're my witnesses."

The throng dispersed, unwilling to get drawn into any potential legal wrangling. The show was over and everyone returned to the business of rubbish disposal.

"If you're so concerned with public health hazards," the tip worker said, "you might have noticed your dog has shat all over the pavement."

Harriet plucked up the turd with the litter picker and waved it in his direction. "This isn't over. I'll tell the papers. I'm an active member of the Echo Facebook community."

He walked away without looking back, raising his middle finger to her to register his feelings on the matter. Amongst the commotion and distraction, nobody had seen Angus slip past the security patrols, across the public zone of the tip and through the gates into the primary landfill site.

He marched with purpose towards the offices and warehouse.

The stench resembled nothing Angus had ever encountered, and he owned cats. Mounds of decaying rubbish steamed in the distance. Mouldy bread, rotten fruit and rancid chicken littered his route, but it didn't deter him. He had a job to do and needed to capitalise on his limited window of opportunity. Seagulls swirled and squawked overhead, landing to feast on whatever decomposing garbage they could fit in their beaks. Fearless, they refused to move for Angus and he walked around them, hoping the workers showed the same disregard for his presence.

Diggers rumbled in the near distance, shifting piles of refuse as a toddler shuffles vegetables on a plate. A constant stream of bin lorries backed onto the site, reverse indicators beeping, dumped their load and headed back out again. Hectic but efficient, everyone busy, getting on with their own roles and taking scant notice of what else happened. Angus needed to blend in, and to blend in, he needed to stand out. He put on the hi-viz bib he'd removed from his bag. Not the standard issue of Maurice Groom's company, yet it was enough to make him appear as if he belonged.

He produced a clipboard and pen. Top of the workers' list of things to avoid was an official with a clipboard. Even with his disguise, he didn't want to push his luck. He positioned himself far enough away from the diggers and lorries, so he'd at least have pre-warning of any challenge. The first pages on his clipboard looked official. Not official enough to pass as an employee, but official enough for his needs.

He stored notes on any wrongdoing in his Palm Pilot. An antiquated piece of technology that the smartphone replaced long ago, but in Angus' world, the Palm Pilot was king. He'd been using it to document his real ale intake for best part of twenty years. If it was adequate for storing vital information, such as the ABV percentage of the half of Golden Ferret Tugger he had in Bolton in 2003, it was adequate for noting the comings and goings on a landfill site.

Recording lorries arriving and diggers trundling amongst the waste wasn't of much use or interest to anyone. He needed to spot something out of the ordinary, and that was more likely to happen nearer to the offices. Angus attempted to position himself somewhere not full of decaying produce or filled nappies and settled on a mound of garden waste.

It wasn't long before the unmistakable Maurice Groom bounded out of the office. He rubbed the head of a worker, jumped in his BMW, and sped onto the main road. Where he was going didn't concern Angus. His mission was to report the facts, not chase after fancy cars. He used his walkie talkie, another object of archaic technology, to alert Karl of the movement. Karl acknowledged the information and seconds later, his Lycra clad figure raced after the BMW, praying the early evening traffic allowed him to keep up with Maurice.

Angus returned to his task, and the second noteworthy event took place. An unmarked transit van arrived, waved through security with no checks, and disappeared into a warehouse. Angus noted the registration plate in the Palm Pilot. Fifteen minutes later it left, but this time he got a good view of the driver, a face he recognised from his recent trip to Amsterdam. Derek Pearson.

There'd been rumours that Jack had let him go from his mechanic's job because of a series of incidents. He didn't know how true this was, or whether Derek had found alternative employment working for Maurice, but he recorded it regardless. Karl was occupied as the only set of wheels, so there was no point in calling it in for someone to follow him.

The fire exit of the warehouse opened and half a dozen men lit cigarettes, furtive glances over their shoulders. They huddled in little groups and whilst Angus was too far away to catch the conversations; they weren't in English. An emaciated lad in a frayed t-shirt broke from the group and ambled toward the fence, putting his fingers through the mesh and giving it a tug. He leapt when an almighty crash caused the railing to shake as a shaven-headed man-mountain took a swing at it with a baseball bat.

"Get the fuck away from that fence." This conversation was in English. He towered over the worker and shepherded him back towards the fire exit. "Who let you lot out, and who the fuck have you been nicking tabs off?" He knocked the cigarettes out of their hands and shoved them into the warehouse.

Angus dived behind a bin bag overflowing with grass cuttings as the tattooed monster had a quick scan of his surroundings before shutting the fire exit behind him.

Angus couldn't record this fast enough, scribbling notes as fast as his electronic stylus allowed.

Until someone interrupted him. "Alright, mate? What you up to?"

Angus almost leapt out of his hi-viz. "Jesus, Mary and all the orphans, where the hell did you come from?"

"Over there." He pointed to a vague spot on the horizon. "What you doing?"

Angus had practised his cover story, but he wasn't so confident of it now. "I'm surveying the land."

"What's that mean, like?"

Angus wasn't sure whether this man doubted his alibi or was questioning the English language.
"This was the site of an ancient battle. I'm studying it for archaeological merit."

"I know nowt about arky... whatever it was you said, but I enjoy my battles. Which one was it?"

If Angus had stumbled across a history buff, his story fell at the first hurdle. He suspected he hadn't. "It was a battle from the civil war."

"Ah, right? Like the Germans and that?"

"No," Angus struggled to hide the contempt from his

voice, "the civil war."

"Nah, a narr this one, man. Civil war that was the Americans, wasn't it?" He bounced on his feet, proud of himself, and gave Angus a playful punch on the shoulder. "Know all about that one coz it's where they invented KFC. Colonel Sanders and that. I'm right, aren't I?"

"Close enough."

"That's class, that is. Champion, right, I'm doing a bunk as it's nashing off time and I want to get home for me tea. Good cracking on with you, mate." He wandered off in the general direction of the buildings.

At that moment, Angus realised, whilst they'd had a Masterplan for sneaking onto the tip; he was clueless how to escape unnoticed.

He couldn't backtrack as the guards were now back on the gate between the public tip and the main one. Several guards, more than expected, manned the front gate, doing sporadic bag searches, although Angus was unsure of what people stole from a rubbish tip. The fences weren't scalable and from the minor incident he had witnessed; the guards kept a closer eye on them than necessary. Angus had to take his chances at the front gate. He remembered the advice he'd received from Jack to act as if he belonged; it was no accident con men got their name for being confidence tricksters. Confidence gained the trust of others. Except Angus was far from confident. He was shitting himself.

He trudged over the mounds of trash, delaying when he had to bluff his way out of trouble. Angus could claim he had become disorientated and wandered in from the public tip, but that made no sense. Why not turn back and leave by the public exit? He had to stick to his cover story no matter what. It wasn't the Hatton Garden Heist; he was only trespassing on a gigantic pile of rotting rubbish.

Angus approached the car park and the biggest warehouse near to him appeared to be the recycling plant, with many people still separating plastics and cardboard with rapid dexterity. The next one along was harder to see, and he didn't want to get too close, as it had tighter security. He heard forklifts reversing and banging and clattering. There was plenty of work continuing after the buzzer had sounded. The final one was set back behind the offices and impossible for Angus to investigate without being seen.

He realised standing still in the middle of the car park was likely to draw attention to himself, so he headed for the exit. Taking deep breaths, he tried to make himself appear taller and more assertive, but he knew he'd crumble if challenged. As he neared the gate, an industrial hooter sounded and lads jumped from their diggers, or stopped working and ran for the gates. A similar evacuation came from the offices, and he hoped to conceal himself within the crowd. Angus noted with interest that nobody left either of the warehouses.

A bottleneck existed by the time he reached the barrier, both a blessing and a curse. He could watch what was happening and plan his approach, but the longer he waited, the more nervous he became. Random bag searches still took place despite the congestion, and Angus edged forward, awaiting his fate. Angus prayed someone in front of him got pulled for a search, but at least half a dozen sailed past before him. He was now at the gate.

"Bag."

"What?" said Angus.

"Show me your bag."

This was it, he was in big bother. He handed it over, lacking the strength to lift it as his arms had turned to jelly. "Here you are."

"Where's your hi-viz?"

Angus pointed at it. "Here."

"Your proper one, that's not regulation."

"Picked up the wrong bib leaving the house this morning, I was rushing."

"Make sure you wear the correct one tomorrow." The guard picked out his clipboard. "What's this?"

"Battle plans."

"The fuck?"

"I'm a history enthusiast. I study ancient battles." He didn't go into his full cover story just yet.

The guard looked confused. "And this."

"My Palm Pilot."

"Speak in English, mate."

"It's for recording notes."

The entire plan was disintegrating.

"Show me."

Angus switched it on and prayed. He pointed at the screen. "This is a Red Mist Stout, heavy on the palette but a steady seven out of ten. The High Force bitter is lively but eminently quaffable."

"Remember the bit about speaking in English?"

"Real ales, I'm off for a pint."

"Eh?"

"I record what I drink and the taste, etcetera."

"What, like nine pints of Carling, mustn't have cleaned the lines because I shat myself?" He got a laugh from the other security guards.

Angus played along with the joke. "That sort of thing."

"Weird." The guard put the Pilot back and returned the rucksack to Angus. "Don't forget your hi-viz"

Angus was past the gate and breathed freedom. He wasn't

sure if he'd survive going through that again.

"Alright, Colonel Sanders," said a familiar voice from behind him. He shouted to the guards. "Daft lad here's been searching for bombs dropped during the Uncivil War, the mad bastard."

Angus didn't wait to find out the security guard's response. Removing his copy of The Art of War from his bag, he threw it at them and made a run for it.

Chapter Eighteen

"Positions everyone." Mr Fitzpatrick tried to attract the children's attention, but they weren't taking any notice. "I said, positions. NOW!" He clapped his hands to hurry them.

The children sniggered, revelling in Fitz's excitable nature, and they knew how to exploit it. Each child took up their marks, just not the ones he instructed them to take.

"Oh. My. God. Do you imagine I'd have these problems with Cheryl Cole? I think not." He placed his palms on one girl's shoulders and manoeuvred her into position. "And you, my little duckling, are no Cheryl Cole."

Ten more minutes of cajoling and manhandling got them where they needed to be. But one child remained. "And who are you?"

"I'm Molly."

"Ah, Molly, the teacher's pet."

"No."

"You're not Molly Ferris," Fitz put on a mock surprised face. "Mrs Ferris's daughter?"

"Yes, but I'm not a pet."

"Of course not, my little treacle pudding, but I'm afraid you're not an actor either," he moved her away with his fingertips, "at least not in this production."

Molly got the message and climbed from the stage as Andrea returned from the staff room. A staff meeting had overrun and her fellow teachers were now racing for the exit. She wished she could join them instead of participating in the farce Fitz was creating.

"Hi, darling," said Andrea, "what's wrong?"

"I'm not in the play."

"We discussed this," Andrea bent, so she was at Molly's eye level. "It's only for this one performance. There'll be loads more."

"Mr Fitzpatrick said I can't act."

"He said what?"

"Said I was a dog."

"I'm sure he didn't say that."

"He did." She turned to her Action Man. "Didn't he, Arthur?" Molly put the Action Man to her ear. "Arthur heard him."

"I'm sure there's been a misunderstanding. I'll have a word."

"So I am in the play?" said Molly, a big grin forming.

"That's not what I meant. The other stuff, the dog… whatever he said. Sometimes we have to make tough decisions, decisions people don't like. On this occasion I decided there wasn't a part for you in the show. It doesn't mean you can't be in the next one."

"I don't care, we'll create our own play." She skipped off to the corner of the hall with her Action Man. Andrea returned to the stage to grapple control back from Mr Fitzpatrick and stop him turning it into a fabulous extravaganza to showcase his own talents.

Molly soon bored with talking to Arthur, and after five minutes of watching her mother get exasperated with Fitz and the feline vocal skills of her classmates, she went exploring. She knew she couldn't go far. The play preoccupied Andrea, but she'd notice if Molly disappeared and had become overprotective since the bus crash. Molly skipped into the store cupboard.

It was twelve feet square, and she'd been in many times before as it stored the PE equipment, and they often asked her to help bring it into the hall. The storeroom also housed Reggie's old lollipop stick. His temporary replacement in the role was proving not to be as popular in the office as Reggie because of a slight body odour issue. The receptionists had hidden the pole in the cupboard, telling the substitute someone had stolen it and he had to source a new one due to insurance concerns. Lies delivered without changing expression, but that was the skill of a receptionist.

Molly entertained herself by jumping from the wooden horse onto the pile of mats that presented an ultra-soft landing. She threw bean bags from one side of the storeroom into a bin at the other. Taking turns for both her and Arthur and keeping score. Molly always won. She danced using the gymnastics ribbon and made a parachute for Arthur from the ribbons and an old carrier bag. Molly tossed him in the air time and time again, watching him sail back to the ground. Although she always did it over the mats, as she didn't want him to get hurt if his chute failed to open.

The sound of raised voices brought her back into the hall.

"Mr Fitzpatrick," said Andrea.

"Fitz."

"Mr Fitzpatrick. I've explained this repeatedly, but we

don't have the budget, the knowhow or the relevant safety certificate for a smoke machine."

"We could design our own."

"That's not happening."

"Imagine, bear with me here, the cauldron at the beginning, dry ice billowing from it, then little Beyoncé here," he points to the smallest child in the class, "bursts out."

"She's got asthma, she's not popping out of a smoking cauldron."

"That's disablist."

"It's not happening."

"Anyone would think you wanted this show to fail. Shakespeare didn't chop his ear off for people not to take his work seriously."

"That wasn't Shakespeare, it was Van Gogh."

"Who? I'm sure you're wrong, but no matter, the point is, this production is a trillion times better with a smoke machine."

"Mr Fitzpatrick, can I remind you that you're a guest in the school. You are here to learn and offer assistance. If you aren't prepared to do that, then you may wish to reconsider why you're here."

"There's no need for the hoighty toighty tone. I'm trying to help."

Andrea realised she shouldn't be having this discussion in front of the kids. She preferred not to have it at all. With everything going on with Jack, the arguments over his business, over Reggie, the last thing she needed right now was an over dramatic wannabe drama teacher.

"I appreciate you're keen to help, but you need to recognise the restrictions we're working in and adjust accordingly."

"A catapult?"

"A what?"

"If Beyoncé can't leap out of the cauldron because of her wheeziness, we can fire her through the smoke. Problem solved." Fitz clapped once and bounded towards the children.

"Give me strength," said Andrea.

Jack sat on the car park wall, unsure whether to go into the school. He'd agreed to meet Andrea and Molly after rehearsals, but things remained frosty between him and his wife. He'd arrived early intending to offer moral support, but was now having second thoughts. After everything that happened with Reggie, disappearing for a lads' weekend in Amsterdam hadn't been his greatest move. Jack had chosen not to tell her the tale of the immigrants escaping on his return, or the fact he'd retrieved Reggie's laptop and visited Harold.

The secrets he kept from Andrea were stacking up. He was a reluctant liar, but had convinced himself it was to protect her. Jack didn't want the children to witness the hostility between them, nor did he want the bonus of encountering Mr Fitzpatrick.

He killed half an hour messing with his phone, but he spent his time contemplating what Harold told him, what Maurice told him, even what Reggie had told him. Everyone told him to stay away, but he wouldn't. He couldn't stand back and let Groom take over his business. The children not involved in the play had long gone, the teachers escaped later than usual, and the office staff before them. Andrea's was the sole vehicle in the car park until the other parents appeared. It therefore surprised him to see a figure skulking near the entrance. A face he recognised, Harold Beeston.

Any other time, lurking outside a school attracted unwanted attention from the authorities, but as most of the children and staff had gone home, Harold hoped to go unnoticed. He was a novelty character to the locals, and Jack was sure the kids had a nickname for him. Whatever he was up to, he could write off as scavenging from the bins, but after yesterday, Jack recognised there was far more to him. He watched as Harold looked for CCTV cameras and ensured he obscured his face. Not that there'd be a problem identifying him from his outfit.

When he slipped inside the entrance hall, Jack dropped off the wall and followed him. If the school office had been locked before, it wasn't now. Jack assumed it was yet another set of skills he had kept from him. Harold knew what he was after and didn't bother checking desk drawers, which he could have unlocked if he had the need. He looked behind the filing cabinets, in the stationery cupboard, and the compact kitchen that led off the office. He checked behind the desks, but to no avail. Whatever Harold was searching for wasn't there, and whatever it was, it must be sizeable if it didn't fit in the desk drawer. He backed out of the office and locked the door, so nobody realised he'd been there.

Except Jack.

"Harold?"

He tried not to look startled. "Jack, are you following me?" The realisation then hit him. "Your wife teaches here. Molly is a pupil."

After recent threats, Jack was less than comfortable with someone on the periphery of Maurice's plot being near to Andrea's place of work and his child's school. He squared up to Harold. "What are you doing here, Harold? What are you looking for?"

"Doesn't matter, it's not here."

"It matters to me." Jack blocked his path as he tried to leave.

"You know what I'm looking for?"

"Do I?" The reply surprised Jack.

"Have you forgotten what we discussed? I warned you to walk away, but I didn't expect you to wipe your memory."

"And I wasn't expecting sarcasm." Then it made sense. "Reggie's camera."

"Exactly."

"But why leave it here? I don't understand."

"Where better? The majority of business takes place here, hiding in plain sight yet again. Maurice is head of the board of governors. He has a free run of the school. When he and his little cronies meet, they nip into the kitchen for a cuppa and have a chin wag in the office."

"Makes sense. Everyone goes home after four and they're sure there won't be interruptions again until morning. Anybody who has eyes on him will watch his business, not here."

"Anybody but Reggie."

"But you didn't search the office. You were in and out in minutes. Reggie's camera could be hidden anywhere."

"Not anywhere. I'm a specialist. This is a specific camera to hide in a specific object."

They spoke in unison, "The lollipop stick."

"Hiding in plain sight again?" said Jack.

"Except it's hiding out of sight now."

"Hi, Daddy."

Jack hadn't seen Molly sneak up behind him. "Hi, love, didn't see you there."

"I'm great at being invisible."

"This is Har—"

"Harry Ramp the smell—"

"Molly!"

Harold laughed and offered his hand. "Nice to meet you,

159

Molly."

"Nice to meet you, Mr Ramp. What are you doing here?"

Jack and Harold exchanged glances. "I was looking for something and I bumped into your dad, so we're having a catch-up."

Molly furrowed her eyebrows whilst examining him, as if deciding whether to believe Harold's cover story. "Okay." It satisfied her.

"How's the play going?"

"Not well, Mummy shouted at Mr Fitzpatrick."

Jack grimaced. "What about?"

"Not sure, firing Beyoncé over a boiling cauldron of fire with a catapult or something."

"At least it's Beyoncé and not me, I suppose. Your mam's not in the best of moods?"

"I wasn't listening. Me and Arthur were playing in the store cupboard." Molly skipped off into the hall.

Jack and Harold swapped excited glances once again. "The store cupboard."

Jack and Harold followed Molly, trying to be inconspicuous and not wanting to run and overtake her on their way to the cupboard. Andrea spotted her husband but didn't understand why he was with the local oddball. At this stage, she was past caring. The children were hyper once more and Mr Fitzgerald wasn't helping to calm them.

Jack and Harold barged into the storeroom. Bean bags and ribbons littered the floor from where Molly had been playing, but it didn't take them long to find what they sought. The lollipop stick rested against the wall to their left.

"I need to see what's on it," said Jack.

"On what?"

"The camera. I'm involved in this, whatever this is, and I'm entitled."

Harold took hold of the stick. "It might be nothing."

"Nothing or not, I want to know. Did it use a microphone?"

"Audio and visual, not much point otherwise," said Harold.

"You're are a sneaky little bugger, aren't you?" Jack picked up a beanbag and lobbed it into the bin.

"It's not here."

"What do you mean, it's not here? You've got it in your hand."

"The camera, it's gone." Harold moved the stick under the lightbulb.

"Gone. How can it be? Who's got it?"

"How the hell should I know?"

"Could it have fallen out?" said Jack.

"I'm a professional, I don't make things that fall out."

"On the off chance your exemplary professional standards slipped for once." Jack knelt. "How big are we talking?"

"Smaller than the end of your little finger. Just big enough for a memory card and it has a separate wire to the battery." Harold joined him on the floor but wasn't hopeful. "It didn't fall out, somebody has it."

They scrambled on their knees for ten minutes until Andrea interrupted them. "What are you doing down there?"

Jack realised there weren't any sensible answers to that question. "Harold lost one of his contact lenses."

"He's wearing glasses."

"That's because he lost—"

"Out, both of you." Andrea pulled Jack up by the collar. "I'll speak to you outside."

Dejected, they trudged towards the entrance hall. "Who has the camera, Harold?"

"Whoever has it, it's unwelcome news for me. Unwelcome news for us."

"What do you think is on it?"

"Could be any manner of things, but whatever is on that camera, they'll piss lava when they discover someone has viewed it."

"Who are they?"

"People you don't want to meet," said Harold. "When they trace that camera back to me, I'm finished."

"How will they trace it back to you?"

"We create our own signatures, people in our trade. Call it arrogance, call it showmanship, call it whatever, but whenever you create a piece of technical genius, the last thing you want is someone else getting the credit."

"That's madness," said Jack.

Harold pointed to his attire. "Did I ever strike you as sane?"

Jack chose not to answer. As they got to the door of the entrance hall, an imposing figure entered via the main door. Maurice Groom.

"Shit," said Harold. "He can't catch me here."

"Why not?"

"You've a reason to be here, Andrea and Molly. I've no business lurking in a school. It might take them a while to work out where the camera came from, but if I'm seen here, he won't need a calculator to add the twos."

"This way, quick." Jack ran across the hall to the fire exit, pushing the bars to allow the doors to swing open.

Harold ran out. "Speak soon."

Jack closed the doors behind him and returned to the entrance hall. "Evening, Maurice."

"Jack, what brings you here?" There was no warmth in the businessman's voice.

"Family."

"Right."

"And you?"

"Me, what?"

"What brings you here?"

"Business," said Maurice, "none of yours." He took a key from his blazer pocket and unlocked the office door.

Jack wandered into the car park, leaning on the wall as he waited for Andrea and Molly to finish. A large Jaguar pulled up, and he spotted another face he recognised. "Noel?"

Noel Cardwell breezed by Jack without acknowledging him. The merest shake of the head was the only acknowledgement he existed.

"Grandad?" Molly was harder to ignore.

"Good evening." Noel considered offering his hand for a handshake, but Molly was hugging his leg. "I have work to do, go and speak to your idi… go and speak to your father."

"Daddy?" said Andrea.

"Andrea." Noel sighed with resignation. He couldn't escape without a conversation.

"What are you doing here?"

"I have an appointment."

"And you didn't think to mention it to me?"

"Why would I? I wasn't aware you were my personal secretary."

"I work here, Daddy," said Andrea, exasperated, "it's Molly's school. If you told us you were coming, we could have met for tea. You know, spend time with your only granddaughter, like normal grandfathers do."

"Dinner."

"What?"

"Civilised people eat lunch and dinner. I see this lot has dragged you down to their level with dinner and tea."

"Dinner, tea? Who cares? Molly hasn't seen you other than when you're on TV."

"I was hoping you'd have gone by now."

"Charming." Andrea shook her head. "Did you see Jack?"

"I passed him."

"And?"

"And what?"

"Did you speak?"

"To that moron?"

Andrea stifled a scream. "He's my husband, your son-in-law."

"You're aware of my views on that. If you're finished with reciting the family tree, I've a meeting to attend." Noel opened the office door.

Andrea spotted Maurice in the office. "What business do you have with Maurice Groom?"

"Nothing that concerns you?"

"But it does, doesn't it? Me and Jack?"

"Keep out of things you don't understand, Andrea. You chose this life, so go back to making cakes out of play dough, or whatever you do with these frightful little people." He shut the office door behind him.

Chapter Nineteen

Maurice was on a call as Noel entered the office. He acknowledged his arrival with a wave and nodded to the cuppa on the desk. Noel looked at it with contempt and pushed it away. He straightened his tie in the reflection in the window and waited, shuffling bits of paper on the desk and straightening the stationery.

"A war investigator? What the hell's a war investigator?" Maurice pointed to the phone and pulled a face as if he was talking to an idiot. "Searching for bombs on our landfill site, our secure landfill site, and not one person stopped the lunatic getting in or leaving, or has the faintest idea who he is?" He loosened his tie. "I'm not interested in your scarecrow-looking mad woman, she's been a public nuisance for years." He shook his head. "A bloke on a bike? How is a bloke riding a bike suspicious? Hold on, I'll ring you back." Maurice ended the call.

"Problems?" said Noel.

"Not sure, don't think so." He peeked through the blinds into the car park. "Just locals acting weird at the landfill."

"And you don't consider that an issue?"

"Locals acting weird around the tip is a custom here, they're bloody crackers." Maurice checked outside again.

"Why do you keep staring out there?"

"The staff reckon there was a cyclist hurtling around near the site for a couple of hours, and now I'm convinced there was one following me on the way here. In his shiny rubber outfit, I assumed he was just a regular cycling dickhead. Is your department responsible for ensuring these public nuisances get a licence?"

"Nobody's making cyclists get licences."

"You should."

"Is this cyclist a problem?"

"I don't think so," said Maurice.

"You don't think a lot of things."

"Maybe they're just locals, but what if they're onto us?" Maurice peered through the blinds once more.

"Who are they?"

"You know, they? Whoever they are. Whoever you tell me I have to fear."

"What I tell you to do is your job. The job you assured us you were more than capable of performing, but I'm beginning to doubt my judgement now."

"I can handle it."

"I need not remind you we're only allowing you a taste of this if you cope with the pressure and come up with the requisite finance. How are we doing with that?"

"It's in hand. I'll have the financials sewn up soon."

"Dare I ask how?"

"Better you don't know."

"This can't come back to us."

"It won't." Maurice glanced at the noticeboard and caught

sight of the staff list. Andrea's name gave him a clue who might be behind the freak army. "One second, Noel, I have to send a warning to someone."

"Don't tell me—"

Maurice held the mobile to his ear. "Nancy. Maurice. I need a favour. Don't want you to dig too deep into this, but a local haulier recently smuggled in half a dozen illegal immigrants via North Shields. Can't say who at the moment, but I need the story front page." He winked at Noel. "I don't give a shit about proof, I'm telling you it's true so it's true; get the story printed. Anonymous source, hint you'll reveal the haulier soon. That's all for now. Get it done."

"Who was that?" said Noel.

"Yet another one who I have in my pocket. You need to assert your authority every now and again, let them know who's in charge."

"I'm sure you don't need reminding who's in charge here? The people you report to won't treat you like your little journalist friend. They won't be removing your dictaphone, they'll be removing your di—"

"I get it, I get it. Everything will be fine."

"It better be Maurice, because if not, you will pay a significant price for your failure."

Chapter Twenty

Jack had kept a low profile from his fellow pigeon club members since the Amsterdam trip, but he couldn't dodge the Annual General Meeting. And he was in the dock. Chief prosecutor was Bill Tindall, club chairman and a man who liked people to know who was in charge. Sat at the head of the table in his trademark v-neck sweater and flat cap.

The meeting hadn't started, but heated discussions raged around the room. Jack was at the centre of most. First up was the Amsterdam excursion. Whilst most had a brilliant time, they were loath to admit it, and reverted to sniping and moaning at every petty thing, including the minor matter of illegal immigrants.

"We're accomplices."

"You can't be accomplices," said Jack, "unless there was a crime, and as there wasn't, we've done nothing wrong."

"You swore us to secrecy, warned us not to breathe a word to anyone."

"That was to avoid the hassle," said Jack, not convinced himself, "imagine the grief you'd get off your lass if you were late returning from Amsterdam because you were being questioned by the coppers."

"We smuggled Uncle Bulgaria and his five mates in the back of the bus, I'd say that was something wrong."

"We didn't know they were there."

"Somebody did. How did they board the bloody bus if nobody knew the buggers were there?"

Even if Jack wasn't aware of the illegal boarders, someone else was. Which led them onto their next issue.

"All those danger strangers," said Bill. "Who invited them?"

"Not this crap again," said Jack. "We agreed, make the numbers up or cancel the trip."

He was regretting not giving in to Molly when she'd asked her dad to stop in and watch a DVD.

"Everyone agreed to a few more lads tagging along, but we weren't expecting your gang. It's like you brought them back to life from a vault in the museum."

"Does it matter? They weren't harming anybody."

"Did you see the plight of them, how they dressed? We've a reputation to uphold."

"A reputation? Have you seen the state of us? When we rolled up, Amsterdam thought 1983 had popped over for a visit."

"And that fat, sweaty mess from your place could have got the lot of us locked up. I'll bet every one of these pint tokens he was smuggling donkey porn. The fear on his face when they checked his passport."

"I've dealt with him."

Jack couldn't prove Derek smuggled the immigrants, but he was ninety per cent sure he caused the bus crash. Most likely through sheer incompetence, although he didn't want to consider the other option.

"That's champion after the event, but we shouldn't have been in that position."

"What position?"

"Your work interfering with pigeon club business. You're putting your own financial concerns ahead of the club."

"That's bollocks," said Jack. He downed half of his pint, winding up for an argument.

"Is it? What about the lofts? You want to stop us selling them in case the dock's expansion impacts your interests. You're looking after Jack Ferris, not the club."

"We can't bloody sell them. We don't own the land, we lease it off the council. If they agree to sell, they'll boot us off without compensation." Jack stood. "The club has built those crees up over decades. Handed down father to son. We've cobbled them together over the years and can't transport them elsewhere. They'd need demolishing. A century of history and heritage flushed down the shitter so some smug businessman can make a profit."

"But the lads might welcome clicking a few quid," said Bill.

"I was thinking of jacking in anyway," said one.

"Our lass says I love them more than I do her. True like, I think more of this pint of bitter than I do of her, but I don't fancy a crack, so it may be time to wrap it in."

"Where's this coming from? I've just explained, we can't sell them. We'll lose every penny we've invested. It's madness."

"Aye, well," said Bill.

"There's no aye, well about it. What will we do with the pigeons, stick them in a fucking pie?"

"They can live in a tree or something, like they're meant to. They shouldn't be caged."

"Caged? They're out flying every day. That's what we're here to discuss, plans for the big race, not this shite." Jack slumped back in his seat.

"Aye, maybe we make the big one our last race. Cash in whilst we still can."

"You can't cash in. What's so difficult to understand?" Jack massaged his temples, fighting off a migraine. "Hold on, have they offered you lot money to go quietly? Who've you been speaking to, Bill?"

"Never mind who I've been speaking to, Jack. You need to remember who's running the show here. I'm chairman, not you, so wind ya neck in."

"This is bullshit."

"I can get you dismissed on a vote of no confidence. You've had your three strikes. The flighty foreigners, the dog touchers on the bus, and now you're trying to block the lofts arrangement, you're on very dodgy ground. We haven't even got around to discussing the whole Reggie business."

"I could have sat at home and had a pleasant night watching a Disney film with the bairn, instead of dealing with this nonoonoo."

Then it came to him, the clue he'd missed. *"Mary Poppins and Dick Van Dyke."*

He leapt from his chair and ran for the door.

Chapter Twenty-One

Jack had barely slept. He'd assumed he'd found what Reggie hinted at when he discovered the USB drive, but what if he was wrong? What if Reggie had been suggesting something else and Jack had missed it? A clue that had been staring him in the face. Jack watched Reggie's home for a while until he was sure nobody was around, and he let himself in. The house had been ransacked.

Whilst there was no obvious sign of a break in from the outside, they'd done a proper job on the place. Sofa cushions slashed, drawers tipped out over the floor, TVs dismantled, all in the search for something. Something Reggie had and somebody else wanted. Something they craved so much they would destroy a dead man's home. But if his hunch was correct, whatever they were looking for wasn't in the property, not exactly.

He went into the yard, and the stepladders lay where he hoped he'd find them. The steps appeared untouched; he was in luck. Whoever had raided the house hadn't found what they were after. Jack was one move ahead.

With one slight problem. He needed to climb onto the roof

to see if he was right, the roof that proved fatal for his friend Reggie. Already shaking when he picked up the ladders, his dread grew each time he extended them. The rattle of metal matching the rattling of his bones. The final extension reached just under the eaves, and he gave them a solid shove to check they were secure. They appeared stable, but he knew this would change as soon as he set foot on them.

The fear had seized him. His vision blurred as his eyes crossed and the pressure on his temples sent shooting pains through his skull. The bridge of his nose felt close to caving in, he sensed a nose bleed coming on, and the inevitable dizziness kicked in. This was before he'd taken his first step. Maybe he should shut his eyes and go for it.

He placed his left foot on the ladder, no turning back, then the right, then he began his ascent. It may not have been Everest, but to Jack, a two-storey house might as well have been. Either the ladders shook because of him, or he shook because of the ladders, but he couldn't stop.

The seagulls circling above didn't fill him with confidence. Far enough away to not be an immediate concern, but near enough to dive bomb at any second if the mood took them. In his experience, they were always in the mood.

He passed the top of the ground-floor windows and realised this was the highest he had ever been on a ladder. Thinking about it made things worse. He had to think happy thoughts about Molly and Andrea. Less so about Andrea at the minute. If she learned he was here, she'd be willing him to plunge to the ground. Jack blanked everything out and kept moving. If he paused, he would freeze.

In a matter of minutes, seconds even, he arrived at the top. Whilst he'd been full of fear, a fear he thought he'd conquered, he realised that getting to the top of the ladders was the simple part. Jack now had to scale the roof. The traditional wooden roofer's ladders remained attached to the ridge tiles. He took another step to reach the bottom rung with his hand. Jack tugged them, and they were secure. He was confident, at least as confident as he ever could be at this height, that they were safe. All he had to do now was pull himself onto the roofer's ladders and make his way to the summit.

"Here goes." He drew himself up from the main steps.

As he was halfway on, he stopped. Not through choice. Something or someone dragged him back. *"Oh, fuck."*

A thousand thoughts raced through his mind. Had Maurice had him tailed? Were the ladders booby trapped? Was the entire house going to crumble, and would he fall to his death? He needed to look down to identify who or what was stopping him. But glancing down would increase his dizziness and could send him plummeting to the same fate as Reggie. With only one eye open at first, as if it would somehow lessen the impact, Jack peeked down, expecting to encounter a hired thug tugging at his leg. But nobody was there. The temporary relief from knowing nobody was yanking him to his death lessened when he realised the actual reason for his halt in progress.

His belt buckle had snagged on the guttering. Reluctantly, he removed his left hand and tried to dislodge the buckle. It stuck fast, hooked on a nail or a fitting of some description. Whatever it was, it wasn't budging. There was nothing else for it. He had to remove his belt.

Removing a belt with one hand was a tricky task at the best of times. Doing it whilst twenty feet in the air, on top of a ladder and shitting yourself from your fear of heights was another challenge altogether. Jack tugged and pulled, twisted and turned, and extricated himself from his belt. He hoped nobody saw what he was doing. Free of the obstacle, but now having to tug at his trousers to prevent them from slipping down, he continued his climb. Flat against the roof, it felt safer than on the ladders that brought him here. He made it onto the ridge tiles in no time.

This presented him with his next challenge, getting to the chimney. If only he possessed the confidence to skip and dance his way there like Dick Van Dyke.Taking hold of a tile with his right hand, he swung his left leg over, so he straddled the roof. He inched along the ridge, keeping his eyes shut this time, until his knees came into contact with brickwork. Jack blinked into the sunlight and took in the view. He could see out across the docks, his yard and the pigeon lofts towards the North Sea. If he glanced over his shoulder, which he allowed himself to do for a second, the vista stretched as far as Penshaw Monument.

Now for the moment of truth.

Jack gripped the TV aerial and hauled himself up. He was now standing on the top of the roof with his hands grasping the chimney pot. And there it was, just as he'd hoped. A rope knotted to the aerial dropped into the chimney. He pulled it up and the other end tied to a JD Sports carrier bag. There was a bit of weight to it, but nothing too heavy.

He didn't want to become distracted by examining the contents from up here. It was breezy, and he couldn't afford for the contents to blow away. The seagulls circled, and he was reluctant to upset them any more than he already had. He slung the rope handles of the carrier over his shoulder and eased himself back into a seating position. Jack didn't bother turning around so shuffled backwards, pausing occasionally to tug his trousers up.

He arrived at the roofer's ladders and swung his leg over, edging down the slates. If he'd assumed the descent would be any easier than getting onto the roof, he was promptly dissuaded of that notion. As his feet reached the guttering, he froze. This had been the straightforward part. Jack had to manoeuvre onto the main ladders before he got to the safety of concrete.

He closed his eyes once again and thought of playing with Molly, dreamed about destroying Maurice. Jack edged his left foot over the gutter and left it hanging. He moved his right hand down another rung and then dangled his right foot out. Both feet hung to the right of the main ladders. He needed to come down, then swing his legs across so he distributed his weight evenly. Difficult to do when your eyes are wedged shut.

He caught the ladders with his left foot and noticed the sudden movement. They were falling. Jack threw his leg out further and dragged them back into position, planting his left foot on one tread. His legs were no longer jelly, they were about to disintegrate.

Once he confirmed the ladder had ceased shaking, and all movement was his own body overreacting, he brought his right foot over. Then, in a monumental leap of faith, he let go of the roofer's ladders and grabbed the main ones with both hands, miraculously not pulling them from the wall. Whether motivated by fear, a desire to find safety or excitement for what was in the JD carrier bag, he wasted no time in racing to the bottom and planting both feet on solid ground. Jack staggered to the door and collapsed onto the step, his legs finished for the day.

On prising open the top of the carrier bag, it surprised him to discover a box from the old board game Battleships. He removed it, removing the lid to find all the pieces still intact. But that wasn't the important part. A brown envelope intrigued him. The envelope contained names of contacts in Amsterdam, links between most of the key players in the deal and the hidden motivation for the dock's expansion. Reggie had covered everything, including the date of a significant drug shipment.

Jack couldn't hang around here. If they found him with this information, he was in genuine danger. He stuffed the lot back into the box, put it into the bag, and left the house. Jack should have checked the coast was clear before stepping outside, but the only person who noticed him was the neighbour. Still in her dressing gown and still smoking a cigarette.

He sprinted back to the car and sped off down the street, the Yorkshire Terrier yapping and giving chase before quitting to pee against a tree. Jack had every piece of evidence he required now. If only he could figure out how to use it.

Chapter Twenty-Two

As desperate as he was to review the documentation, Jack needed to show his face at work. He'd spent the day with his mind not on the job and left as early as reasonable without drawing attention to himself. When he got home, he locked himself in his office and worked through the information he collected. He dumped the Battleships behind a pile of old paperwork so Andrea didn't stumble across it and ask him what it was.

Reggie had been watching Maurice's crew for a long time and gathered a mountain of material on them, but the narcotics shipment was the game changer. Another USB drive contained audio files and emails. He fished a pair of earphones from his desk drawer and plugged them in. Jack didn't recognise every voice, but a couple were familiar and the discussion exposed the true extent of the operation.

This wasn't merely a land grab and an endeavour to profit from the dock's expansion. They intended to control the port and everything that came in and out, legal or otherwise. Whilst the drugs shipment appeared to be the headline news, it became a side note, a raindrop in the Atlantic compared to future developments. They discussed existing routes and how problematic they'd become. How they needed somewhere new that they controlled from top to bottom, including their preferred hauliers, Ferris Haulage. They had an unspecified temporary distribution centre up and running. And whilst it didn't state it explicitly; it suggested everything from guns, to drugs, to people filtered through there. The scale of things dawned on Jack. Maurice had been right. It was far bigger, and far more dangerous, than he ever imagined.

Maurice's voice peppered the audio, his part little more than that of a dogsbody. Someone used for his local connections and trying to cling on to the coattails of the big boys. The dominant voices smacked of Eton and Eastern Europe. Two worlds coming together and using Sunderland as their new gateway into Europe.

Nobody objected to business expansion and the jobs it brought to the region, and they could subcontract the role of keeping locals in check to someone like Maurice. They didn't need to worry themselves with people complaining about pigeon lofts, and God help those protestors if they ever intervened. Jack was in so far now, his feet touched the bottom of the ocean and he was wearing cement filled wellies.

But he had an advantage. He had the evidence. He made copies of emails, recorded the date of the drug consignment, albeit with little detail, and he had the audio recordings. This had to be enough to sink Maurice's development. If only Jack knew where to deliver the proof.

He knew Maurice paid off detectives, and DS Sidra Ramsay had it in for him. The newspapers were in his pocket and Noel Cardwell's presence showed even Government ministers weren't afraid to get their hands dirty. The fact Noel Cardwell was

Andrea's father only added to the complications.

How could he tell Andrea her father was facilitating smuggling and enabling criminals? How could he share evidence that might imprison her dad? He imagined the impact on Molly seeing her grandfather behind bars.

It wasn't a simple case of handing over the evidence and washing his hands; he needed to weigh his options. Whatever he did was risky, but was it bigger than the risk of doing nothing? Of selling up and pretending none of this happened. Could he live with himself if he not only allowed someone to snatch his business away from him, but feigned ignorance to criminal behaviour that brought misery to thousands?

While he owned the incriminating information, the opportunity remained to do something. What that was, he hadn't a clue, but it was preferable to have possession of the proof than to not be aware it existed. Unless somebody discovered he had it.

He lost track of time as he dug deeper into the documents and files that Reggie collated. Reggie's role became clearer. He wasn't collecting evidence to hand over to the police; he was never a grass as his family was at pains to point out at the funeral. Reggie gathered intelligence on behalf of his criminal associates down south. People with a vested interest in alternative smuggling routes, smuggling routes that may disrupt the power balance.

Jack wasn't sure how much information Reggie handed over, but the USB stick and the documents sitting in his desk drawer could be worth serious money to the right people. Or the wrong people.

Jack heard a sickening scream; from Molly's room.

He ran to the door, struggling to open it until he remembered he'd locked it to keep Andrea out. He wrestled with the key, then launched himself up the stairs, taking them three at a time. Andrea had reacted quicker and was comforting an inconsolable Molly.

"What's wrong? What's happened?"

"This is your fault, Jack." Andrea slapped him on the shoulder, then went back to pulling Molly's face into her belly.

"What's my fault? What have I done?"

"You've brought them into our house, Jack. Into Molly's bedroom. I told you to give in, but you refused to listen."

"Who's been in her bedroom?" Jack scanned the landing to see if anyone was still lurking. "What are you going on about?"

"That." Andrea pointed to Molly's bed.

A horse's head perched on the pillow. To be more precise, it was the rubber horse's mask Jack had thrown in the skip a week ago. They were watching him, and this was their way of letting him know.

Chapter Twenty-Three

Jack stormed past the personal assistant and straight into Maurice Groom's office.

"What the hell is this?" Jack threw the horse mask across the desk?

"I'm not sure." Maurice picked it up with the tips of his fingers. "And I'm not convinced I want to find out."

"You know." Jack had been awake through the night, comforting Molly and Andrea. He was tired, he was angry, and he wasn't letting Maurice get out of this one.

"I don't know what you're accusing me of." He waved away his PA, who was hovering at the door. "Or what you hope to gain by marching in here, but you're not in any position to be shouting the odds."

"Molly's bedroom, they came into my daughter's bedroom and left that in her bed."

"I'm unsure what the rules of engagement are in whatever perverted sex clubs you go to, but you want to be having this discussion with them."

"Perverted sex clubs? This was your people. You're behind this." Jack leaned on the desk, looking Maurice straight in the eye.

"Apart from the odd flutter on the Grand National, I have no interest in equine pursuits." Maurice took a sip of tea from a china cup. "I'm bemused at how you've connected this horseplay to me."

"You know where I found that mask. Have you forgotten why I had it?"

"So the mask is yours?"

"I dumped it in a skip that your refuse disposal company empties."

"We empty hundreds of skips and thousands of bins every day, do you think I ask for an inventory from each one?"

"If you assume this will scare me into selling my business, you're very much mistaken." Jack pointed at Maurice's face. "And tell your crooked mates to back off."

"Crooked mates?"

"I know what you're up to."

Maurice paused for a moment, considering the extent of Jack's discovery. "I've only met one crooked person," he slid open his desk drawer, removing several photos, "and that's you, Jack."

Jack studied the photos of him on the bus steps as a group of illegal immigrants ran to the trees. "But they, they had nothing to do with me."

"There are witnesses." Maurice passed over a copy of the local paper. "And the press have uncovered the story."

Jack scanned the article, which didn't mention names, nor were there any photos, but any idiot could join the dots. "This is bullshit."

"Maybe, maybe not. It's not for us to decide. I have

friends at the station I could pass it onto, and they could speak to their colleagues in immigration."

"Your pals down the nick, just like your mates in the press. You have everything sewn up, don't you?"

"At least my friends are still alive."

"If I find out you were involved in Reggie's death—"

"Hold on a minute there, Jack." Maurice rose and towered above him. "You've come into my office, flapping your lips and making ludicrous accusations. Now you're blaming me for your mate's suicide."

"Suicide?"

"You've got a vivid imagination, I'll give you that, but you need to remember who you're addressing here."

"I know exactly who I am talking to."

"I don't think you do, Jack. You don't understand at all." He leaned back in his chair. "I'm aware of your little gang of misfits sniffing around the tip, I even heard you were playing Miss Marple at Reggie's house yesterday. No doubt trying to find evidence of a crime that didn't happen. I've tried to be nice, I've tried to warn you, but now you've become an irritant."

"I'm glad I'm making you itch."

"You're a nobody, Jack. You'll never amount to anything resembling noteworthy, but that doesn't mean you can't be useful to us."

"Of use? To you?" said Jack.

"You're going on another little boat trip."

"Not for you, I'm not."

"Argue as much as you like, but you are." Maurice picked up the photos. "You've proven you have particular skills."

"Skills? I didn't know they were there."

"Plausible deniability, even better." He replaced the photos in the drawer. "You're off to see the tulips again, Jack."

"I'm going nowhere."

"After all this, you still believe you have a choice? You're still in control?"

"And you're in control, are you, Maurice? You might delude yourself that you're big time, that you're making the decisions, but you're not fooling anybody else. You're just another Harvey Oswald being lined up to take the fall for the big boys."

"You still don't get it, Jack. I'm a respected businessman and philanthropist. Admired in the community and beyond. If I want something to happen in this city, it happens, and nobody, especially you, can stop me."

"I get it, I get far more than you realise."

"Jack, you're a truck driver who attempted to plough his mate over in a bus carrying your own daughter. After your friend died, instead of grieving, you sailed off on a jaunt to Amsterdam and smuggled in a busload of illegals. Who will believe a word you say?"

"We'll see. I'm not going on any trip, Maurice."

"You are, Jack. I see you need a touch more persuasion, your stubbornness is not an attractive trait."

"It is from where I'm standing."

"Your choice, Jack, but whether I have to twist your testicles further, you're heading back to Amsterdam."

Jack didn't wait long for Maurice to flex his muscles. He'd been back at the yard an hour when there was an official sounding knock. Two men in hi-viz jackets entered and flashed their identification.

"Mr Ferris?"

"Yes."

"We're from the Health and Safety Executive. We've had reports of unsafe practices on site and we're here to carry out an inspection."

"Reports from where?"

"Intelligence can originate from a variety of sources, but that's not important." He peered over his glasses at his clipboard, then pushed the spectacles back up his nose. "What is important is that we safeguard the wellbeing of your staff and reassure the public."

"I take safety seriously."

"I believe you were involved in an accident recently. Is that correct?" He lifted his glasses onto his head as he waited for an answer.

"But that's been dealt with."

"Dealt with? I wasn't aware the criminal investigation had concluded."

"I mean dealt with here," said Jack.

"How so?"

"The individual responsible is no longer here."

"You've preempted the police inquiry?"

"No, the person responsible, who I consider responsible," Jack fiddled with the collar of his shirt, "there were other issues, we had to let him go."

"Other issues?"

"Nothing connected to Health and Safety."
Jack didn't want to get into a conversation about Derek and his suspicions.

"It won't look great if you were seeking to keep someone away from the investigation."

"It's not like that."

"Isn't it?" He raised his eyebrows.

"Remind me again why you're here," said Jack.

"Routine inspection."

"Routine? You said there'd been reports?"

The inspector dropped the spectacles from his head onto his nose and read his clipboard. "Yes, reports. Do you have the relevant paperwork to hand?"

"And where did these reports come from?" Jack came from behind his desk.

"The reports are none of your concern if everything is in order."

"Maurice sent you, didn't he?"

"Maurice? I'm not aware of any Maurice."

"What a load of shit," said Jack, shaking his head. "He's pulling your strings the same as he's trying to pull mine."

"Mr Ferris, we've explained why we're here and what we wish to inspect. You can try to make it difficult for us if you choose, but you're only making things worse for yourself."

"Let's see your ID again."

"Are you sure you want to do this? Appear difficult?"

"I'm sure."

Both inspectors handed over their badges. They looked genuine, but Jack wouldn't know.

"You're welcome to phone the Health and Safety Executive to verify our credentials, but any reasonable man would assume you were stalling for time." He removed his glasses and put them in his pocket.

Jack handed the badges back. "What's the point?"

Jack opened the filing cabinet to retrieve the documentation, then switched the kettle on as they inspected the files. He didn't offer them a cup.

There was a second knock, and Ted wandered into the

office. "Jack, there're blokes downstairs. Official types."

"Official?" He turned to the inspectors. "There's more of you?"

"Just us two. We'd love a cuppa if you're making one. Paperwork is thirsty work, that's what we always say."

"Who are they, Ted?"

"Immigration, Jack, they say they're from immigration."

Jack peeked through the blinds. Several uniformed men swarmed the yard and guarded the entrance. "What do they want?"

"Asked to see my papers," said Ted.

"Your papers?"

"Aye, to show I had leave to remain in the country or some such shite."

"Leave to remain?"

"I'm sixty-odd-year-old and haven't stepped out of Sunderland in forty years. Not got a passport because I've never needed one. Not been abroad, apart from back in seventy-nine when our lass dragged me to Scotland. Full of midgies, so we spun the car around and drove home. Never again."

"They singled you out?"

"They're asking all the lads, they're having a proper snoop around."

"Shitting hell. I'll find out what they're after. Keep an eye on the Two Ronnies here whilst I'm gone." He slammed the door behind him.

"How do lads?" said Ted.

They didn't reply.

Jack raced down the stairs into the yard. "Who's in charge?"

An official pointed towards the garage and another clipboard.

"Jack Ferris?"

"Who are you?"

"Immigration." He brandished a badge. Again, Jack couldn't tell if it was real, but they'd gone to a lot of trouble if it wasn't.

"Immigration?"

"We've had reports."

"Where've I heard that before?"

"You're reported often for illegal workers?"

"Illegal workers?"

"Illegal immigrants, people without the relevant credentials."

"No, never." Jack had to tread carefully. He didn't know where this was leading, or how much Maurice had revealed.

"We need to validate everybody's papers, have a look around and check everything's in order."

"Of course everything's in bloody order. I don't employ foreigners."

"Don't employ foreigners? That's not very enlightened in the current climate."

"Illegal ones, you understood what I meant." Jack got in the officer's face. "You asked Ted for his leave to remain for fuck's sake."

"Your point is?"

"He's nigh on a pensioner, and he gets nose bleeds if he leaves Ryhope for too long. He's as British as they come."

"There shouldn't be any problems then." The officer opened the door of the lorry cab. "Do many trips overseas, Mr Ferris?"

"It's our core business."

"Ever have issues with illegal boarders?"

"Illegal boarders?" Jack tugged his collar again. "Not sure what you mean."

"Immigrants trying to hitch a lift without you knowing. Bet you get it all the time at Calais."

"Not so much." Jack wanted to change the subject. "I guess you'll still want everybody's paperwork?"

"We will, yes."

"Step into the office," said Jack, heading for the stairs, "join the queue."

Chapter Twenty-Four

The passage across the North Sea had been smooth, and Jack sailed through customs with his paperwork in order. He pulled into the warehouse on the outskirts of Amsterdam, as dull and innocuous as any other. The labourers unloaded the trailer of its nominal load, premium recycled waste from Maurice's recycling depot. An uncomplicated delivery, a perfect trip. The return journey promised not to be so straightforward.

This formed the easy part, a legitimate shipment to a company with no notion of the next step of the plan. Jack asked to use the bathroom and sat in the trap, guts churning, wondering how he'd got himself to this point. Despite the evidence Reggie collected, Maurice and his cohorts still held not just the cards, but the whole casino. They owned proof of Jack's people-smuggling, albeit inadvertently, and had direct lines to government departments who made life difficult for Jack.

Worse than any of the threats to Jack himself, they proved they could walk into his house and threaten his family, and he had no way of stopping them. He didn't doubt they'd take it further if they saw fit.

There was no point fighting. He'd sell the company. Andrea had been pushing for the sale and the horse's head put the ink in the deal signing pen. Jack had stormed into Maurice's office full of rage, but in the back of his mind, he knew he'd bend to Maurice's wishes, giving him the business. But that wasn't enough for Mr Groom.

Maurice twisted the screw, reasserted authority over people he still controlled. Jack reminded him how insignificant a player he was in the larger scheme, and Maurice returned the favour. He could have taken his chances and refused, but the horse in the bed wasn't a playful warning. It was a reminder they'd been watching him and they weren't only targeting Jack; Molly was in danger. Here he sat, in a filthy toilet cubicle in a vast, anonymous warehouse outside Amsterdam. Knowing his next move took him so far into the criminal world that there was no turning back.

Trailer and bowels unloaded, and paperwork taken care of, Jack fired the wagon's ignition and checked his destination on the map. The truck had sat nav, but they'd warned him not to use it for this stage; they didn't want a trackable record of his visit. Another twelve miles, another innocuous warehouse on a dull industrial estate, the only obvious distinction being the heavy Eastern European contingent. And an intimidating armed presence.

The gunmen ordered him to wait in the office while they loaded the wagon. The trailer didn't belong to him. He'd collected it along with the load at the landfill site. He assumed they'd customised it for whatever merchandise he brought back. On the face of it he was delivering used machinery parts, and that's what the documentation showed. But they hid a secondary cargo in the hold and nobody advised him what it was, or even acknowledged its existence. He tried to ask, but none of Maurice's men answered.

The less he knew, the better.

Maurice hinted it was people-smuggling, again, but it could be drugs, it may be guns, it might even be bombs. He wanted to burst out of the office and run all the way to the ferry, but before he set foot on deck, they'd harm Andrea and Molly. He couldn't risk it. So he waited.

He felt he'd been there for hours when they gave him the paperwork and told him to be on his way. Jack asked them to warn him of any complications regarding the shipment. If people holed up in the trailer, did they have enough food and water? It was a long slog home with a fifteen hour ferry journey. They ignored his question and talked amongst themselves in whatever language they spoke.

The weather turned by the time he arrived at the port at Ijmulden. The rain lashed, and the wind had picked up. It promised to be a bumpy crossing. Jack sat in the queue of wagons waiting to embark, edging ever closer to the point of no return. Once he passed the checkpoint, that was it. He was a criminal, a smuggler, and even further under the thumb of Maurice and his crooked masters. The sweat streamed out of him. Jack's wipers were running at full speed, keeping rain off his windscreen. He needed a pair for his forehead.

Maybe it was possible to turn around, abandon the wagon and board the ferry by foot. Nobody would realise until the consignment didn't arrive at the other end. By then, he'd have a small window to get Andrea and Molly to safety before the gangsters reacted. Where could they go? He had no family to speak of and with Andrea's father implicated in the plot; he was no help. Andrea and Molly didn't deserve this. Jack had created this mess. He placed his head on the steering wheel and sobbed.

A knock on the glass startled him. "Shit." Jack wiped his

eyes and wound down the window.

"Papers, please?" The Dutch customs official cheerier than expected for someone in his role and in complete contrast to Jack's mood.

Jack passed over the paperwork.

The official inspected it, but everything was in order, and he handed the documentation back to Jack with a smile. "You're in for a rough crossing. Hope you get through it okay."

"It's going to be choppy. Who knows whether I'll survive to the other side?"

Parked in the hold, Jack stepped from his cab and resisted the urge to check on his cargo. He performed a perfunctory check of the wagon to make sure everything was secure and listened for any noises or clues whether it was a human consignment as he suspected. It was a fifteen hour crossing on choppy seas. Jack expected it to be rough in his cabin, despite en-suite facilities. If there were stowaways secreted somewhere in the trailer, how would they manage? He was unsure whether they had adequate provisions and they didn't have toilet facilities. He didn't want to consider how they'd cope.

His stomach heaved again. He looked to see if there was anyone he could hand himself into, admit his wrongdoing, and throw himself at the mercy of the law. Saving the wretched souls in the hold. Deckhands busied themselves securing freight, truck drivers parked and carried out their business, passengers arrived in their cars. A people carrier pulled in opposite him. A girl, a similar age to Molly, smiled at him and waved. He ran up the steps to the deck, gasping for air. Grasping the handrail, he vomited onto the jetty.

"Struggling to get your sea legs. We haven't even set off

yet, mate," said a fellow truck driver sneaking in an illicit fag break.

Jack wiped his forehead with his sleeve and retired to his room. He couldn't face other people.

He lay on his bunk, staring at the ceiling. What had he become? All because he was too stubborn to give up a business for which he now realised he couldn't give a toss. He checked his watch. The ship should have set sail an hour ago, but they were still in dock. A voice came over the tannoy, first in Dutch, then English, announcing a four-hour delay until the weather improved. Jack thought of his load and ran to the en-suite to be sick again.

Once they left the dock, the ship lurched and rolled, throwing Jack from his bunk on more than a couple of occasions. He'd been on many a rough sea crossing and considered himself to have strong sea legs, yet he'd heaved his guts multiple times on this trip.

When things calmed after five hours, Jack shuffled his way to the upper decks to contemplate food. Whilst still queasy, he'd brought up so much that he was starving and needed something. He glanced at the hot food, but the merest whiff of curry made him nauseous. He saw other passengers making the most of the trip, oblivious to the conditions, drinking, laughing, stuffing their faces. How could they? He bought a sandwich and a bottle of water and staggered to his cabin.

He managed one half of his sandwich and put the rest to one side. After a couple gulps of water, he lay back and tried to sleep. The rocking of the boat and the turmoil in his head prevented him from drifting off despite being shattered. Progress was slow and when the ferry docked in North Shields, a fifteen hour crossing had become twenty-one hours. Jack was tired and unwell and the thought of what lay ahead did nothing to help his general wellbeing. If he hadn't brought up every morsel in his stomach earlier, he'd have been ill once more.

Diesel engines roared into life as the bow door opened and disembarking begun. Jack approached customs with an impending sense of doom. He lowered the window, handing over his passport and paperwork.

The customs official checked Jack's photo and then his face, then back at the photo again. "Are you okay there?"

"Yes, thanks."

"Your face is a different colour to the one in your passport. Rough crossing?"

"You could say that."

"Mind if we look in the back?"

"Be my guest." He stepped from the cab and trudged to the back, opening the doors, not knowing what sight would greet him.

The customs official clambered aboard with his torch and climbed over crates, checking every nook and cranny. Jack leaned against the wagon, his legs making hard work of supporting him.

The official climbed back down and handed Jack his paperwork. "Thank you. Hopefully, the rest of your journey isn't so unpleasant."

On arriving at the landfill site, they waved Jack through and directed him to a warehouse further back, out of sight to the others. The shutter rolled up for him and closed the moment he was inside the warehouse. There was a flurry of action, forklifts reversing and removing the pallets containing the machinery. Nothing appeared untoward. Perhaps this whole exercise had been to test Jack, to see if he'd do as they told him.

Once they unloaded the legitimate cargo, a second gang of workers climbed aboard and removed panels beneath where the pallets had been. Pairs of eyes emerged from the bowels of the

HGV. The stench was horrendous, even from where Jack was standing. Puke and shit, urine and fear. Girls as young as thirteen, covered in their own mess, crying. The gang leader pushed them to one side as he counted, taking an occasional blast from his asthma inhaler. Faces scratched off a list. Once validated, a worker led them away.

Voices rose as they checked the inventory, and there were shouts from deep in the trailer. They deposited a further young girl to the ground, sporting a filthy Justin Bieber t-shirt, her broken leg at right angles to where it should have been. Then a dull thud. A body hit the concrete. An auburn-haired skinny woman, not much over twenty-years-old. Dead.

"Mr Ferris." The man with the inhaler approached Jack. "You have delivered damaged goods."

"The conditions on the crossing were horrific. How can you pack girls in like that and expect them to survive? It's inhumane." His legs gave way, and he crumbled to the floor, sobbing.

"Your job was to deliver the goods intact." He wheezed and took another blast. "You have failed, we're two short."

"I did as they told me."

"You owe us for two missing items, Mr Ferris."

"You can't hold me responsible for the poor girl dying."

"We can and we will." He produced a gun from his inside pocket and shot the injured girl in the forehead. "For both."

Chapter Twenty-Five

The events of the previous evening left Jack unable to face work. He'd dropped the wagon off on his way home and tried to sleep, but the images of the two girls never left. Eyes closed, eyes open, lights on, lights off. Their faces still haunted him. Andrea asked him what was wrong, but he couldn't tell her. He'd never let her in on his pain. He caused the death of two young women. Jack may not have arranged it, he may not have carried out the act, but the responsibility lay with him. He'd never lose the sickening feeling at the pit of his stomach whenever he thought about it, which was every tick of the clock.

Andrea left for school, taking Molly with her. Jack sat in the kitchen in his boxers and a t-shirt, cradling a cup of coffee. He'd eaten nothing. Whenever he heard a car go past, he expected it was the police coming for him. Or somehow the girls' families tracked him down and wanted revenge. Jack had no way of making this right. His conscience pulled him towards handing himself over to the authorities and confessing his crime. But the sole reason he got involved, the one reason he made the fateful trip in the first place, was the threat of what they'd do to Andrea and Molly if he spoke to the police.

Maurice controlled various coppers on his payroll, and Jack hadn't sussed out where DS Sidra Ramsay sat. But he knew she didn't sit on Jack's side. He could storm into Maurice's office again. Rant and rave, draw a fraction of the hurt out of him and put it on somebody else, but Maurice didn't care. It would achieve nothing. The remorse haunted him. Stuck with the knowledge his own stubbornness and stupidity had dragged him into this.

The evidence he'd collected, that Reggie collected, lay in front of him on the kitchen bench. The one thing putting him in jeopardy and the only thing keeping him safe. Whilst he had it, he was always a target. They only knew he'd been to Reggie's house, not that he'd found the information. As long as they remained unsure of what he had, and didn't know what he had planned for the evidence, they needed to treat Jack with a modicum of caution.

He had to sell. That was without question. Andrea was right, he should have done it long ago. He'd gift the business to Maurice if it protected his family, but it wouldn't be enough. Jack could hand it to Maurice with a solemn vow never to mention any of it, but he'd witnessed a murder on Maurice's premises by someone he assumed in Maurice's employment. They couldn't allow Jack to carry this knowledge around with him. He was on borrowed time.

A well established smuggling enterprise, with routes, vehicles and cargo sorted. The trip would have happened without Jack. But they were teaching him a lesson, leaving him in no doubt who was in control. It wasn't him.

He caught a whiff of himself and realised he stunk. Jack hadn't showered on the ferry, too busy fretting about his cargo, and he'd headed straight to bed when he returned home. Edging himself from the stool, he went for a shower. Whilst the scalding hot water cleansed his outside, his inside needed it more. He'd never cleanse himself of this. Whether guilty in the eyes of the law, despite mitigating circumstances, he wasn't sure. Jack wasn't religious, so wasn't fussed over how he looked in the eyes of the Lord. But in his mind, what he thought of himself, the guilt was on him and he deserved punishment.

Jack dried himself and got dressed. Whilst he didn't feel up to working, he had obligations to his workers, individuals such as Ted who'd worked for the Ferris family for decades. How could he tell Ted he was selling to a bunch of criminals? And if Ted didn't lose his job, he'd more than likely be implicated in a criminal conspiracy?

Whatever Jack did, it harmed someone. Innocent people who merited none of this. Reggie was dead. Andrea and Molly were in danger. Ted might lose his livelihood, or worse. And two unnamed Eastern European girls lay dead somewhere. All because Jack wouldn't back down, refused to accept that every argument wasn't his to win.

His phone rang, he was reluctant to answer. Whoever was calling wouldn't be bringing good news. He checked the screen; Bill Tindall. Jack rejected the call. With everything that was happening, Jack had forgotten there was a race meeting today. After Reggie died, Jack paid a couple of lads in the pigeon club to look after his birds. He didn't have the time himself, and he'd lost interest. His bird topped the favourite's list in the event. He didn't care if it won or not. Things important two weeks ago no longer mattered.

The phone buzzed again. Bill wasn't going away.

Jack hit the green accept button. "Bill?"

"Jack, you need to get yourself down to the lofts."

"Bill, I've too much on, mate. I'm needed at the yard and I've got shitloads to do."

"It's important, Jack."

"Sorry I forgot the race, but I've loads happening. If the bird's won, give the prize money to the lads, they've earned it."

"Not calling about the competition, Jack. They've gone."

"They've gone? What's gone?"

"The lofts, Jack. Somebody's burnt the fucking lofts down."

Jack arrived at a scene of chaos and confusion. Two fire engines and their crews were finishing up, the flames gone, but the embers still smouldering, acrid smoke burning Jack's nostrils.

The pigeon club had assembled the lofts over decades, with multiple layers of varnish and paint, many stretching back to when they nicked it from the shipyards. Jack suspected most of it to be unsafe by today's standards, and the fumes being given off would not be healthy.

Most of the members were there, and they all backed Bill as he rounded on Jack.

"This is your fault."

"Me?"

"I said you should sell the yard." Bill pushed Jack in the chest. "But you had to be stubborn. Mr self fucking righteous."

"Selling the business has nothing to do with the pigeon lofts."

"Bollocks, is it nowt to do with the lofts. It's connected and they want you gone. They want us gone. We could have walked away with no drama, set up somewhere new, but you had to argue the toss."

Bill removed his flat cap and ran his hand through the few hairs remaining on his head.

"You can still relocate."

"With no fucking birds?"

"The birds? The pigeons were at home? I thought they were out racing?" Jack tried to get to where his loft was.

Bill dragged him back. "We only sent the top ones to the race. Weather forecast was ropey, and we didn't want to risk the young uns, scared we might lose one or two in the storm. Ended up losing every bastard one now." Bill was crying. "I've been doing this my entire life, Jack. What am I going to do now?"

"We could—"

Any words he uttered were pointless. Jack placed a hand on Bill's shoulder, but he shrugged it off.

"You're out, Jack."

"Out?"

"Of the club. We've had a vote, you're too much trouble."

"How can you call a vote without holding a meeting?"

"Don't make it difficult," said Bill. "You're not wanted, let us rebuild in peace."

"You can't chuck me out."

"I'm being as fair as I can, Jack. The lads don't want you around, but your subs are paid up till the end of the month. We'll let you compete in one final race. You've still got birds out there." Bill pointed skywards. "Most of us aren't so lucky."

There was no point arguing. Jack brushed past Bill and inspected where his loft used to stand. It was little more than a pile of ash, his younger birds roasted to a crisp. He picked up a bone. Death surrounded him.

"Mr Ferris, do you care to give us a statement?" Nancy Whitworth shoved a microphone in his face.

"Where the shitting hell did you spring from?"

"Where there's smoke, there's fire. As a journalist, I'm trained to sniff these things out."

"You're not a journalist, you're just a mouthpiece for whoever is paying you."

"I am a journalist, I was highly commended—"

"Yeah, you mentioned it once before. Maybe you should consult your paymasters about the blaze."

"My sources tell me it was teenage vandals."

"Sources? You've got no sources."

"Teenagers frustrated at the lack of job opportunities in the city."

"Get that away from me." Jack slapped the mic from her hand. "What happened to reporters jotting things in a notepad?"

"The world's moved on, Mr Ferris, you should do the same."

Jack walked off without acknowledging her. He sought to comfort the lads, but they shunned him.

Hard as nails men, who'd fight anyone down the Queen's Head, were in tears at the loss of their pigeons. Jack didn't antagonise them further. He needed to sort this. How he sorted it was a mystery, but it had to end.

As he passed the fire engines, Jack noticed a face in the bystanders, the rubberneckers getting off on the excitement. Most with their phones out, no doubt posting pictures and videos to social media, not contemplating the devastation it had caused to people's lives. One face stood out. It stood out because Derek Pearson was smirking.

Jack grabbed him by the windpipe and pushed him through the crowd. "You best pray you had nothing to do with this, Derek."

"You're not the boss of me." He struggled to loosen Jack's grip. "You can't push me around anymore."

"I'll push you over this fence and into the fucking river if you're responsible."

"What if I was? You won't do a thing."

"You'd burn down these lofts, kill everybody's pigeons, because I sacked you?"

"Best thing that ever happened to me. You reckon I'm bothered about being sacked by you?"

"Why did you do it then?"

"I have a new gaffer, Jack. One who recognises my talents and doesn't belittle me."

"What talents?"

"See what I mean?" Derek wrestled Jack's grasp from his throat. "My new boss appreciates me, understands my skill set."

"Skillset?" Jack let out an involuntary laugh. "I know who you work for, Derek. We've seen you lurking around the dump. A place well matched with your capabilities."

"I don't work at the tip, Jack. My brief is far more wide ranging."

"I realise what's happening there, and the characters involved, I understand why they'd prefer to keep you away."

"You think that's the only place they run operations? They have plenty more specialised locations. And guess who they've put in charge?"

"You're not even in charge of putting on a splash of deodorant in the morning. Nobody trusts you."

"You'll regret those words, Jack. Just wait, wait until they come back to bite your pompous arse."

The fire engines left the scene, their work done. The lofts were now a pile of damp ash, and the lads picked through the remains. There was nothing to recover. They destroyed everything.

Jack sat on a nearby rock and watched them come to terms with their loss. The pigeon crees weren't just bits of wood and nails. They represented something, something that had lasted decades. Whatever had happened in Sunderland over the years, the miner's strike, shipyards closing, the football team forever disappointing, the pigeons had been a constant. But now they were dead, and Jack was to blame.

The club could rebuild elsewhere, but they'd lost something they could never get back. Jack looked down the hill to his yard, his father's yard before him. He was about to surrender his link to the past generations. If he wasn't careful, he'd lose all links to the present one.

DS Sidra Ramsay spoke to the lone PC left at the site and made a beeline for Jack.

"Mr Ferris?"

"Just what I need," thought Jack. "DS Ramsay, what a lovely surprise."

"Bit of a mess, isn't it?" she pointed towards the remnants of the lofts.

"Certainly is."

"Any suspects?" said Sidra.

"Isn't that your responsibility?"

"Hoped you might join a few dots for me."

"Dots?"

"I don't normally bother myself with vandalism. Little more than kids playing with matches when they should be at school. But there've been several suspicious incidents recently, and there's one thing that links them together."

"What's that?"

"You, Mr Ferris."

"I link nothing, DS Ramsay, just a victim, same as

everybody else." He stood and wiped the muck from the seat of his jeans.

"My offer still stands," said Sidra.

"What offer's that?"

"Tell me what's in there." Sidra tapped his head with her biro. "We both know you've not been telling me the truth, not the whole truth."

"I'm afraid you know nothing."

"Yeah? I'm afraid of that." She put the pen to her chin. "Reggie Higgins looked after your pigeons, didn't he?"

"How did you know that?"

"I'm a detective. And you mentioned it the last time we spoke."

Jack had forgotten what he'd told her and what he hadn't. In the past, he worked on a policy of honesty. Then you'd never get caught in a lie. Those days were long gone.

"He used to," said Jack, "not anymore."

"And you think the two things are connected?"

"Do you?"

"That's what I'm seeking to establish, Jack. Could Reggie have been hiding something in the lofts?"

"Hiding something? Like what?"

"Drugs, evidence, anything." She rubbed her calf. It was cramping up again.

"Believe me, Reggie wouldn't hide stuff anywhere so straightforward."

Sidra jotted a note in her little black notebook. "But he would hide stuff?"

Jack shrugged. He didn't want to get into this. "He was more complex than he appeared, that's all."

"So I gather."

"What does that mean?"

"Nothing, nothing much. Are you aware of Reggie's occupation?"

"Lollipop Man, best we've had."

"His previous occupation?"

"Yeah." There was no point in lying. "I suspected he had a past when I encountered the congregation at his funeral."

"Can you put names to any faces you recognised?" Sidra said, poised with pen and pad in hand.

"Afraid not. Although one of your mates was there, he might be able to help."

"My mates?"

"Detective, from Southwick nick, Stoker ."

Sidra paused for a moment. "I noticed. You wouldn't know the connection between him and Maurice Groom?"

"Sorry, until a fortnight ago, my interaction with the local constabulary was non-existent. Can't get rid of you now."

"Yeah, we're a bugger to shake off." Sidra placed her pen and notebook in her bag. "You realise that I'm trying to help you, Jack?"

"I'm sure you are, DS Ramsay." He brushed by her. "But I'm way beyond help."

Jack dropped to his haunches and inspected the spot where his loft used to be. Apart from tiny bones, there wasn't a hint of what once stood there. It may have been the dust from the ash, but he had tears in his eyes. He worried that if he started crying now, he might never stop. He composed himself, wiping his eyes with his sleeve.

"Did DS Ramsay have any news?" Nancy Whitworth was back.

"Shouldn't you be asking her?" said Jack.

"She won't speak to me."

"Wise woman." Maybe DS Ramsay wasn't as bad as Jack thought.

"That's not nice, Mr Ferris. I'm only doing my job, it's tough being a journalist."

"It's tough owning a haulage business or racing pigeons. Nothing's easy in this life. You'll learn that one day. It's time you grew up and got in the real world."

"Why is everyone so horrible to me?" Nancy was nearer to tears than Jack. "I worked hard at university, I was highly—"

"Highly commended, you said."

"But when I try to do my job, everybody swears and bullies me. Apart from the odd person who gives me a tip off, nobody wants to help a journalist."

"I'll help you, just this once." Jack crouched to her eye level. "Take a closer look at the people who are helping you, the ones giving you the tip offs. Ask why they're doing that rather than getting upset at victims who don't wish to talk to a nosey little bugger when they're full of emotion." Jack walked away, leaving Nancy more confused than ever.

There was a flutter of wings above him. Jack's champion homing pigeon was home. Except he no longer had one.

Chapter Twenty-Six

"Talk to the police, Jack." Andrea threw the tea towel onto the bench.

"It's not that easy."

"Isn't it?"

"Sell the business, find a job, go to the coppers. Everything's so bloody straightforward."

"Yeah, because my life is straightforward? The parents and teachers question my integrity daily at work and because of that, my daughter now hates me because she's not in that stupid school play."

"Molly doesn't hate you."

"Feels that way. It's okay for you, Jack. You can jump in your lorry and disappear, but I'm the one at home, holding things together."

"And I enjoy being away from home?" Jack dumped his mug in the sink.

"Don't you?"

"Of course not. I have to go away, so I've got a home to

return to, so we've got a home."

"There's no *have to* about it, you've never considered other possibilities."

"I'll sell the business, Andrea. I don't give a shit anymore, I'd throw the bugger away, but it's gone past that, way past it."

"Let them have it and we can begin again."

"You're not listening, it's complicated."

"How?" Andrea grasped her hair in frustration. "What's so difficult?"

"I know things, they know things. They won't give up."

"What do you mean, they know things? What have you done, Jack?"

"Nothing, not deliberately. It's best I don't tell you."

"Don't hide stuff from me, I need to figure out what's in that head of yours."

"I'm trying to keep us safe."

"And how's that strategy working out for you so far? They've torched your pigeon lofts — "

"It might not be them. Maybe it was an accident."

"They've been in our house, Jack. In our daughter's room. How is that keeping us safe?"

Jack walked into the sitting room and switched on the TV. "I'm trying, Andrea, I really am, but it's not enough."

Andrea snatched the remote from him and turned it off again. "That's why you must talk to the police. We need to talk to someone, we can't carry on like this."

"I can't speak to the police, we can't speak to anyone until I can figure a way out of this."

"What's next, Jack. The intruder, the pigeon lofts, the accident, don't tell me the bus crash was them as well?"

Jack shrugged. "They, I don't—"

"Molly was on that bus." Andrea slumped onto the sofa. "What have you dragged us into?"

"I'll get us out."

"Who are we dealing with, Jack? Maurice Groom is slimy, but intimidation, is he capable? What do they want from us?"

"It's me, they want something from me."

"Give it to them. Put an end to this."

"I can't." Jack was now looking at the floor.

"Why not?"

"Because it might be the only thing keeping me alive."

Andrea stormed out of the room and Jack heard her footsteps stomping up the stairs. He should tell her the truth, but how could he admit he'd caused the deaths of two young girls? How did he explain he was now in the sights of a serious criminal gang who'd stop at nothing to get what they wanted?

How could he confess he possessed the evidence that might just put a stop to this, if only he worked out where to deliver it?

Andrea banged and clattered upstairs, opening and slamming every door.

"JACK! JACK!"

He was up the stairs in seconds. Andrea was on the landing, hand covering a face drained of colour. She handed him a note. "They've taken Molly."

Jack's head spun. He grasped the bannister to prevent him from tumbling back down the staircase. The pain returned behind his eyes; he felt he might pass out.

"Who've, what…" He grabbed the note from Andrea. It was old-school letters cut out from newspapers and stuck on the paper with glue. Three simple words spelled out. **YOU WERE WARNED.**

Andrea ran into their bedroom and returned with the phone. As she dialled, Jack grabbed it from her. "What are you doing?"

"Dialling 999." She attempted to snatch it back from him.

"We can't."

"Jack, what bit of this don't you understand? They've taken our little girl. Our beautiful ten-year-old girl. We have to get her back."

"We will, I promise, just not the police."

"You've had your chance, Jack. Every decision you've taken up to now has brought us to this point." She made another swipe for the phone. "I'm making the decisions now."

She bolted for the stairs. Jack blocked her path. "Let me explain, Andrea. Let me explain so you realise what bringing the law into this will do." He led her into the bedroom and sat her on Molly's bed.

He placed the phone out of Andrea's reach and tried to take her hand. She snatched it from him and took the pillow, putting it to her face, savouring Molly's scent.

"I found information on Maurice and his friends. On how he planned to seize the yard and the lofts."

"You've told me this, Jack. This isn't bringing Molly back."

"I hoped I could use it as leverage, make them back down."

"Again, information you've already shared with me."

"You don't understand. You don't understand why they need the docks and the business."

"I don't understand because you won't tell me."

"I'm telling you now."

"Get to the point because they have my daughter and I need to bring her home."

"They're dangerous, Andrea, very dangerous."

"Jack, they've kidnapped our little girl. I'm well aware they're bloody dangerous."

"It's bigger than I thought. They want the docks as part of an illegal smuggling operation."

"You've got evidence of this."

"Yes."

"So why don't you give it to the police?"

"It's not that easy," said Jack.

"Don't start that again, I'll smother you with this pillow."

"The detectives are in on it. Maurice is paying them off."

"There'll be other police, ones who aren't bent."

"But we don't know who they are. If we speak to the wrong ones, we'd be putting Molly in more danger."

Andrea stifled a scream in the pillow. "How can she be in more danger?"

"It's not only Maurice mixed up with this gang, it involves your father."

"My father?"

"His political connections are smoothing everything over, he'll be taking a huge cut."

"My father wouldn't allow them to kidnap Molly. We'll speak to him, he'll get her back."

"Your father is interested in nobody but himself. He disowned you when we hooked up because I'm beneath you and would bring trouble to the family."

"I wonder what gave him that impression."

"He sees Molly as an extension of me, he doesn't care."

"That's not true, Molly's his granddaughter."

"He's a sanctimonious prick. A typical Tory who'd sell his own grandkids to make himself a few quid."

"That's not fair, you've never liked him."

"And he's never liked me, so we're all square."

"This isn't getting Molly back, we must call the police."

"We can't."

"Why not?"

"Because I'm involved, Andrea, they hold stuff on me. If they go down, I go down."

"What stuff? What could they hold on you?"

"Smuggling." He avoided looking her in the face and instead stared at the unicorn pictures on Molly's bedroom wall.

"Smuggling?" She clutched his shoulder and dragged him so he was facing her. "Smuggling what? Tobacco? Drugs?"

"People."

"Jesus…" Andrea put both hands to her mouth. "Why, Jack? Why on earth would you involve yourself in people smuggling?"

"It was by accident," he attempted to take her hand again, but she swiped it away, "at first."

"What have you become, Jack?"

"I hoped it was a path out, assumed if I went along with it they'd leave me alone, leave us alone."

"We can still go to the police. If it wasn't your fault, I'm sure they'd understand. Tell them everything, strike a deal."

"It's not as easy as that."

"Jack—"

"People died because of me."

Andrea ran from the room.

When she came back, Jack was still on Molly's bed. "I

don't care if you end up in prison, Jack. I only want my daughter back, so you do what you like, but I'm going to the police."

The doorbell rang.

The doorbell rang again, then a firm knock. "Molly!" They raced to the bottom of the stairs, Jack getting there ahead of Andrea. He opened the door.

"Mr Ferris?"

"DS Ramsay?"

"Do you know—" said Andrea.

"No, we've yet to prove who started the fire," said Sidra, "that's why I need another word with your husband."

"Not the fire, about—"

"About the bus crash, Andrea was wondering when they'd sort the insurance." Jack shot Andrea a glance and gave her a slight shake of the head.

"Sorry, not my department. Can I come in?" Sidra had a boot wedged in the door, despite Jack trying to pull it around.

"Yes, please do," said Andrea as she snatched it open.

Jack and Andrea sat in armchairs, Sidra on the settee.

"Have you any ideas about who may have done this, Jack?"

"Jack has a few theories." Andrea glared at him.

"Care to share them, Mr Ferris."

"Vandals." Jack was sweating. "It'll be bored teenagers, usually is."

"Usually," said Sidra, "not always." She rubbed the back of her calf. It was still tight.

"It's where I'd be looking."

"Luckily, it's not your responsibility to look. I wouldn't be doing my job if I didn't explore every avenue."

"Isn't it the most obvious suspect in ninety per cent of cases?"

"It's the ten per cent that interests me, Jack. Do you have any other theories?"

"Not off the top of my head." He wiped his sweaty palms on the arm of the chair and hoped Sidra didn't notice. "Vandals."

"No enemies?"

"We're a pigeon club. Other than hardline animal rights activists, I'm not sure who we could upset, and I doubt they'd kill a hundred pigeons to make a point."

"I was thinking about you rather than the club. Anybody you've annoyed?"

Jack looked towards Andrea, then back to Sidra. "Not that I'm aware of."

"Returning to the pigeon club, I understand they've expelled you."

"Not expelled, a parting of the ways, a difference of opinions."

"About what?"

"Emotions were running high after the blaze, things were said. Things people didn't mean."

"Like what?"

"Nothing specific, just blokes letting off steam, it's how we are."

"I'd considered pigeon racing to be a gentile sport, maybe I'd underestimated it."

"It's a grand sport, pastime of the common man and kings alike."

"I might pop along to watch one day."

"Not much to see since the lofts have gone."

"A couple lads said your expulsion wasn't related to the

arson, something regarding Amsterdam, any idea what that's about?"

"Lads on tour nonsense. People do stuff when they're away, they'd prefer folk at home didn't discover. Amsterdam's criminal for that sort of behaviour."

"You know things about individuals?" Andrea butted back into the conversation. "Things they don't want made public?"

Jack glowered at her. "Something like that."

Sidra sensed the tension. "Molly not here?"

"She's—"

"In bed." Jack cut Andrea off.

"I'll just go and…" Andrea left the room, struggling to hide her tears.

"Sorry, to disturb you, Mr Ferris. I'll leave you and your family to it, but if there's anything you need to speak to me about, anything at all. My phone is always on."

Jack closed the front door, his fingers rested on the handle, as if he was unwilling to go back inside and face whatever was taking place.

Andrea didn't allow him that luxury. "Jack, she could have helped."

"How can we be sure she's not involved?" said Jack. "She's landed just after Molly has disappeared. What if they sent her in to study our reactions?"

"Not everyone is part of your conspiracy, Jack. Not everybody works for Maurice Groom."

"Even if she doesn't, she won't believe us. If she accepted our story, we have the issue of them knowing we've gone to the police. We didn't have a choice."

"What's your suggestion then, Jack? You seem to have it

all worked out. How are we planning to rescue our daughter from these gangsters who, as you've just informed me, will execute people worthless to them?" She made a lunge for the door. "I'm getting that detective back."

Jack grabbed her and dragged her from the door. "We can't Andrea, we can't."

Andrea fought him off, but as she got outside, DS Ramsay's car was leaving the estate.

The realisation hit Jack, and he slid down the wall, crying.

"You've done this, Jack. You." Andrea slammed the door and ran up the stairs to Molly's bedroom.

Jack gave it five minutes until he'd composed himself, then followed Andrea upstairs. She was lying on Molly's bed, sobbing into her pillow.

"I'll bring her back," said Jack.

"How? Everything you've done up to now has resulted in disaster. How are you going to save Molly?"

"I'll give them what they want."

"Which is what? What do they want, Jack?"

"The evidence and our silence. I'll hand it over to Maurice."

"You think it's as simple as that? We'll hand over a few memory sticks and they'll return our daughter and pretend this never happened? You're deluded."

"It's our only option. They're ruthless, but they won't kill Molly and risk drawing too much attention on themselves."

"Have you heard yourself? Talking about killing Molly as if they are deciding on what curry to have at the Indian's." She threw the pillow at Jack. "You've put Molly in danger, and I can never forgive you for that."

Jack would never forgive himself. Things had corkscrewed

out of control to the point where he no longer thought straight. Return the documents, go to the police, come up with an elaborate plan to rescue Molly. Whatever he did was full of danger, and there was no obvious course of action.

Perhaps he should let Andrea take charge. She was right. Every single thing he'd touched up to now had ended in tragedy. He had brought them to this point. Jack placed his arm around her shoulders. Andrea shrugged him off.

"I'll bring her home, Andrea. I accept you can't forgive me, but I'll do everything in my powers, everything, to get her back to you."

Andrea left the room without acknowledging him. Jack had to pass the evidence over to Maurice, but there was no harm in covering all bases, he needed help.

Jack posted a group WhatsApp message to Karl, Angus, and Harriet. He hadn't known them long, and didn't know how much he could trust them, but they'd proven themselves up to this stage. Jack swore them to secrecy, told them what had happened, and asked for them to do some discrete snooping. Follow the primary targets, check out the usual haunts and find any sign of Molly. Requesting they were discrete was a big ask, but he couldn't risk spooking Maurice. They responded within seconds, keen to help. They'd jump onto it straight away.

Jack needed to tackle the far trickier task of placating Andrea. He found her on her iPad, typing a post on Facebook, alerting the world to Molly's disappearance. Maybe she was right, maybe social media was the best approach. Go public and see how the cards fall. But this wasn't a game of poker, and Molly wasn't a bargaining chip. Her life was in peril. Jack took the iPad from her and deleted the post. Andrea didn't put up a fight.

"We'll find her," said Jack. "They're dangerous but not

stupid. Harming Molly will be counterproductive."

"We don't know that. They're evil. We don't have the slightest comprehension of what they're capable of."

"I'll speak to Maurice."

Jack sent him a message saying he'd be around later to deliver the documentation. He wanted to phone in case he could pick up any clues from what Maurice said, but a message at least permitted them breathing space.

**

Jack and Andrea didn't speak. Jack gathered the evidence, ready to give to Maurice. Andrea scrolled through social media sites, praying she'd spot a picture of Molly safe with a friend. Instead, she received an endless stream of food photos, inane rambling and pictures of other people's kids. Every child happy and safe.

Then Twitter and Facebook buzzed with breaking news. There was a trickle of posts at first, and then a flood. Details were sketchy, but the lure of blue flashing lights had drawn out the amateur reporters with their camera phones. Something was happening. Something big. At the tip.

"Jack, you need to see this." Andrea flicked through the pictures of police cars with a growing sense of horror.

Jack raced into the room. "What is it?"

"The police, they're at the tip." She put her hand over her mouth. "They've found a body."

Chapter Twenty-Seven

Neither Jack nor Andrea remembered how they got to the tip. They'd both been in a haze. Jack driving and Andrea frantically refreshing Twitter for further news, both of their minds in turmoil with the scenarios. The gangsters were killers, but murdering a child that was way beyond their comprehension.

As they pulled up to the police cordon, Andrea prayed the body was anybody but Molly. Jack wished the corpse was his. There was already a crowd, and it was growing as social media spread the story. Jack couldn't understand why people wanted to be there to witness such a grizzly scene, yet here he was himself, clamouring for information.

"Who is it?" he said as he pushed through the throng. "Do they know who the body is?"

Everyone had a theory, nobody had any facts. Speculation was rife amongst the fevered imaginations of the crowd, with many willing it to be the worst outcome, so they could say they were there. Jack's elbows got him to the front and Andrea followed in his wake. A young PC guarded the tape dividing the public from the scene.

"Have you identified the body?" said Jack.

"We have no information at this time."

"But you've found a body?"

"I can neither confirm nor deny."

"It's not a little girl, is it? Tell me that."

"I'm sorry, sir. I need you to step back."

"Just tell me for fuck's sake."

"You're not helping matters, sir. Swearing at a police officer is a criminal offence."

"Don't be so fucking ridiculous." Jack was getting an audience. Phones were coming out and camera apps were being opened.

Andrea dragged him away. "He won't tell us. Let's find someone who will."

They elbowed their way back out towards the parked police cars. They recognised one, a BMW that had left their drive only hours beforehand. DS Sidra Ramsay was putting on shoe covers before entering the crime scene.

Jack made a beeline for her until a WPC blocked his path. "Sorry, sir. This is a restricted area."

"I need to speak to DS Ramsay."

"She's busy."

"She's there, I can see her. Can you call her over please?"

"Sir, you're interfering with a crime scene."

"I'm not interfering, I need her for two minutes."

"Please step back, sir." She pushed Jack in the chest.

As the WPC wrestled with Jack, Andrea marched straight past her and up to DS Ramsay. "Is it true they've discovered a body?"

"Mrs Ferris? I'm surprised to see you here."

"Is it true?"

"We're trying to establish the facts."

"It's a simple yes or no."

"I'm sure you can understand—"

"I can't understand why you can't answer a simple question. Have you found a body?"

"Why are you so interested?"

"Simple answer, yes or no. Have you found a body?" Andrea raised her voice and was fighting to stay calm.

The WPC arrived and tried to drag her aside. Andrea shrugged her off with her elbow.

"That's assault," said the WPC

"You'll learn what assault is if she doesn't acknowledge a simple bloody question."

"That's it," said the WPC, "I'm arre—"

"No, you're not," said DS Ramsay, "I'll take it from here." She glared at the WPC, who walked away, huffed at her authority being undermined.

"Can you please answer my question?" Andrea steadied herself by placing her hand on the roof of the BMW.

"Mrs Ferris, I've been asking you and your husband questions for days and neither of you are forthcoming. Why should I answer yours?"

"Because we're desperate," said Jack. "I wish I could say more, I do, but please, do us this one favour."

Sidra looked at the frantic couple and checked nobody else was in earshot. "I'm not sure why I'm telling you this, and I don't want it repeated, but yes, we have discovered a body."

"Oh, God," said Andrea. Jack sought to comfort her, but she brushed him off.

"This body," said Jack. "Is it a chi… is it an adult?"

"We believe the victim is an adult male, and that is as much as I can say at present."

"Oh, Jesus." Andrea grabbed the side of the car to stop herself from collapsing. Only then did she allow Jack to hug her.

"Do you have an idea who the victim might be?" said Sidra.

"We don't," said Jack. "But thank you, thank you so much."

"Don't go anywhere," said Sidra, "I need to get to work, but I've answered your questions and I think you should answer mine."

Jack didn't respond and clung onto his wife.

DS Sidra Ramsay walked towards the crime scene, but hoped she could spend more time with Jack and Andrea. There was a lot more going on than they were saying, and whilst they claimed no knowledge of the body's identity, their behaviour was far from normal. Whoever the body was, the Ferris family would be at the centre of her investigation.

Jack and Andrea blended back into the crowd and edged back to the car. They needed to return home in case there was any news about Molly.

There was a tug at Jack's arm. It was Karl still clad in Lycra, albeit in more subdued colours than usual. "We might have a problem."

"A problem?" said Jack.

"Who's this?" said Andrea.

"It's Karl, he's a friend, he's helping us look for… what did you mean a problem?"

"I discovered who the dead bloke is."

Jack didn't like where this was going. "Who?"

Karl shook as he spoke. "Harold Beeston."

Jack's legs gave way, and he collapsed to the floor. Andrea followed him.

Jack and Andrea staggered back to the car, yet neither was in a fit state to drive. They sat in stunned silence. Another body. Another death linked to them. They dumped Harold at the tip. The warning was clear. They had no idea where Molly was, or if she was safe. What if Harold had uncovered something, and they held her captive here? The police swarming over the place may encourage her captors to release her, or place her in more danger.

At present, the investigation concentrated around the council end of the tip. The landfill area was where Jack suspected illegal activity was taking place, but he couldn't alert the police without giving away both his evidence and his involvement. He sent a WhatsApp message to the group and called off the search. He refused to put anybody else at risk. This was his mess, and he had to get out, he had to get Molly out.

The crowd thinned out as the lack of any concrete information led folk to become bored. Only the diehard rubberneckers hung around, hoping to be the first to glimpse the corpse.

Jack and Andrea were sitting in their car, feeling like they should go home in case of any news. But they sensed Molly was here and they could rescue her if only the police looked beyond the confines of the council tip. There was a knock at the window. DS Sidra Ramsay. Jack wound the window down.

"Still here?" she said.

"Looks that way," said Jack.

"I'm not sure what brought you here, but I can assure you there's nothing to see and you should head home."

"Nothing to see?"

"No foul play, we're wrapping things up, just a tragic set of circumstances."

"That makes no sense."

"How so?"

"Harold, he was—"

"Hold on," said Sidra, "Harold? I didn't give you any names."

"It was the rumour circulating in the crowd."

"You know the deceased?"

"We met recently."

"What business did you have with him?"

"None, not as such. He was Reggie's acquaintance."

"Reggie Higgins and Harold Beeston were acquainted?" Sidra took out her notebook.

"Sort of, but you can't give up here."

"Why not, Jack? What have you heard?"

"Enough to realise you're missing something."

"It was an accident. At first, we suspected suicide, but it appears the deceased was scavenging. He's well known for it. We assume he slipped and caught his neck in the cabling."

"That's impossible."

"How? What aren't you telling me, Mr Ferris?"

"You've seen the body, and that's what you think has happened?"

"I wasn't first on site," she pointed to another detective, "my colleague looked into it and they're not concerned with the cause of death."

Jack recognised Stoker, and knew he could make the scene look any way he wanted. What he didn't understand was how involved DS Sidra Ramsay was.

"Tell her, Jack." Andrea spoke for the first time.

"Tell me what?"

"Nothing, there's nothing to tell. Like you say, just one big tragic set of circumstances."

"Mr Ferris, you've been hiding something from me from the moment we met. It will be easier if you tell me what that is rather than me having to find out myself."

"Easier for you."

"Easier for everyone." She leaned into the window. "That's two of your friends who died in unfortunate accidents."

"Harold wasn't a friend."

"Two of your acquaintances died in mishaps. I'm not a great believer in coincidences, and I don't want you to lose anyone else close to you. If you have information, it's better you share it with me now."

"There's nothing," said Jack.

Sidra shook her head. "And you, Mrs Ferris? Do you have anything you'd care to share?"

Andrea and Jack glared at each other. She looked away from Jack and towards Sidra and shook her head.

Sidra stepped back from the car. "I'll be in touch."

Stoker watched from a distance and approached Sidra as she walked back to her BMW.

"Why didn't you explain about Molly?" said Andrea.

"Why didn't you?"

"This is insane, Jack. Molly is missing, she could be here, the detective is offering to help and we say nothing. What is wrong with us?"

"Look at them," said Jack, pointing to the detectives chatting by Sidra's car. "One is in Maurice's pocket and I'm unsure about the second. We can't risk it."

"What's left to risk, they've taken the single thing precious to us. Nothing matters but Molly, we have to bring her home."

"We will, I promise."

"How can you promise, Jack? Everybody you come into contact with dies. Reggie, Harold, the anonymous immigrants you won't discuss. DS Ramsay is right. None of this is a coincidence, it's cause and effect. If you'd sold the business when I said, those people would still be alive." She wiped her eyes with her sleeve. "And maybe our gorgeous daughter would be tucked up in bed instead of lying terrified somewhere in this godforsaken shit hole."

Jack started the car. "Sod this."

"Where are we going? We can't leave."

"I'm getting the evidence. I'll see Maurice to sort this out once and for all. This has gone on long enough. I'm bringing Molly home even if it kills me."

He screeched away as the two detectives watched on, wondering what Jack Ferris would do next.

Chapter Twenty-Eight

Deep bags shadowed Jack's eyes. Having not showered, and wearing the same clothes he'd worn last night as he dozed in the armchair, he wasn't looking his best when trying to smooth talk Patricia, Maurice Groom's personal assistant.

"Mr Groom has back-to-back appointments," she said without glancing up from her PC.

"It's urgent. I have something he wants, something he needs."

"Like I said, he's in meetings."

"You don't understand how important this is."

Nobody could understand how important it was to Jack. He'd not told anybody Molly was missing. Nobody knew his life was in jeopardy other than those killing off his friends. And the other stuff, the immigrants, and the shooting. He took that to his grave.

"I don't wish to be rude." Patricia's tone expressing the opposite impression to her words. "Everybody who wishes to see Mr Groom thinks their need is more important than the individuals he is meeting. If you tell me what your request is, I'll check if he can fit you in next week sometime."

"I've explained, it's urgent. I've got something he needs."

"If you give it to me, I'll make sure he receives it."

Jack could rush past Patricia and burst into Maurice's office, but he didn't know who was behind the door and drawing attention to himself helped nobody.

It opened, and a gentleman in an expensive suit gave Jack the briefest look of disdain. A gentleman he recognised from Reggie's funeral.

"Can I book you a taxi?" said Patricia, wanting to appear useful.

He ignored her as he buttoned his overcoat and strode out.

Maurice appeared at the door, red in the face and more flustered than normal. "Jack?"

"I told him you were busy," said Patricia, "but he refused to leave."

"Come in, Mr Ferris," said Maurice.

"I assume there's a small window in your diary," said Patricia, annoyed he had overruled her authority, "seeing as your meeting has finished early."

Maurice glared at her and slammed the door.

"Friend of yours," said Jack, "Bloke in the posh threads?"

"What do you want, Jack?"

"I want Molly back."

"Well, she's not here." Maurice swept his arm around the room. "I'm not sure what you're expecting." He slumped into his executive leather chair.

Jack remained standing and tried to stay calm. "You kidnapped a ten-year-old girl over a piece of land."

Maurice shook his head, poured a whisky from the crystal

decanter on his drinks cabinet and indicated for Jack to sit.

"And you assume walking in here resembling a Harold Beeston tribute act will bring her back?"

"I've got what you need."

"I very much doubt that."

Jack hoisted two carrier bags onto the desk and emptied their contents. Paperwork, memory sticks, laptop, everything Jack had found at Reggie's house. "It's all there."

"What's this?" Maurice looked unimpressed.

"Evidence."

"Of what?"

"Your conspiracy. Plans to obtain the docks, the real reason you're taking over the port."

"Which is?"

"Smuggling, people, drugs, whatever," said Jack. The enormity of it dawning on him.

Maurice nodded. "And where did you discover this?"

"At Reggie's house."

"That's quite the reconnaissance mission he's been on."

"It is, but that's everything."

"How do you know?" said Maurice.

"How do I know what?"

"That it's everything? How are you sure Reggie didn't uncover more than he's revealed?"

"The law would be kicking your door down if he'd already turned it over to them."

"He's given nothing to the police, Jack. That's not what worries me. It's what he's passed to the men who employed him."

"Who did he work for?"

"You don't have a clue, do you? Despite your bravado and your bluster, despite all that has happened to you and your associates these past few weeks, you still underestimate those you're up against."

"I'm not afraid of you, Maurice, I just want Molly back."

"You don't need to be frightened of me, Jack. I'm not the threat here." Maurice took a sip of whisky. "The organisations I represent, they're a different matter."

"And who are they?"

Maurice smirked. "I imagine Reggie's employers won't be overjoyed with you now you've tipped this rubbish over my desk. You're making dangerous enemies, Jack Ferris."

"I'm not interested in enemies. I only want Molly back. To take her home to her mother where she belongs. What happens to me after that… well, we'll see."

"You still haven't grasped it."

"Deliver the papers and I'll sign the firm over to you." Jack leaned in towards Maurice. "For free. I don't want any money. The business and the evidence for Molly, that's the arrangement."

Maurice swivelled his chair to face the window, scanning the city rooftops. "How can we be certain you didn't produce copies?"

"Of what?"

"This. The evidence, as you call it, although it's not clear what evidence is there, it could be a work of fiction by Reggie Higgins."

"I wouldn't copy it. Do you think I'm that stupid?"

"Your behaviour up to this point suggests that you are."

"I haven't. I swear on Molly's life."

"And you consider yourself in a position to swear on her life?"

"Tell me where she is Maurice, and I will walk away.

You'll never hear from me again."

"It's too late for that."

"Too late for what?" The bile rose in Jack's throat. "What do you mean by too late?"

"Don't worry, Molly isn't in danger." Maurice swung back around to face Jack. "For now. She's nothing but a holding pattern, keeping you in check until I get all my parrots on a perch."

"A holding pattern?"

"You've been an irritant, Jack. No more than a mosquito bite, but enough of a pain to cause me problems." Maurice poured another whisky. "Putting this deal together isn't straightforward. You think you're crucial to it, but you're the smallest cog in the machine. I needed you to back off, yet despite many warnings, you continue to be a thorn in my arse."

"That's why I'm here. To call a truce, to put an end to it."

"You don't get to call truces, Jack. I demand your silence, and I need you to behave. My colleagues handle things differently, more efficiently, but I have a reputation to uphold in this city. I'm the one person keeping you, and Molly, alive."

"How do you mean?"

Maurice came from behind the desk. "All this." He pointed to the documents. "It's very kind of you. And I believe you when you claim no copies exist."

"They don't."

"Even you aren't that foolish. But the information is stored up here." He ruffled Jack's hair. "You've read it, you know who's involved, and whilst you understand nowhere near as much as you think you do, that's the knowledge that puts you in the ground."

The realisation dawned on Jack. "How come they haven't killed me yet?"

"Public relations, the optics don't look good at the moment

if you died."

"Optics?"

"A lonely old lollipop man and a reclusive hoarder. They can disappear without making much of a splash. If I take over the business of somebody recently deceased, especially if it's something as tragic as a joint suicide with his little daughter, it won't do wonders for my public profile."

"Joint suicide?"

"These men are professionals, more than professional. Leaders in their field. They can make it appear how they like."

"But, Molly, none of this mess is any of her fault."

"Does it matter? I'm spinning a lot of plates, Jack, and if one has to come crashing to the floor, it'll be you. Your only hope is doing what I say and maintaining silence until my ship comes in. Then, and only then, will Molly be safe."

"And me?"

"Wheels are in motion. You've done well to survive this long. I have a little influence. I might even allow you the opportunity to say goodbye to Molly, but you've upset too many people."

Jack was white, the nausea replaced with a blankness, a knowing, the realisation he had days to live, if that. "You give your word that Molly will be safe?"

"You have my word I won't do anything to harm her. You have my word. I will try to persuade my associates it's not in their interests to hurt a ten-year-old schoolgirl. After that, it's out of my hands."

"How long?"

"How long for what?"

"How long before they come for me?"

"Few days, enough time to get your affairs in order."

Jack nodded. "Keep Molly safe." His legs shaking as he shuffled towards the exit.

"I'm sorry it's come to this." Maurice ruffled Jack's hair again.

Jack brushed his hand away. "So am I."

Patricia attempted to catch Jack's eye as he left the office. "Would you like me to—"

"Fuck off," said Jack.

He stood by the lift, one arm on the wall, keeping him upright. His phone rang, it was Andrea. He rejected the call.

Descending three floors was akin to the descent into hell. Sweat dripped from every pore. Thoughts swirled through Jack's brain. The elevator doors pinged open, and he stumbled towards the exit.

A cool breeze mixed with the stale stench from the landfill hit him as he stepped outside the offices. Jack struggled to remain standing and fought the overwhelming feeling of nausea rising in his stomach. Workers went about their day, unconcerned about his predicament.

He sat in the car, attempting to regain his composure before leaving. Jack looked in the rear-view mirror at the large warehouses, the ones Angus had told him about. Not only were illegal activities going on inside, if Harold had been searching the tip, Molly could be in there somewhere. He wanted to snoop around, see if he could find her and make her safe, but it was futile. How easy would it be to find a tiny child on a site so huge? If Maurice caught him, it signalled the end for both Jack and Molly.

It was pointless, hundreds of workers. They couldn't all be criminals. If a schoolgirl was being held against her will, someone had to speak up. Jack spotted a face he recognised. Derek Pearson. His fat sweaty head beaming as he shouted at a young lad before jumping into a battered old transit van.

Derek was enjoying his new role much more than he enjoyed working in the garage. Jack had done him a favour by sacking him. One of the rare decisions Jack had got right. On reflection, the only one. None of this had gone as he'd expected. He took his phone from his pocket and considered calling Andrea. But to say what? What could he say? Jack had promised he'd hand over the evidence and return with Molly. Instead, he'd delivered the evidence and received his own death sentence.

How much could Jack trust Maurice to keep his end of the arrangement? Not that he was offering a lot. Maurice needed Jack's silence for now, but his life wasn't safe and he wasn't convinced Molly's was. He wasn't convinced he had a plan on how to change that. Maurice had been nothing but deceitful up to now. Jack had no reason to believe him when he said he'd ensure Molly's safety. Even if Jack wasn't about to survive this, he had to at least keep Molly out of harm's way.

He removed the card from his wallet and turned it over in his hand. Creasing the corners, toying with it, knowing the thing that may be his only chance, Molly's only chance, could be the one thing that ended it for both of them. The name embossed on the card, DS Sidra Ramsay.

She and Jack had not hit it off. She disliked him, and he didn't trust her. Was she yet another copper in Maurice's blazer pocket, or was there something more about her? If Jack went to her with his account, how likely was she to believe him, and how likely was it her next phone call would be straight to Maurice Groom? He picked up his phone again and dialled the number, his finger hovering over the green call button.

He pressed call, and she answered within two rings.

"DS Ramsay."

"Hi, it's Jack Ferris."

"Mr Ferris, what can I do for you?"

"I have information." He stared up at Maurice's office window. "About a conspiracy."

"A conspiracy to do what?"

"It's complicated."

"I'm in the station right now if you'd like to pop in for a chat."

"I can't come to the station."

"Why not?"

"They can't see me speaking to you." He scratched his head, wondering how much he wanted to reveal. "There are officers who might be involved in the conspiracy. And one who is definitely connected."

"Can you provide names?"

"No, sorry."

"A conspiracy theory without names will be a little tricky for me to investigate."

"I have names, don't worry about that, just not every one."

"Would you care to share any names you do know?"

"Not over the phone."

"Not over the phone," said Sidra, "not at the station. You're not making this easy."

"I can meet you somewhere. The pulled pork van in B&Q car park, to look like we'd bumped into each other."

"A Muslim at a pulled pork van, I might stand out."

"Okay, the lay-by behind B&Q, can you get there in half an hour?"

"I'll see you there, Mr Ferris." Sidra hung up.

Jack was wary of her, and his suggestion of a meeting in

the car park meant there'd be plenty of people around. Even if they took no notice. In the lay-by, they were out of sight to the public, and if he was wrong in trusting DS Ramsay, he could disappear without a trace. It was a chance he must take. He left the tip and headed to B&Q.

Sidra's BMW was parked in the lay-by. If she was trying to be discrete, she wasn't doing a great job as she was leaning on the bonnet, stretching her calf muscles. He pulled in behind her.

She climbed back in her car and indicated for him to get in the passenger seat. "Jack, thanks for coming. What did you want to tell me?"

"How do I know I can trust you?" said Jack.

"How do I know I can trust you?"

"A fair question, but I asked first."

"Simple answer is that you don't. I find it difficult for anyone to trust me. Nobody in the station trusts me. I'm not even sure my husband one hundred per cent believes me when I say I'm working late." She bent to massage her calf. "If this plot of yours involves coppers at Southwick nick, I'm as far from being on the inside as it gets."

"Okay." Jack couldn't tell if she was telling the truth, but he had come this far.

"Can I trust you, Jack?" She straightened up and grimaced at the pain in her leg. "You haven't exactly been forthcoming with me until now."

"I've got nowhere else to go. You're my last hope. I'll tell you what I uncovered, and what you do after that is up to you. But if you can't or won't act on the information I'm offering you, I'm a dead man."

"Now I'm interested." Sidra took out her notebook.

"No notes, this needs to be off the record."

"If we're to trust one another, Jack, you must understand nothing is ever off the record with me."

He nodded, unconvinced. "Maurice Groom wants to buy my business and the real estate it sits on."

She didn't write it in her notebook. "I'm not convinced any of this information is news."

"It's why he wants it, that's the news."

"Docks expansion. It might not be in the public domain, but it's common knowledge." Sidra still wasn't taking notes.

"It's the reason he wants to expand the docks."

"Which is?"

"Smuggling. He plans to control what comes in and out of the port, or at least the criminals he works for do." He glanced in the wing mirror to check nobody was watching. "Once they own the docks, the haulage company and the surrounding land, they can come and go as they please without rousing suspicion."

Sidra nodded but still wrote nothing. "How do you know this, Jack?"

"Reggie Higgins."

"The Lollipop Man?"

"He was more than a Lollipop Man."

Sidra nodded. "Go on."

"He'd been watching them, collecting evidence. He advised me how to recover it in the event of his death."

"What evidence?"

"Emails, documents, taped discussions, it's damming stuff."

"And how does an ageing Lollipop Man obtain such intelligence? And why?"

"He was undercover," said Jack.

"Police?"

"For a criminal syndicate in London."

She tapped her pen on the top of her notebook. "This is who Maurice works for? On whose behalf he plans to run the docks?"

"No, as far as I can gather, they're rivals." Jack hadn't thought this bit through.

Sidra raised her eyebrows. "Okay. This still doesn't explain how Mr Higgins got this material."

"He had help."

"From who?"

"Harold Beeston."

"The hoarder?"

"Yes, although there was a lot more to him than it seems at first glance."

"There are multiple characters with hidden depths in this tale. What was his role?"

"He had a background in technology. Possibly even a spy."

"A spy?"

"I'm guessing at that part. What I'm saying is that he was very skilled at what he did. He made bugs, hacked into things, designed tiny concealed cameras."

"There's video?" Sidra's interest piqued.

"Yes, at least I think so. I haven't seen them."

"But they exist?"

"There was a camera hidden in Reggie's lollipop stick, but when we went to retrieve it, it had gone."

"They realise they were being spied on?"

"I guess so."

"They're aware the snooping involved Reggie and

Harold?"

"Reggie definitely, I'm not sure about Harold."

Sidra rattled the pen between her teeth, then spoke. "And you have this evidence with you today?"

"No." Jack realised where this was going. "I don't have it anymore."

"Who does?"

"Maurice Groom."

"Why does Maurice Groom have it?"

"He threatened me."

"With what?"

Jack thought about Molly and considered his response. "He threatened to kill me."

"Did you make any copies?"

"No."

"Why not?"

"I said I wouldn't."

"That was incredibly honest of you."

Jack shrugged. "I don't enjoy lying."

"Let's see if I've got this." Sidra looked at her notebook, although she had taken no notes. "Your business rival, Maurice Groom, wants to acquire your company, and conveniently, you discover he is complicit in a major smuggling conspiracy?"

"Conveniently?"

"The evidence which could send him down is no longer in your possession, if it ever was. And you gave it to the man you're accusing without making copies."

"What do you mean by if it ever was?"

"Two other men could corroborate your story, a Lollipop Man and a reclusive hoarder, unfortunately both died before they could back you up."

"There's nothing unfortunate about it, they killed them."

"Unfortunate for them. I'm not sure whether they entered this tale of yours before or after their deaths, but it's somewhat inconvenient, or convenient depending on your point of view, that they aren't here to confirm your story."

"That's my point. They murdered them because they knew too much, and I'll be next." Jack gripped the dashboard in frustration.

"I need more, Jack. What, why, when, who? Up to now you've offered me nothing but tittle-tattle regarding a business competitor."

"Tittle-tattle? My life is on the line here, my family's lives."

"Your family?"

If he mentioned Molly now, it left Jack's hands, left Sidra's hands. She'd need to escalate it, and neither of them could control what happened next. "They've made threats, they've been in the house."

"I need more," said Sidra.

"The immigrants." Jack was incriminating himself, but it was his last move.

"What immigrants?"

"The dead ones."

"What are you talking about, Jack? Tell me about the dead immigrants."

"They already operate a smuggling route, bringing them in via North Shields and taking them to Maurice's warehouse at the landfill."

"Go on." Sidra made notes.

"I'm not sure if they work, live or get processed there, but they all go via the warehouse. These men are ruthless, DS

Ramsay."

"Ruthless in what way?"

"If the girls aren't of use to them anymore, they'll execute them. No hesitation, no questions, a bullet in the skull there and then." Jack wound down the window for fresh air, again checking the mirror that nobody was around.

"Why should I believe this, Jack?"

"I've seen it with my own eyes."

"Let's be clear here, you've witnessed a murder."

"Yes," said Jack.

"Who carried it out?"

"Some asthmatic Eastern European thug. Didn't catch his name. They controlled things within the warehouse."

"This took place on Maurice Groom's property?"

"Yes."

"You saw it?" Sidra was no longer writing and looked Jack straight in the eye.

"I replay it every time I close my eyes. Or when I spot anybody of a similar build or look to the young girl, I see it every second of every day."

"This is the part I'm struggling with. What were you doing in Maurice Groom's warehouse?"

Jack stuck his head out of the window and drew a deep breath in through his nose before speaking. "It was me who brought the girls into the country. It was me who drove them to their deaths."

"You're part of this smuggling operation?" Sidra leaned in towards Jack.

"Not part of the smuggling. They tricked me, forced me into cooperating."

"You realise that not only have you advised me you

witnessed and could be an accessory to a murder, you also confessed to the serious crime of people-smuggling?"

Jack nodded. "I need you to believe that what I've told you is true."

"You remember the bit at the beginning of this conversation where I said nothing is off the record?"

Jack nodded again. "I told you I didn't enjoy lying."

"You realise I must arrest you?"

"You can't, not now."

"I can't ignore your confession, Jack. Coerced into it or not, it's a serious crime."

"I realise that. I expect punishment for what I've done, but there're people who don't deserve to pay for my mistakes and I have to get them out of this."

"Get who out of this, Jack? Who else is involved?"

"I've declared everything I can for now. Please, just give me a couple of days and I'll slap the cuffs on myself, but I need to sort this out."

"I can't do that." She knocked her pen on the steering wheel, thinking.

"I'll get you the evidence you need. Enough to lock up Maurice and his associates a hundred times over, but if you take me in now, I'll deny everything. All you'll have are the ramblings of a bitter man about to lose his business."

Sidra shook her head. "Jack, that isn't how it works."

"I'm afraid it has to be." Jack slipped out of the passenger seat and ran to his own car.

She opened the driver's door to chase after him. Sidra was quick, she'd chased down many a winger in her rugby playing days at uni, but her calf twinged and she reconsidered.

Jack sped off, and she considered calling it in, but he had a point. What did she have at present, other than the mutterings of a madman? She'd let him go for now, but DS Sidra Ramsay planned to keep a close eye on Jack Ferris.

Chapter Twenty-Nine

Andrea stood at the front window, hoping against hope that somehow Molly's with her fiery red hair would come bounding around the corner. The phone in her hand was a last resort, her thumb poised on the dial button for the past five minutes. She pressed it.

Lottie answered after six long rings. "Hello?"

"Mummy, it's me."

"Andrea, I thought we'd discussed this. You can only ring at the agreed times."

"Says who?"

"You know who. If he finds out we're talking, that will be the end of it. No more conversations, no more Molly updates. The end."

"I need to speak to him."

"Oh, darling, you know that's out of the question."

"I saw him, you know?"

"Saw him, when?"

"At school," said Andrea.

"Your school? Your father went up to Sunderland to visit you?"

"He had a meeting. I'm sure he had no intention of meeting me or Molly."

"He met Molly? Noel met Molly?"

"He never mentioned it?"

"Well, of course he hasn't bloody mentioned it." Lottie placed her gin glass on the side table and perched herself on the arm of the sofa.

"Is he there? This is important."

"I'd say it's bloody important. Your father's been to visit our only granddaughter, a granddaughter I am forbidden from seeing, and he hasn't thought to mention it."

"Why are you still with him, Mummy?"

"You know why. For better or worse. Those words used to mean something. They must mean something to you because I can't see any other reason why you're still with that horrid little man."

"I love Jack, and Jack loves me. You may not approve, but people in glass houses—"

"Don't start that with me. Your father, your father—"

"Is he there? I really don't have the time to be discussing the relative merits of our marriages."

"He's at the constituency office, or at least he says he is. He could be hotfooting it up to Sunderland for all I know."

"Have you got a number for the office. This is a matter of life and death."

"He won't speak to you. You know that. You won't get past his receptionist."

"I'll find it myself." Andrea ended the call and launched her phone across the room.

**

Jack joined the queue for the tip. Even during the week, it went halfway along the road. He wanted to get close enough to observe where Molly could be without drawing attention to himself by pulling up outside the landfill site. He'd thrown a few rubbish bags in the boot of the Yaris to make it appear as if he had a reason to be there.

As he edged closer to the entrance, he realised his trip was futile. He lacked a decent view, one he couldn't get without being spotted. Jack needed a drone for an aerial perspective, but even that wouldn't go unnoticed.

He made a call on his hands free. "Bill?"

"Yes."

"It's Jack."

"What do you want, Jack? I'm busy."

"I'm in a spot of bother, and I need help from the pigeon lads." He only had the vaguest of plans. It included finding a camera at Harold's house and fitting it to a bird.

"Not interested, Jack, we're finished with you."

"I'm desperate. I'm asking you to run it by the committee. The club owes me that much. I've been a member for years, my dad for decades before me."

"The club owes you nothing. The crap you've brought to our doorstep, you've near as hell ruined us. If it wasn't for the rules and your subs being paid up, I'd be buggered if I even let you anywhere near the big race. You're lucky we're giving you that."

"Don't be a twat, Bill. It's a small favour, if you'd just ask the lads."

"Not a chance, Jack. You're poison. Most of the lads

bailed because of the lofts fire, and that's all your doing. Nobody owes you a thing." He hung up.

Jack removed his bluetooth earpiece and threw it in the glovebox. In hindsight, his proposal was ridiculous. Even if he got a miniature camera, how could he train the pigeons to fly slowly over the tip to get a proper view of what was going on? *"Idiot,"* he thought.

He realised that being sat in the queue did him no good either. Jack spun the Yaris around and headed back down the hill. His phone rang. Maybe there was news on Molly, or Bill reconsidered. He pulled onto the pavement, allowing a speeding motorbike to pass, and bent to grab his mobile from the passenger seat. As he did, he heard small cracks behind him and something whizz past his head and another crack, followed by shattering glass and a motorcycle accelerating away.

He kept his head low for a second, wondering what had just happened, then rose, shaking the broken glass from his hair. Both the driver's and passenger's windows shattered, and a bullet lay embedded in the telegraph pole beside the car.

Jack opened the driver's door and vomited onto the tarmac. Pulling it shut, he raised his head again; the motorbike was long gone. He was past the end of the row of waiting cars and he assumed no one saw what had taken place. Jack should call the police, he should phone DS Ramsay. But how much of a coincidence was it that this happened minutes after he spoke to her. Who had she told? He was on his own.

As he tried to regain his composure, a thought struck him. *"What if they're heading to the house? What if they've gone after Andrea?"*

With his legs shaking, he barely had the strength to push the clutch pedal, yet he had to drive. He sped off and hoped he got there in time.

Jack skidded to a halt on the drive, ran inside and shouted for Andrea.

"What is it?" she said as she vaulted the stairs. "Is it Molly?"

"No." He staggered into the sitting room, slumping into the armchair. "Someone… someone has tried to kill me."

"Tried to kill you, how?" Andrea sat in the chair next to him and took his hand.

"Are you okay? Nobody has been here?"

"I'm fine. Are you saying I'm in danger?"

"I'm not sure, I'm not sure of anything anymore."

"This has to end, Jack. Go to the police." She squeezed his hand.

"That's the problem, Andrea. I have."

"You've been to the police?"

"After I spoke with Maurice, I realised he wouldn't help us, so I had to act." Jack unhooked his fingers from Andrea's and placed his head in his hands. "I did what you said, I did what you thought was right."

"The police want you dead?"

"I met with DS Ramsay, told her everything."

"You told her about Molly?"

"Almost everything, but I confessed to the people-smuggling. I'm going to prison, Andrea." Jack punched the arm of the chair. "If they don't kill me first."

"It wasn't your fault, you can't go to jail."

"It doesn't matter anymore, the only thing that matters is getting Molly back, and nobody is locking me up, or killing me before I've rescued her." Jack jumped from the seat, but Andrea dragged him back.

"Calm down, Jack. Don't go rushing off again, I need you here."

"I can't just sit here Andrea, I need to do something."

"Look where doing something has got you."

"You told me to give the evidence to Maurice. You advised me to speak to the police. I've done what you said and now someone is making a colander out of the car window."

"Don't put this on me."

"I'm not, but it makes no odds what we decide. Which direction we turn, they have us cornered. There's nowhere left to run, Andrea. Our only hope is you and Molly come out of it unharmed."

"We need you with us," said Andrea, now pacing the room.

"I'm sorry, but one way or the other, I'm finished. Whether I end up in a prison cell or a shallow grave, I don't care, I have to get Molly back."

Andrea wandered over to the window and sniffed. "How did we end up here, Jack? We had such a nice quiet life."

"Seagulls and pornography brought us to this. It'll be something to carve on my gravestone." He tried to laugh, but it was hollow.

"Jack?" There was panic in Andrea's voice. "It's that woman again." She adjusted the blinds. "DS Ramsay is outside."

"Quick, move away from there." Jack dragged her back, then crawled to the window himself and peeked through the blinds.

Sidra got out of her BMW, stretching her calf. She noted the missing driver's window in the Yaris, then the broken glass on the seat and the shattered passenger window. She looked towards the house and noticed the blinds flicker.

"Jack, what are we going to do?"

"Run upstairs and hide under Molly's bed. Don't come out, no matter what you hear. I'll try to get rid of her."

The doorbell rang. Andrea sprinted up the stairs, hoping Sidra didn't spot her through the frosted glass.

Jack composed himself. Prepared for his fate, and answered the door. "DS Ramsay."

"Jack, can I come in?"

"Anything you have to say can be said here, in full view of the neighbours."

"I thought you wanted to be discrete."

"I think that ship's sailed now, don't you?"

"What happened with the car?" She pointed towards the Yaris.

"As if you don't know."

"I'm detecting hostility here, Jack. Do you want to tell me what's changed since our earlier conversation?"

"I trusted you."

"And you still can."

"So how do you explain someone putting a bullet through my window after I talked to you?"

Sidra glanced up and down the street, then pushed Jack. "We need to get inside, right now." She wasn't taking no for an answer and shut the door behind her.

"What happened, Jack?"

"You tell me."

"Are you suggesting I had something to do with it?"

"I'm not suggesting. It was you. Why else would somebody be trying to shoot me?"

"You haven't made yourself popular, Jack. It could be for any number of reasons. Perhaps handing over the evidence you had ended any leverage you had and they want rid of you."

"Bloody hell, I can't do right for doing wrong."

There was a scream from the top of the staircase, and a giant polar bear hurtled towards them. "Get off him!"

Initially shocked, Sidra's martial arts training soon kicked in and she side stepped Andrea, tripped her and then pinned her under the over-sized cuddly toy she was brandishing. Jack grabbed Sidra's sleeve, but she shrugged him off.

"Will you two stop attacking me? I'm here to help." Sidra let Andrea up. "A polar bear?"

"First thing I grabbed." She had no fight left in her and was no longer considered a danger.

Sidra hobbled to the stairs and perched on the first step, massaging her calf. "I'm stating the obvious here, but these are dangerous men, very dangerous."

"You think?" said Andrea as she dusted herself down.

"I've done a little discrete digging. As you suggested, we're unsure who we can trust. Reggie Higgins worked for ruthless people, he was ruthless people. GBH convictions, rumours of carrying out gangland hits, he was an information gatherer and enforcer of considerable repute. He has quite the reputation in London."

"How did he end up in Sunderland?" said Jack.

"That part is up for debate. It looks like he was aiming to create an alternative future, escape from his past. His last conviction involved serious stuff. Children got hurt, albeit through collateral damage. After he served his time, he tried to escape it all and make a new life for himself up North."

"That went well."

"You never escape that life. His employers let him leave with their blessing until they needed him."

"Gathering information on Maurice?" said Jack.

"Looks that way. They caught wind of what Maurice, or at least what his associates were up to and asked Reggie to look into it."

"He got too close? That's why they killed him?"

"We have no evidence of murder. What we've learned is that you haven't merely stumbled into a conspiracy, you've marched right into the middle of a turf war."

"I don't do things by halves."

"Things have escalated, Jack. I have to bring you in, keep you safe."

"You mean well, but don't be offended when I say the last place I feel safe is in your hands, especially not your colleagues."

"Point taken, but you're not protected here. You got lucky with the shooting."

"Lucky? They put two windows out and parted my hair."

"They won't miss a second time. You need to keep your family safe." Sidra looked up the stairs. "Where's Molly?"

Jack and Andrea exchanged glances. "Sleepover at her friend's," said Andrea. "With everything that's happening, we considered it best to keep her away from the turmoil."

"Wise move," said Sidra, standing. "I accept why you're not coming with me now, Jack. I wish you would, but I understand your reservations. Promise me you'll keep your head down and stay alive long enough for me to sort this."

"I'll try my best."

"Have you got family you can go to?" she said to Andrea.

"Ha, you don't want to know."

"Go somewhere, anywhere but here. I'll be in touch soon, but, please stay safe."

Jack and Andrea watched her hobble along the path.

"Why didn't you tell her about Molly?" said Jack.

"You're right, we can't trust anyone, and there's one more option I want to try."

"What do you mean?"

"Like DS Ramsay said, I have family." Andrea snatched the car keys from the table and headed for the door.

Chapter Thirty

With both windows missing, it was an arctic drive to North Yorkshire for Andrea. As she arrived at her father's constituency office, only numbness remained in her ice white fingertips.

She wished he lived closer, but pompous Tories got the pickings of a dog in Sunderland. Noel's safe seat in the more affluent part of the country where Andrea grew up suited him. Trees lined the street where his office stood in a converted church building. Very quaint.

"Sorry, we've just finished up for the day," said the assistant as Andrea breezed into reception.

"I need to speak to my father."

"Your father?"

"Noel Cardwell, is he here?"

The assistant looked confused. "He never mentioned a daughter."

"That doesn't surprise me." She stormed into Noel's office.

He was on the phone, but hung up as soon as he saw her.

"Andrea?"

Noel waved away the assistant, closing the door behind her.

"I need your help, Daddy."

"Little late for that. I offered you help many years ago."

"You offered me money not to marry the man I loved. How was that helping?"

"And everything is okay in your marriage?" He allowed himself a condescending smirk.

"I've no time for your smugness, Molly is in danger."

"Perils of marrying beneath yourself, Andrea."

"Not from Jack, from your friends."

"My friends?"

"Your less than salubrious partners. We've evidence of your cosy deals around the docks and Jack's business."

"That's the one bonus of my only daughter marrying a cretin. It sparked the idea of buying the docks. If it wasn't for your idiot husband's business, Sunderland wouldn't receive a second glance as a destination for an import export enterprise."

"You admit you're involved."

"Admit it, don't admit it, it makes no difference. You can't do a thing to stop it. The port is expanding, your husband's company is defunct, and you get to lie in the bed you made."

"Daddy, it's Molly, they've kidnapped your granddaughter."

"Really?"

"You don't sound surprised."

"Nothing surprises me with what you lot get up to in those northern backwaters."

"It's nothing to do with how we behave, it's your friends who've kidnapped her."

"They're no friends of mine. My reputation is sacrosanct."

"You know who has her?"

"What do you want, Andrea?"

"I want you to get Molly back."

"You think it's that simple?"

"She's your granddaughter, you're a government minister, it is that simple. You could have the entire weight of the security forces brought on them if you wanted."

"Have you any comprehension of what that level of public exposure could do to my career? Do you have no notion of what I've sacrificed for this job?"

"This is your granddaughter we're discussing. Your job is irrelevant. They've snatched Molly to keep Jack quiet."

"Don't be so naïve, Andrea. Your pathetic little spouse is irrelevant."

"What?"

"They've taken her to keep me in line. They're labouring under the misapprehension I give two hoots about your sad little family. I'll let them believe that for now, might even benefit me in the long run."

"Unbelievable. You're doing nothing to save your only granddaughter?"

"This conversation is over, Andrea. I've a function to attend." He brushed past her, leaving Andrea stunned and more convinced than ever that she'd made the right choice in choosing Jack over her father.

Chapter Thirty-One

Jack put his pint on the beer mat and pulled up a stool.

"What are you playing at, Jack? This is pigeon club business," said Bill Tindall.

"It is, and whilst my subs are paid up, I'm still a member."

"Aye, but." Bill shuffled in his seat. "This regards the future of our club and you'll have no part in it."

"That's as maybe, but we'll be discussing the big race and I'm very much a part of that. I'll hang around if it's all the same to you."

"Aye, well." Bill took a gulp of his pint. "But you'll not be able to vote on the future stuff."

"Whilst I remain a member, my vote counts the same as anybody else's."

"Don't be awkward, Jack. I can postpone the vote until after you've gone."

"And I can invoke an extraordinary motion."

"You know the rules as well as I do. You'll need someone to second it, but nobody at this table will back you." He scratched his head under his flat cap. "Isn't that right, lads?"

There were murmurs of agreement. Nobody looked Jack in

the eye. They liked Jack, but Bill intimidated them, and a few had clearly taken a similar backhander to keep quiet about the takeover of the club's land.

"I'll back him." A booming voice from the door. In marched Ted, the mechanic from Jack's haulage yard. His pint of Guinness dwarfed by his shovel-like hands. "Evening, lads."

The welcome for Ted was a friendlier than the one for Jack. A popular, jovial man, his grandfather was a founding member of the pigeon club and Ted had a lifetime family membership. He couldn't commit to the time spent racing, but he still had a keen interest.

"Ha'way, Ted," said Bill, "you know your membership is honorary."

"Best honour it, then. My granddad didn't start this club so gobshites could make a few quid from flogging it to crooks."

"That's not true."

"Isn't it?" said Jack as he placed a carrier bag on the table. "I have fascinating documents here, emails, phone records, bank statements. They paint a very interesting picture."

Bill fiddled with the neck of his jumper. "Where did you get those?"

"I didn't, Reggie did. It appears our recently departed friend was digging into corruption and he found intriguing information on how much you pocketed to sell the club down the river."

"It wasn't just me, there's plenty here who accepted the cash."

"They'll have an opportunity to do what's right, but I don't need to call an extraordinary motion for everyone to recognise your position as chairman is untenable."

"This is outrageous, it's a coup."

"A coup in a pigeon coop, if you will." Jack edged the bag towards Bill. "You can resign, on health grounds, family reasons, whatever, or we can discuss the contents of this carrier and have them a matter of public record in the minutes. Your choice."

The reporter, Nancy Whitworth, walked into the room. "Mr Ferris, you said you had a story for me?"

"Yes, if you'd take a snap of our departing chairman, Bill Tindall, please."

"Your departing chairman? I thought you had a scoop, not the comings and goings of a pigeon club."

"It's far more than that, Nancy."

"I'm not here to do your publicity," said Nancy.

"No, but when I tell you the truth about the people who've been peddling you propaganda, you'll wish you had been covering pigeon club committee meetings. Take the photo."

She reluctantly got her camera out and captured a shot of the fuming Bill Tindall.

Bill downed his pint, glaring at the faces around the table. "Bollocks to the lot of you." He disappeared without saying another word.

"Thanks, Nancy," said Jack.

"That's the story? Angry pigeon chairman ousted from his position?"

"The trouble you're in, you should be grateful to be writing the bus timetable. Wait in the bar whilst I have a quick chat with these lads. I'll update you soon. Trust me, it will be worth your while."

"I was highly commended at university, you can't treat me like this."

Jack nodded to the door, and she left, huffed.

"Anybody else?" Jack looked towards a couple of lads he

suspected of taking the money.

One spoke. "I took the cash, I'm not going to lie. Bill didn't leave us much choice, and I needed it. I'm on the bones of my arse. But I don't want to leave, Jack, give us a chance."

"I'm not forcing anybody out, but from this point forward, I need everybody's help. This is far bigger than the lofts being set alight. I need your help to keep me alive."

Jack introduced new guests to the group. Not Pigeon Club members, but some recognised Karl and Angus from the Amsterdam trip. Mumbles of resentment were less than welcoming.

"A lot of you aren't happy with me for various reasons, not least for bringing strangers into our meetings. This has moved beyond a committee meeting, it's much more important." Jack took a gulp of his pint. "What I tell you, and what I ask you to do, is dangerous."

"More dangerous than buying a ticket for one of your buses?"

The joke lightened the mood and allowed Jack to ease into his tale.

"What I need from you is silence. That's why I've sent the reporter to the bar. If you can't keep what I'm about to say a secret until it's over, please leave now."

Nobody moved.

"I'm going nowhere. I've got half a pint left," said Ted, winking.

"Okay." Jack took another mouthful. "Most of you were on the Amsterdam trip and saw our stowaways. Someone put them on the bus to blackmail me, as I'd uncovered evidence that incriminated prominent local figures."

"Spill the beans, mate."

"All in good time. I won't burden you with that information right now."

"Ha'way man, we love a bit of gossip."

"This knowledge has got me into shed loads of bother, and those responsible took my daughter."

"Say that again." Ted's jovial demeanour had gone.

"They've kidnapped Molly to buy my silence."

"Tell me who took her and I'll smash their fucking skulls," said Ted.

"Appreciate the sentiment, Ted, but they're ruthless. Yesterday they shot my car window out and near as shit blew my head off."

Ted finished his pint in one go. "Not your biggest fans, then?"

"They won't stop until I am dead. There's not much I can do to prevent that, but I'm buggered if I'm letting them harm my little girl."

"You need to inform the police."

"I have, sort of. They're in on it and I don't know who I can trust. I let one of them into what I'd discovered and next thing, my car was getting new air conditioning."

"If you can't trust the police, what makes you think we can help?"

"I have to find Molly, and I'm sure she's at the tip, but that's too obvious. I need you to dig around for clues, be discrete, but see what you can uncover."

"That's it?"

"The big race."

"What about it?"

"Everyone knows the club's booted me out, and it's my

last race. I can't be there, so need someone to guide my pigeons home."

"Aye, we can do that, but it wasn't worth a meeting."

"Fair point, but the reason I can't be at the finish is that I expect the gunman will try again."

"You can't spend your life looking over your shoulder, mate."

"No choice," said Jack, "at least until Molly is home. After that, who knows? But she is my one and only priority."

"We'll get her back," said Ted.

"Sorry for putting this on you, I had nowhere else to turn." Jack fidgeted with his sleeve.

"Let's get to work, lads." Ted stood, his authority in the group clear, and the rest followed.

Jack received handshakes and words of encouragement, yet despite this gang of friends stepping up to help, he'd never felt so alone.

"Are you going to tell me what is happening?" Nancy Whitworth had returned to the room, her face suggesting she'd been sucking lemons whilst sat at the bar.

"Grab a seat, Nancy." Jack pointed to a spare stool. "Do you realise you're being used?"

"Are you calling my journalistic integrity into question?"

This wasn't the time for accusations. "Not at all, but you may have been a tad naïve."

"I'll remind you that as a journalist, I take great pride in my work and I am far from naïve."

"Nancy, have you any idea what Maurice Groom and his associates are up to?"

"I didn't become highly commended at university without doing my homework. They're planning to develop the port and take over your business and the land where the pigeon lofts are. I assume that is why you dragged me here tonight?"

"Do you understand why they want to expand the docks."

"To improve the city's employment prospects for generations to come."

"That's the official line they've given you?"

Nancy hesitated. "It's the truth."

"You believe that? What are your journalistic instincts telling you?"

"They're telling me I should be on the settee in my pyjamas with a glass of wine." She packed her camera and notebook into her backpack. "You brought me here on the pretence of giving me a big story, and so far all I have is a resigning Pigeon Club president."

"There's this." Jack slid over the carrier bag he'd presented to Bill Tindall.

"What's this?"

"The reason Bill resigned."

"Why would I care about a Pigeon Club chairman?"

"Look inside."

Nancy opened the bag and had a peek. "A pile of magazines?"

"Yes."

"Copies of Pigeon Fancier's Monthly."

"What does that tell you?"

"That you're wasting my time."

"You're a journalist. Why does someone resign his position that he's held onto for years, without even checking what was in the carrier?"

Nancy retrieved her notebook from her bag, the penny dropping. "I still don't understand why it interests me."

"Because there's an enormous pile of evidence out there, and it incriminates a lot more than Bill Tindall."

She clicked her pen and began jotting notes. "You've seen it? How big are we talking?"

"Big enough to make your career."

"And you'll get it for me?" said Nancy, scribbling away.

"No, you will get it for me."

Maurice Groom had no time for Nancy Whitworth. She was a minor irritant at the local newspaper who he had used to his own advantage. Her desperation to be on the inside left her easy to manipulate. He'd thrown her many an 'exclusive' that was little better than free advertising for whatever he was promoting. Nancy was too naïve to see it, and her editor unlikely to challenge Sunderland's most prominent business owner.

The arrangement was that whenever he wanted something printing; he rang her, and she came running. That's how it worked. Yet here she was, in his office, demanding to talk to him. With everything that was going on at the minute, he didn't need an overenthusiastic trainee journalist sniffing for a story. But Nancy claimed she had a story for him. A story that couldn't wait, and one that got her past Maurice's unflappable and impassable Personal Assistant.

"I'm sorry, Nancy," said Maurice from his executive leather chair. "You've forced your way in here with breaking news, and you're telling me it's the ousting of the chairman of the pigeon club?"

"That's right."

"Have you mistaken me for the flying vermin correspondent at your shitty little paper? Have you any idea how busy I am? What on God's green earth has this got to do with me?"

"They mentioned your name."

"My name gets mentioned everywhere. I'm a local celebrity."

"They said you were the reason they removed Bill Tindall from his position. Suggested he'd taken payments from you."

"Switch that off." Maurice pushed Nancy's phone towards her. She'd set it to record. "I've never heard of a Bill Tindall, and even if I had, I'd have no reason to pay the flat cap wearing, whippet bothering idiot."

"You're denying it?"

"Denying what? There's nothing to deny, Nancy."

"They suggest there's something underhand involved."

"Who's this mysterious they you are referring to?"

"Jack Ferris."

Maurice snorted with laughter. "Jack Ferris? Take no notice of a word Jack Ferris says. He's a bitter little man."

"He seemed convinced."

"Like I say, he's bitter. In his tiny little mind, every inconvenience is a conspiracy against him. Makes him feel better about his inadequacies."

"He was very determined."

"Determined to do what? Must I remind you how this relationship works? I give you the articles, you don't come looking for them."

"Something involving the big race on Saturday."

Maurice paused. "One second, Nancy, there's something I'd forgotten to get Patricia to do." Maurice went out to his Personal Assistant and closed the door behind him. Maurice's raised voice reverberated through the thick wooden door, but Nancy was unsure what was being said. He returned to the office, still talking to Patricia. "I don't care where they are, I need to speak to them now."

"Everything okay?"

"World of waste management, I'm afraid, if it's not one thing, it's another." He left the door open and perched on the end of his desk, his six-foot five frame towering over Nancy. "Was there anything else because I am a tad busy?"

"I don't mean to be pushy, Mr Groom. I appreciate the stories you have given me."

"But?"

"But they've all been low-level fluff pieces and as a journalist, I want more. I was highly—"

"Commended at university, yes I remember you saying."

"I want to do proper features, something substantial, something exclusive."

"You won't find those sniffing around pigeon club meetings," said Maurice.

"I thought—"

"A significant event is happening in the next few weeks, a major announcement. When it happens, I'll get you in the front row and will give you an exclusive interview afterwards." He ruffled her hair. "Can't say fairer than that."

"I guess not," said Nancy. "Sorry if I came across as obnoxious, it's my journalistic training."

Maurice guided her into reception and past the glaring Patricia. They both watched her leave.

"Never allow that Press Gang wannabe in my presence again." Maurice slammed the office door and picked up the phone. Jack Ferris was becoming much more than an irritant, and he needed silencing.

Chapter Thirty-Two

"You sure you should be here?" said Ted, glancing up from the bus engine he was fixing.

"No place I'd rather be, mate," said Jack.

"After what you told us last night, I thought you were keeping a low profile."

"I am, but I've got a couple issues to resolve first."

"Any news on Molly?"

"Nothing as yet. The lads are clearing the lofts away today." He pointed up the hill towards the decimated site where his pigeons once lived.

"Good excuse for multiple trips to the tip."

Jack nodded. "If owt untoward is happening, they'll uncover it."

A big truck rumbled through the main entrance. It was the pigeon transporter used to take the birds to the starting points of races.

"What's he doing here?"

"Need a favour, Ted. Any chance of making some urgent

modifications before we send this down south for the big race?"

"No problem, what sort of modifications?"

"Not much, just planning ahead."

Ted wiped his oily hands with a rag. Nodded, then jumped onto the back of the truck. "Let's have a gander at what you need."

Jack explained what he needed and left Ted to it. He returned to the office, and he hadn't been there five minutes when he heard footsteps clattering up the metal staircase. Karl stumbled in the door, kitted out in another dazzling Lycra outfit, and with his cheeks as colourful as his clothes, he was gasping for breath.

"How are you so knackered?" said Jack, "You're fit as a lop."

"I was racing a motorbike." Karl slumped into a chair.

"A motorbike?" Jack peeked into the yard.

"Aye." He mopped his forehead. "I avoided the tip, not sure why you think I'd stand out, but anyway, I did what you said. I've been doing circuits, up near your house, down to the lofts, just inconspicuous low level reconnaissance."

"Inconspicuous, good." Jack tried not to smirk.

"Second pass of the lofts. I noticed the bike. He sat back from the road, behind a tree, but he didn't look right."

"How's that?"

"He has his visor up and was having a blast of one of those asthma things."

"Sounds like Vlad the Inhaler. Our paths have crossed before. Could be a coincidence, could easily just be some wheezy old grandad out for a ride."

"But after that he had binoculars, and he was looking straight down the hill at your yard."

Jack wandered to the window and stared through the blinds and towards the lofts. "Is he still there?"

"Get away from the window, for fuck's sake." Karl made a grab for Jack and dragged him onto the sofa.

The door to the Portakabin opened. They had heard no one coming up the stairs.

"Interrupting something?" It was Ted, laughing at the sight of a Lycra clad Karl lying atop Jack.

"How does someone your size move so quietly?" Jack shoved Karl away.

"Years of practice," said Ted, "have you ever tried sneaking in the house past our lass after eight pints on a Sunday afternoon?"

"What's up?" said Jack.

"Nowt, just letting you know there's not much work required for the adjustments. Three hours tops. Need to jettison a pigeon basket or two and it won't stand up to too much scrutiny, but should be enough for your needs."

"Cheers, Ted. From what Karl has been telling me, we might need it a tad sooner than anticipated."

"Oh aye, you two planning on eloping?" Ted opened the door. "I'll leave you two lovebirds to it."

"You have to disappear, Jack," said Karl, "if the hitman is watching you, he could be here any minute."

"You've got a point, make yourself scarce."

"Make myself scarce? Where are you going?"

"I'm not going anywhere."

"We could create a diversion."

"I'm sure you could, Karl, but that won't be necessary. You've done more than enough already."

"You said it yourself, Jack. These are dangerous criminals, you should be in hiding."

"If there's one thing I've learned through this fiasco, it's that it's better to hide in plain sight." He nodded to the exit and indicated for Karl to leave.

He watched as Karl's bright red skintight suit sailed up the bank, getting his second wind.

There was no sign of the motorbike or its rider, but Jack knew he wasn't far away. He took an old computer monitor that had been gathering dust, something else that could have gone to the dump, and placed it on his desk. Jack plugged it into the extension cable, which added to the tangle of wires on the floor. He poured himself a cuppa, sat in his office chair and waited.

As much as he expected the visit, the door creaking open was still a surprise. The assassin being as light on his feet as Ted. He strode into the office in full leathers, with his visor shut and the pistol pointed straight at Jack's head. He wouldn't miss a second time.

"I've been expecting you, Vlad." Despite Jack's bravado, he was in real danger of soiling himself.

"Mmmm." The muffled voice from under the crash helmet gave little away, and he didn't appear perturbed as he cocked the trigger.

"I'm assuming you're a professional," said Jack, "so I'll be quick and you can get on with what it was you came here to do."

"Uuuhhh?"

"You might consider yourself efficient at protecting your identity with your visor down. But I'm not certain how much your employers have shared with you about why they want me dead."

"Ehhh?"

"I have information on them, information we gathered via innovative technology. Technology such as this." He patted the top of the monitor that, not even being flat-screened, looked far from cutting-edge. "We have cameras everywhere and we've been following you."

Vlad tilted his head, but remained mute.

"When you lifted your visor to use your inhaler at the brow of the hill." Jack pointed out of the window. "We got a close-up of your iris."

Vlad moved a chair aside and stepped closer to the desk.

"And all the time you've been here," Jack pointed to various spots around the room, "our discrete body shape monitors have been creating a 3D model unique to you. These two pieces of data will identify you in the result of my death."

He shrugged and moved around to Jack's side of the desk, the gun still pointing at his face. And Jack unleashed the full power of technology on him.

Jack pushed his chair backward on its castors, dragging the extension cable and the tangled wires beneath his desk, until they wrapped around the gunman's leg and tripped him. His gun span out of his hand as his helmet clunked off the floor. Jack leapt from the chair and reached for the gun, but a leather-clad hand gripped his ankle and he tumbled to the ground, the pistol just out of reach. Jack kicked out at the helmet with his spare foot and attempted to scramble to his feet once more. Another tug brought him crashing to his knees again.

The two men wrestled on the worn carpet tiles and the realisation hit Jack that this was as far as his Masterplan took him. Tattered wires attached to an old monitor wouldn't stop a professional killer. He kicked out again and grabbed the monitor, smashing it onto the hitman.

Jack inflicted no permanent damage but had loosened his grip. He grasped the edge of the desk and hauled himself up. The revolver was beyond Vlad and Jack didn't want to risk stepping over him, so dodged around the opposite side of the desk; he had to make a run for it. His parting gift was to tip a heavy filing cabinet over onto the hitman's legs. Again, not enough to cripple him, but enough to hamper his chase.

Jack darted outside and cleared the metal staircase three steps at a time. The yard was quiet as he'd expected trouble and sent everyone but Ted home. There was no sign of Ted, he assumed a victim of the assassin. Another friend to add to the list of those that have perished because of Jack's stubbornness. He didn't have time to dwell on it as a shot rang out from the top of the staircase; the bullet ricocheting off the tarmac at Jack's feet.

Seagulls that had been resting atop the flat roof of the garage were now swirling and screeching, reacting to the sudden noise.

Jack rolled under the pigeon lorry and gave himself a brief reprieve from the line of fire. He looked towards the port where everyone worked away, oblivious to the gunfire. He edged along to the cab of the lorry and glanced through the window to the wing mirror on the far side, where he could see the gunman approaching.

Jack waited until Vlad stepped towards the rear of the truck and he feigned the opposite way. He darted across the yard towards the garage, where he hoped to earn a few seconds to plan his next move. Another gunshot scuppered that. It missed again, but put a clean hole in the metal shutters across the garage window. Jack dived behind a large toolbox, wondering if there were any useful weapons in the box. There was no point. The hitman had him pinned in the corner. He couldn't miss again. Vlad raised the gun as a seagull swooped and shat over his visor.

The gunman's temporary blindness gave Jack a small window of opportunity. He sprinted again, wishing he was as fit as

Karl as his heart was beating out of his shirt and sweat cascaded down his back. His only chance was to race to the gates and sprint up the hill. The unsurmountable task became impossible as he stumbled on a discarded water bottle from Karl's bike and ended in a heap on the floor.

He awaited his fate. Everything was silent. The sound of the docks below disappeared. The seagulls had settled back to their lounging on the garage roof, and all Jack heard were the rubber-soled footsteps of the assassin as he approached.

And a huge clunk as Ted took a gigantic wrench to the back of his crash helmet.

"Jesus, do you have to sneak up on folk like that?" said Jack.

"Are you complaining?"

"Guess not." Jack stumbled to his feet. "Where've you been? I thought you were—"

He produced a copy of The Mirror from the back pocket of his overalls. "Been for a visit." He nodded towards the toilet. "Thought I heard a commotion."

"A commotion?"

They dragged Vlad into the garage and tied him to the shelving. Jack removed his helmet and confirmed his suspicions. He was still groggy, wheezing, but awake.

"I'll keep this simple," said Jack, "you're going to tell us where Molly is, or my colleague here will take that wrench to your head again." He pointed his thumb at Ted. "But this time you won't have the protection of your safety helmet."

The massive wrench looked little more than a spanner in Ted's shovel hands, but it was intimidating enough.

"No English," said Vlad in an accent that may have been Croatian, may have been Hungarian, may have been improvised on the spot. Jack wasn't buying that he didn't speak English after their previous meeting.

"That's your first and last wrong answer," said Jack.

Ted tapped the wrench on the toolbox.

"I know nothing of your daughter."

"But you know Molly is my daughter?"

Vlad shrugged at his mistake. "Is she?"

Ted smashed the wrench into his left kneecap. The sound of crunching bone coming just before the piercing shriek of pain.

"Ted. What are you doing?" said Jack, feeling nauseous.

"No time for fucking about. He knows where Molly is and we're getting her back."

"I don't, I don't," said Vlad.

The wrench descended on his right knee. Another scream, another crunching bone.

"You sure? Ankles next, then hands, then your knackers." Ted lifted the wrench above his head. "By the time I get to your face, you'll be crawling there on your stumps to save her."

"The idiot," said Vlad.

"The idiot?" said Jack.

"The idiot has her."

"The idiot?" said Ted. "Who's the idiot?" Ted looked at Jack.

Jack looked at Ted, and the recognition hit them both. "Derek Pearson."

With Vlad tied up in the secret compartment of the pigeon truck, Jack set off to find Derek Pearson. Since Jack sacked him, he'd been working for Maurice Groom and hadn't hidden the fact. Whilst the world was full of idiots, Jack was convinced Derek was who Vlad referenced. He checked in with Angus and the pigeon lads who'd been visiting the tip. None had seen Derek or anything suspicious that pointed to Molly being on the site.

Derek was a creature of habit. He never strayed far, so Jack had a fair idea where he'd be. His hunch proved correct when he walked into the Ship Inn and found Derek at the bar. He was sleazing over the barmaid, so didn't notice Jack come in, and he wobbled on his stool when Jack gripped his shoulder.

"Derek, I need a word."

"Have it with someone else."

"It's important."

"I don't care, you're not the boss of me now." Derek straightened his Reactolite glasses and sipped his pint of Fosters.

"It's your new boss I need to talk about."

"What's there to discuss, Jack? How much more he pays me than you did. How he trusts me and gives me responsibility? You sacking me did wonders for my career."

"You want to have this conversation here, in front of everyone?" Jack looked around the bar, but it was early. Only diehard alcoholics were in, and they weren't interested in Jack and Derek. The barmaid took Jack's arrival as an excuse to escape from Derek and moved to the far end of the bar under the guise of washing glasses.

"Crack on if you like, Jack, but I've nowt to say."

Jack caught the barmaid's eye as if he wanted serving, and when she was in earshot, he faced Derek. "I have to ask you about a missing little girl."

Derek was flustered, sweat forming on his brow, his face reddening. "Don't know what you're talking about." He downed his pint.

The barmaid had her phone out, not sure if she was witnessing an intervention from an online vigilante group. She took a snap of Derek, who was attempting to cover his face with a copy of The Sun.

"I know you're involved, Derek. Tell me where she is."

Derek stepped from the stool. "Stay away from me, I've got nothing to say to you." He marched to the exit as fast as his stumpy legs would carry him.

"Don't come back, you're barred," shouted the barmaid who'd made up her mind regarding Derek, "you dirty fucking paedo."

Jack chased after Derek, who was already in his battered van when he reached the door. By the time Jack got in his car, Derek was gone.

He was more convinced than ever that Derek was implicated, but he needed to act quick to find him and rescue Molly. Jack spooked Derek, and the barmaid's intervention meant his face was doing the rounds on social media and a vigilante squad mobilised.

Jack didn't mind that so much, but he couldn't risk Derek going further underground, or worse still, fear forcing him into doing something stupid. If Molly was in danger before, the situation had become critical. Jack sent a group message to everybody concerned in the mission.

Derek Pearson is our number one target. Last seen heading west from the Ship Inn in his rusty van. Report any sightings as a matter of urgency.

He gave details of the van and prayed someone spotted it soon.

**

Karl was resting against a tree when he read the message from Jack. He was disappointed at being ruled out of the visits to the dump, so he'd done circuits hoping to see something interesting.

He didn't have long to wait as Derek's van sped past. Karl jumped on his bike and gave chase. He was back in the game.

Staying out of sight whilst clad in head to toe skintight red Lycra wasn't easy. He banked on Derek being preoccupied and not being aware of him as he weaved in and out of buses and cars, keeping Derek in his eye-line. He prided himself on being a safe cyclist, always following the highway code, and highlighting the regulations to drivers when they didn't. But this was an emergency, and rules were going out of the window. Derek passed a light changing from amber to red.

Karl didn't hesitate and pedalled straight through the stop sign, ignoring the beeps of angry motorists having their cyclist preconceptions solidified. Derek hadn't been so lucky at the next lights and sat at a red. Karl didn't want to waste valuable seconds taking his cleats out of his pedals, so rested his hand on the car behind Derek's, keeping his balance.

The driver took exception to this and wound down his window. "Get your fucking mitts off my paintwork, it's just been waxed."

"And I've just waxed my legs so I can pedal faster, so I'm not wasting time putting my feet on the tarmac."

Karl's argument made little sense, but before the driver could articulate a response, the lights were green and Derek was off again. The seconds saved came in handy as he clung to Derek all the way to his destination. Harold Beeston's house.

Karl sailed past him as he parked, but doubled back around and hid behind a bush on the corner of the road. Derek squeezed out of the driver's seat, his face scarlet and sweaty, glanced up and down the street, not noticing Karl, and let himself into Harold's property.

Karl fumbled for his phone and made the call.

Chapter Thirty-Three

No sooner had Karl hung up than Jack was pulling up alongside him, he'd wasted no time sticking to the rules of the Highway Code.

"He's in Harold's house?" said Jack.

"He had a key and walked straight in."

"I don't get it. What's he doing in there?"

"Is it where they're hiding Molly?" said Karl.

"I hope not. The place is such a shit tip, she'll have contracted cholera by now."

"But if she is, we've found her."

"You haven't seen the inside of that hovel, it's impossible to find anything."

"Only one way to find out, Jack."

Jack was procrastinating. He was desperate to find Molly, but terrified of what he might discover. "Okay, I'm going in. You stay here and keep an eye out. Give me a yell if you spot anything suspicious."

"You're not calling the police?"

"They can't be trusted," said Jack as he crossed the road, "and we don't have time."

As he closed the gate behind him, it dawned on Jack that Derek might not be alone. Karl had seen him enter the house, but he didn't know who was lurking behind the door. He rummaged in the garden's undergrowth and struck lucky. There was an old cricket bat nestled amongst the weeds. It had spent so long outside that a couple of solid boundaries would splinter it into a thousand pieces, but it filled the brief for Jack's immediate needs.

He crept to the door and gave it a nudge. Derek, as lazy and clumsy as ever, hadn't locked it behind him. Jack edged it open and peered into the darkness and dustiness of the passageway. The same decrepit boxes and ancient cabinets were there from his last visit. He paused and listened. There were voices coming from the kitchen, male and female. He couldn't figure out what was being said or how many opponents he faced, but they outnumbered him. He contemplated calling the pigeon lads for back up but he may not have time to wait and needed to act. Would he go in swinging and pray the bat held out? Or burst in and use it as a threat only to discover they had guns? Jack's bravado and plan were ebbing away. Until he heard the scream.

He launched himself to his feet and sprinted into the kitchen with the bat above his head, confident he'd at least take out a couple before they tackled him. But Derek was alone. Derek stumbled out of the kitchen chair, dropped his phone and cowered beside the 1980s Hotpoint as Jack stood on the opposite side of the table. A can of half-drunk Fosters spilled over the formica tabletop as the voices and the screaming continued. Jack scanned the room in case anyone was hiding in the corners, but he spotted Derek's phone and the porno he'd been enjoying as Jack surprised him.

"Where is she, Derek?"

"What was that shit in the Ship, telling the barmaid I was a paedo?"

"I didn't tell her. She took one glance at you and made up her own mind. Where's Molly?" Jack edged around the table, the bat still held aloft.

"I don't have a clue."

"You do. Is she here?"

"I'm just paid to watch the joint."

"Who'd pay you to babysit a dead man's house? Why's this place any of Maurice's concern?" said Jack.

"It's a good property to hide stuff."

"Hide what? Molly?"

"Just stuff." Derek straightened himself up, satisfied he wasn't in imminent danger of the bat crashing into his skull.

"I won't ask again, Derek. Where's Molly?" He swiped at the table and knocked the spilt Fosters can across the room.

"That's a waste, I was enjoying that." Derek lifted himself with the aid of the fridge handle opened the fridge door. "I'm getting another. Do you want one?"

"No, I don't want a fucking can of Fosters."

"Want this instead, then?" Derek was pointing a pistol straight at Jack's head.

He was getting used to the feeling. "You don't know how to use that?" said Jack.

"You want to test your theory?"

"Don't be stupid, Derek?"

"Stupid am I? Stupid Derek? Thick Derek, that's how you see me, isn't it? Derek the dickhead. Dumbo Derek. Dimwit Del. Derek small dick."

"Impressive list of aliases you have there."

"Dipshit Dez, Derek the Dildo. I've had them all, ever since I was at school."

"Have you ever considered taking the hint?"

"I'm not the stupid one. I'm the one holding the gun. Who's stupid now?"

"It's still you."

"You don't take me seriously, do you? You never did, but Maurice does. That's why he trusts me to guard this house."

"Derek, I could swipe that gun from your fat fingers before you worked out where the safety was, don't be an idiot."

"Yeah? And I'd pick up another one, I've got a house full. You think you're such a smart arse. Think because you smuggled in half a dozen foreigners, you understand the business? You understand fuck all."

"I'm not interested in the business, I only care about Molly."

"You know why I tricked you into smuggling them foreigners? Yes, it was me, not so stupid now, eh?"

"I guessed it was you. It was hardly a secret."

"It was a distraction, so you'd assume a handful of illegal immigrants was our entire operation, but it's more than that, much, much more."

"Guns."

"And the rest."

"And they trust you to look after it?"

"Part of it, there're safe houses same as this across Sunderland."

"Why Harold's place? Why this house?"

"Our goods stay hidden. It'd take months for anybody to find The Ark Royal in this shit hole."

"And Harold allowed it?"

"Maurice and his friends, they know everything. Harold

had no choice."

"Everything?"

"Let's say they performed due diligence on the residence."

"Due diligence?"

"We know where the bodies are buried."

"Maurice was blackmailing Harold?"

"He tried. Turns out old Harold was a stubborn bugger. Not one to give into blackmail. That's why he ended up on the tip."

"Why there? Surely that was bringing attention on Maurice?"

"Live in a tip, die on a tip. It's what he'd have wanted. We covered it up, made it appear an accident."

"I still don't understand why Maurice would take the risk."

"It was a warning to you, Jack, but you're another one who doesn't listen."

That still didn't answer the question of where Molly was, and Jack was tired of talking. He took a swing at Derek's hand and slapped the gun clean out. It cracked against the kitchen window and plunged into the murky depths of the washing-up bowl. "Enough talking, where's Molly?"

Derek was looking around, hoping to discover another gun, but Jack cornered him.

"She's not here."

"Where is she?"

An ear-piercing shriek distracted both of them. The porno playing out on Derek's phone had just arrived at its climax. Derek seized the opportunity and bolted for the back door. Jack followed and chased him through the undergrowth, hopeful he could catch him before he reached the fence. But Jack stopped in his tracks.

As he came to an open piece of grass, the one tended patch

of lawn, the one that contained a small cross bearing the name Mrs Beeston. Beside it, he discovered a second, freshly filled-in grave. He fell to his knees as Derek clambered over the fence and made his getaway.

Jack slumped on the grave and cried. "No, Molly, what have I done?"

Jack dug. With his bare hands and his fingernails, he tore at the soil. Terrified at what he'd find, but unable to live with himself without knowing. He dug until his fingers seeped blood. Then dug again. Hair snaked out of the ground, blonde, not red-headed like Molly, but he needed to be certain. He swept the soil away until the face of Justin Bieber stared at him. The face on the filthy t-shirt he'd seen the young immigrant girl wearing before they shot her in the head. Jack didn't need to see any more. He didn't need to see the bullet wound he caused. It wasn't Molly, and that's as much as he could handle right now. He scuffed soil back over the body and returned to the house.

The phone rang. It was Karl saying he'd given chase when Derek left, but he'd lost him. They were no closer to finding Molly and may have pushed them further underground.

The phone sounded again, except this time a different ring tone chimed. It wasn't his phone; it was Derek's, and it was Maurice calling. Jack picked the phone from the floor and considered answering, but he had nothing to say to Maurice. They weren't returning Molly, no matter how much he begged. He suspected he knew why Maurice was calling and checked social media. His suspicions proven correct. The barmaid wasted no time in sharing pictures of the 'Pub Paedo'. Derek's face was plastered over Twitter and Facebook, and the lynch mobs would be out soon. Vigilantes didn't care about facts.

The only question was whether the lynch mob or Maurice's men found him first, and he assumed Derek was safer in the hands of the former. If Maurice's associates were looking for him, Harold's house would be top on their list of locations of interest. Jack had to leave. But not before he'd messed with them a bit. If Derek was telling the truth about the guns stashed in the house, Jack could steal them, denting their profits whilst pointing the finger at Derek. Not that he needed any more fingers pointing at him.

He looked in the fridge where Derek retrieved his gun, but it only contained seven more cans of Fosters. Jack emptied containers in the kitchen and in the passageway, but remembered what Derek said, it'd take someone months to discover them in there. Disappointed, Jack unlocked the front door, but one final thought halted him. Running into the kitchen, he rummaged through the kitchen cupboards until he located the Weetabix box. It was reassuringly heavy.

He pulled out the laptop and fired it up, viewing the CCTV footage from the last few days, hoping to watch the guns being delivered and hidden. Jack didn't have much time, so rewound the film at speed until he noticed movement, then studied it in more detail. Nothing much happened. Then he spotted Derek's chubby frame in the passageway, messing with the newel at the end of the balustrade of the stairs.

Jack raced along the passage, lifting the top of the newel and the filing cabinet slid out, revealing a door to the cellar. Harold's engineering skills once again. If he was quick, he could get downstairs, grab the guns and flee before Maurice's men arrived. He struggled to find a light switch so used the torch on his phone. Jack took the stairs at a steady but cautious pace. He couldn't afford to fall now.

Arrival in the basement proved his suspicions were correct, but he'd seriously underestimated the smuggling operation. Wall to wall boxes, not tatty old cardboard affairs that littered the floors upstairs, wooden crates containing guns and ammunition. Too many to shift alone. His only tactic now was to escape. As he put his foot on the first step, he sensed something behind him. Jack wasn't sure what, but it sounded like a sniff. He turned slowly, expecting someone to point a gun at his head. His torch shone in the general direction of the noise, but there was no gun, just a shock of red hair.

"Molly!"

Jack ran over and grabbed her in both arms. Molly tried to hug back, but a heavy chain attached to the wall prevented her. He removed the gag from her mouth, unable to speak. She just sobbed.

"I'll have you free in a second, love." Jack wasn't sure how, but his determination to free Molly overrode any difficulties as trivial as a lock and chain.

Whilst rummaging in one box for a gun, he had visions of shooting the locks off as he'd seen in hundreds of films and thought better of it. Jack took a weighty shotgun from the box and told Molly to lean away. Jack smashed the chains from the wall with the stock of the gun. His first swing proved fruitless, but this was an old house. The walls may have been strong enough to hold a ten-year-old girl, but not a desperate father. He banged at it a second time and after a few blows, the first one was loose. Jack made short work of the second and scooped Molly into his arms again. He kissed her on the forehead and raced up the stairs, back into the light.

As he got to the top of the stairs, Molly spoke. "Daddy?"

"Yes, love?"

"Arthur's still down there."

The temptation to run out and pretend he hadn't heard was strong. But he had heard her, and after everything she'd been through, he couldn't deny Molly. "Back in a jiffy, love." He placed her on the floor.

His second descent into the basement wasn't so cautious. Jack leapt down the stairs, running to the corner where Molly had been, shining his torch. He located the Action Man figure and snatched it. "Thank fuck for that."

"Was that a bad word, Daddy?" said Molly from the top of the stairs.

"It will be if we don't get the fuck out of here."

Jack scooped her up again and legged it through the door. He skipped past the obstacles on the garden path and had just got Molly in the car when he saw two Range Rovers come around the corner. Jack panicked but realised they were searching for Derek, not him, and they hadn't spotted him. He jumped in the driver's seat and eased away, avoiding a dramatic wheel spin that would draw attention to himself.

Once he was a safe distance away, he stopped to make two phone calls. The first to Andrea to let her know her daughter was safe. The second to DS Sidra Ramsay to let her know she may want to take an armed response unit to Harold Beeston's place.

Chapter Thirty-Four

Andrea was at the end of the path waiting when Jack pulled onto the drive. She ran to the passenger door and lifted Molly out, tears of relief streaming down her cheeks.

Once in the house, Jack locked and checked every door, shut the blinds, then called Ted to tell him Molly was home and to call the lads off the search.

"I'll bring a couple of lads to sit outside in case anybody turns up," said Ted.

"There's no need."

"Ha'way, Jack, you're hardly capable of looking after yourself, never mind the family."

"About earlier—"

"It was nowt. Quite therapeutic, taking the wrench to his head."

"Not that. I wanted to have a word with you about the excessive time you spend on toilet breaks."

"Health and Safety, Jack. Place would get evacuated if anybody thought the stench of scorched rubber was coming from one of our trucks."

As the two men laughed, Jack realised it was a long time since he'd been able to relax and, despite clattering a would-be shooter, many problems remained unresolved. The big lass hadn't warbled yet.

"What's the plans for Vlad? We can't leave him in the pigeon truck?"

"Already taken care of."

"Taken care of?" Jack feared what Ted may have done to him in his absence.

"Deposited out the back of Southwick Nick with his gun. Won't take them long to find him, even by the quality of our coppers. It won't be the first time that gun's seen action."

"Thanks again, Ted. Not sure how I'd manage without your help and dexterity with a massive spanner."

"Just keeping my mates out of bother. We'll be there soon, so don't be alarmed if you see cars outside the house, it'll be us."

"I appreciate it."

"Speak soon, Jack."

Jack was confident they weren't in immediate danger. There'd be no point in taking Molly again, and Maurice's gang had bigger things to occupy them if DS Ramsay followed through after his call.

Despite being unwashed and still frightened, Molly appeared unharmed.
Jack and Andrea expected there'd be psychological issues to overcome, but for now, they were ecstatic to have their little girl home. Andrea had a hundred and one questions.

"Did they feed you? Were there toilets? Did anybody hurt you?"

Jack placed his arm around her shoulder. "Let her settle in.

Let her get her bearings, we can ask her later."

"Are you telling me how to—" She was ready for a fight. It was Jack who had dragged them into this mess, but she knew he was right. Arguing in front of Molly helped nobody.

"Would you like something to eat, love?" said Jack.

Molly nodded.

"I've got all your favourites," said Andrea, "pizza, should I put a pizza in?"

Molly nodded again.

"And chips? Do you want chips? And beans?"

Molly nodded.

"At least she has her appetite," said Jack.

"She's not eaten for ages, poor thing." Andrea hugged Molly, trying not to grimace at the stink from days of not washing. "We'll need to get you in the bath after your tea."

Molly nodded.

"Do you fancy some ice cream?" said Jack.

Molly looked at Jack, then Andrea. "Before my pizza?"

"If you want," said Andrea.

Molly smiled. It would take time, but they were getting their daughter back.

Andrea rushed off to get the ice cream, and Jack handed Molly the remote control. There were questions they needed answering, but normality is what Molly needed, and if he had to suffer CeeBeebies or YouTube, then that's what he'd do.

Once fed, bathed, and in her pyjamas, Molly cuddled up to Andrea and Jack on the sofa. "Daddy?"

"Yes, love?" Jack kissed her on the top of the head.

"I'm sorry."

"What have you to be sorry about?"

"For making the nasty men angry."

"You didn't make them angry, it was me they were unhappy with and they took their frustrations out on you."

"I didn't tell them where it was."

"Tell them where what was?" Jack glanced at Andrea.

"The camera," said Molly.

"What camera?"

"From Reggie's lollipop stick."

"You took it?" said Jack, unable to hide his surprise.

"I'm sorry."

"You don't need to apologise for a thing." He pulled her in tight and gave her a cuddle. "Nothing at all."

"Arthur kept it safe."

"Arthur?"

Molly held up her Action Man she'd clung onto since she left Harold's. "He didn't tell anyone."

"Not daft, our Arthur, is he?"

Jack took the doll from Molly. There was an opening in the back where she'd secreted the camera, the lens poking out of his left eye.

"It's been there the whole time?" said Andrea.

"Yes."

"Was it switched on?" said Jack.

"Sometimes." Molly showed Jack the switch that operated the Action Man's Eagle Eyes.

"Genius," said Jack as he gave Molly another hug. "Do you mind if I remove it?"

"You'll need to ask Arthur."

"Do you mind, Arthur?"

Molly put Arthur to her ear. "He says okay."

Jack removed the camera as Andrea fetched the laptop. They gave Molly another bowl of ice cream to distract her, and they settled down to watch the contents of the memory card.

Everyone from Maurice to Mr Shakespeare, to shady Eastern European criminals, and Andrea's father, Noel Cardwell, starred in the damning movie. Impromptu meetings in the school office caught in high definition with crystal clear audio. Jack fast forwarded to Harold's house, concerned with what he might see. He'd never thought to grab Harold's laptop when escaping, so it could be destroyed or in the hands of the police now. He didn't know whether there were cameras in the basement, but Molly had captured the comings and goings.

Derek, whilst clearly the dogsbody being bossed around during the guns delivery, wasn't shy in building up his part when speaking to Molly. Not only had he confessed to a multitude of crimes, he'd incriminated everybody else in the food chain. This stuff was dynamite, and better still, nobody was aware they had it.

"What are we going to do?" said Andrea.

"I don't know," said Jack, leaning back in his seat.

"The police?"

"Eventually, we need to know we can trust DS Ramsay." Jack picked up his phone and had a look at Twitter. "I see she acted on my last tip." He handed his phone to Andrea.

Twitter was awash with photos of an armed raid by police, and guns being retrieved from the scene.

No mention of the bodies or the laptop. Those revelations would follow in time.

"So we go to her?" said Andrea.

"Not just yet, I must be one hundred per cent sure that when it's out there, they can't cover it up."

"Mummy?" Molly glanced up from the TV.

"Yes, love?" Andrea plonked herself on the settee and hugged her.

"Am I still banned from the school play?"

"You were never... of course not, you can have a starring role." This scuppered Mr Fitzpatrick's plans, but from now on, as it always should have been, Molly was Andrea's one and only priority.

Chapter Thirty-Five

With Molly safely home, Jack wanted nothing more than to skip work for the day and spend it cuddled up with her and Andrea on the sofa. Whilst he still owned it, he had a business to run. He needed to get into the yard and hope he could tidy the stray bullets before his workforce found them. Jack was therefore shocked to arrive at the gates to find several news crews there. He'd been out of the loop since the shootout and hadn't considered how a cache of guns being discovered linked back to the incident. It was foolish to assume nobody heard the gunshots. He drove past them without drawing much scrutiny. Nancy Whitworth was front and centre. She spotted Jack but turned her back to him.

Ted was already in the garage.

"What's happening, Ted? Has anyone spoken to you?"

"How's Molly? Is the bairn alright?"

"Yeah, she's great thanks." Jack patted Ted on the shoulder. "Thanks for everything yesterday, I can't ever repay you."

"No bother, mate. As long as the little un's okay, that's all that matters to me."

"Sorry to drag you into this." He pointed at the news crews. "Have the press been questioning you about the shootout?"

"They're nowt to do with us, just as well, because I've not had my hair done. There's a news conference about the port or something. The view's better from up here."

"News conference?"

"Big announcement apparently. They've even wheeled in some dickhead Tory politician to make it."

"Cheers, Ted."

Jack fought his way past the scrum of reporters until he found who he was looking for, Noel Cardwell.

"Noel, we need to talk."

"Mr Cardwell is busy." An aide pushed him away and a less than discrete member of his security team blocked his path.

"I'm his son-in-law."

"As I said, he's unavailable. This is an important statement."

"Noel, I have a message from your granddaughter."

This caught Noel's attention, and he excused himself from the reporter to who he was chatting. "One moment whilst I have a quick word with this gentleman."

"Noel, what brings you to this impoverished neck of the nation?"

"What is it, Jack? I'm a busy man."

"Aren't you going to ask how Molly is?"

"Like I said, I'm a busy man."

"You truly don't care that they kidnapped her for your little scheme?"

"Little scheme?" Noel guided Jack away from the throng of reporters. "Have you any concept of how big this thing is?"

"Painfully aware."

"Then you'll understand nothing can stop it."

"Nothing?" said Jack.

"Not even your little stunt yesterday."

"Little stunt?"

"Leading your little Muslim busybody friend to the gun stash. I expect whoever that belongs to may take umbrage with your activities."

"As if you don't know who it belongs to. I doubt I'm at the top of many people's Christmas card lists at the moment."

"Do yourself a favour and stay out of things that don't concern you."

"Don't concern me? They're taking my business, my pigeons, snatched my daughter, your granddaughter, and possibly killed two of my friends. If it wasn't for wayward gunmanship, I'd also have a bullet in my skull. I think it concerns me."

"You've no idea. All your actions have done is bring the announcement forward."

"How come?"

"We saw yesterday's raid on the criminal empire of the recently deceased Harold Beeston as an opportunity."

"He had no criminal empire."

"That's how we'll spin it. A stockpile of arms in his house, a shady background, and two murdered illegal immigrants in a grave beside his illegal immigrant wife."

It all made sense now, 'we know where the bodies are buried'. Burying the murdered girls in Harold's garden left him with no choice. If he reported it, the police would desecrate his wife's resting place. "You can't keep this quiet forever."

"We control the media, we control the police. Your little friend ventured off-piste, but she will pay for that. As will you.

We're making the announcement today to highlight the need for increased docks security. And what better way than a multi-million pound investment?"

"That's ridiculous. The same criminals doing the smuggling are the ones expanding the docks."

"I guess you have evidence of that, do you?" Noel shook his head. "I heard all about your little stash of documents and emails. How quaint. Even if they got into the public domain, in the era of fake news, we could make them look fabricated. Who will believe you?"

"When I back it up with video evidence? A fair few, I imagine."

Noel paused. "Video evidence?"

"Whilst you may not care about your granddaughter, she took a keen interest in you. And your friends."

"You're walking a very dangerous path here, Jack."

"Do the decent thing, Noel."

"This can't be stopped."

"It can, and you can be the one to stop it. You know what you need to do. If you don't, I'll introduce these news crews to a cute and photogenic ten-year-old girl, with her copper curls and tales of abduction and abandonment by her politician grandfather. Whichever way you try to spin that, they'll remember you as the Tory who traded his family."

Noel stormed off, snatching the copies of the press release from his aide.

**

Jack and Ted settled down in the office and switched on the news on the TV in the corner. They sipped their tea as they went to a live broadcast from Sunderland docks.

"I'm in Sunderland today to make two announcements,"

said Noel Cardwell. "First, I would like to announce plans to expand the scale and operation of the docks in Sunderland. Both increasing the capacity and delivering a well-needed jobs boost to the city."

"The fucking prick," said Ted, slamming his mug on the desk.

"Wait," said Jack, putting a calming arm on his shoulder, "it's coming."

"But," said Noel, "an expansion of such magnitude does not come without risks, as yesterday's gun haul shows." He loosened his tie and the top button of his Saville Row shirt. "I will therefore refer the planning to the Secretary of State for consideration."

Bulbs flashed and numerous reporters shouted out questions at once.

Noel put up his hand to calm them. "Second, my recent visits to Sunderland reminded me how I've been neglecting my family in pursuit of building a stronger and safer country for everyone. It is with a heavy heart, my duty to inform you that once I've referred this to the Secretary of State, I will retire from politics for the foreseeable future."

After the barrage of questions, photographs, and filming, the news crews began filtering off, leaving Noel shell-shocked and bewildered. Even his own aides disappeared, realising political life was short and, with Noel's now dead in the water, he was of no use to them. Jack watched him from the window with no regret. Noel had it coming, and lots more besides, but he was Andrea's father, Molly's grandfather, and he was a broken man. Noel caught Jack's eye and marched across the yard, storming up the stairs and bursting into the office.

"Have you any idea what you've done?"

"Can you give us a minute, Ted?" said Jack.

"No bother, Jack," said Ted, tapping his wrench on the desk, "give me a shout if you need anything." He left, giving Noel a dismissive shake of the head.

"What I've done?" said Jack. "From where I'm sitting, this has all been of your making."

"I'm ruined."

"Like I said, it's your own doing."

"You still have no notion of who you're dealing with." Noel slumped into the chair Ted had vacated. "They'll go after the Secretary of State next, and everyone who works for him. These people are ruthless, you won't be able to stop them."

"We'll see."

"Losing my job won't satisfy them. They will make me pay for this. Don't be surprised if I turn up in a staged suicide. Molly could lose her grandfather over this."

"She never had one, Noel."

"And you, they'll come after you. Sitting in your little Portakabin thinking you've taken on the big boys, you don't have a clue. You are in their sights."

"I have been for a long time."

"We're finished, both of us." Noel leaned across the desk towards Jack. "I don't care about you. I hope you get one in between the eyes, but Andrea doesn't deserve to suffer for your mistakes."

"My mistakes?"

"I warned her she shouldn't marry beneath herself, but she wouldn't listen."

"This is your fault, Noel. Don't pin it on me."

"Get Andrea and the child far away from here, somewhere

they can't be found. They are coming for you, Jack, and they won't stop until they've extracted their revenge."

"Their enterprise is being dismantled bit by bit, they've bigger things to focus their minds."

"You think the gun haul was more than a minor blip? Did you hear of any arrests at the raid?"

Jack wasn't aware of anyone apprehended at the scene. Strange, considering several men had appeared on the scene minutes before the police. "Not that I've noticed."

"It's because they knew they were coming. Why do you think there's been no mention of the police finding a laptop left on the kitchen table that contained incriminating CCTV footage? It vanished before the police arrived. They're monitoring your phone calls, and your little Muslim mate. If you think you can call in a favour from her, they'll always be one step ahead of you."

Noel's phone rang. He checked the name on the screen. "Oh, Christ." He answered. "Noel Cardwell."

Jack couldn't pick up what they said on the other end of the line. Raised voices thwarted any attempts by Noel to interrupt or apologise. "Personal reasons," being the only words he muttered before hanging up.

"Party chairman. Not a happy chap. PM peeved I didn't give him the heads-up." Noel massaged his forehead. "A rather inglorious way to end my career."

Noel's phone rang once more. Any colour he had remaining in his face drained away. He answered again. There was shouting, but Noel didn't interrupt. When the call ended, he was shaking. "They're coming for me, Jack. They'll never forgive me for this." He stood to leave. "Or you. If you have a scrap of decency left, get my family away from this mess." He barged out of the door into the searing early morning sunlight and stumbled down the metal staircase. For the first time in his life, from prep school to his career in politics, Noel Cardwell didn't know where he was going next.

Noel was right, Jack was in danger. The criminal fraternity wasn't a forgiving bunch, but he couldn't go on the lam forever. He'd put Andrea and Molly through enough. Jack had to resolve this before somebody resolved him.

Chapter Thirty-Six

Despite being way past Molly's bedtime, neither Andrea nor Jack wanted to put her to bed. They never wanted her to leave their sight again. She'd said little about her spell in captivity, and they didn't want to push it. She'd tell them what happened in her own time. Their wish for her to fit back into a routine and normal environment, whatever normal was, overruled their desperation to know. A family of three sitting in a pigeon transporter in the Kent countryside was very far from normal.

Despite their recent arguments, Andrea took little persuading when Jack suggested he'd launch the birds for the big race and take his wife and daughter with him. It was the perfect cover, and they persuaded Molly that they deserved a little family holiday after what she'd endured. Normal could wait when normal meant that gangsters might break into your home and attack your family. Jack assured Andrea that Molly was no longer in danger, but he didn't sound so convinced himself. A little time away to regroup and contemplate the next steps was what they needed.

They'd left in the middle of the night to avoid prying eyes.

Shoving a few essentials in a bag and telling Molly to bring whatever toys she could squeeze in her unicorn rucksack. They'd made decent time on the motorway and settled in for the evening, ready for the release of the birds in the morning.

The modifications Ted made to the truck meant Molly had a full size bed, with light, to sleep in whilst Jack and Andrea roughed it in a small tent. They had access to the shower block in a camp field next door, and Ted loaned them various bits of camping equipment he used when fishing. They sat at a picnic table sharing a can, neither wanting to get tipsy and drop their guard.

Molly played in the rear of the truck, tired and a touch agitated, but with no desire to go to bed herself. When she used the bathroom, Andrea and Jack had to do everything in their powers to stop themselves standing guard outside the toilet. Normal environment. The pigeons cooed, resting up for the big race ahead and with the sun low in the sky, it was the most peaceful either of them had been for weeks.

Molly had been quiet for a short while and both Jack and Andrea wondered which one would say it, which one would 'Go and check.'

They heard shuffling coming from the truck and they curbed their sighs of relief when she walked around the corner.

"Can we play this, Daddy?" She brandished a battered cardboard box.

"What is it?"

"I found it in your office."

It was the Battleships box he'd recovered from Reggie's chimney, the one that contained the information that got them into this trouble in the first place.

"I'm not sure all the pieces are there, love."

"Awww."

"No harm in looking though." Jack took the box from her and emptied the contents onto the table.

"Have you ever played this?"

Jack wasn't sure he remembered the rules. He'd not played it since the eighties and never this electronic version he'd always coveted. First, he checked the batteries, surprised to find new Duracells. He skim read the rule book, although not convinced Molly would be interested in playing it as the manufacturers intended. They laid out their pieces and let Molly go first. The game was more fun than he expected, and he allowed Molly a peek of his pieces when he pretended to read the rules.

It wasn't long before she was destroying his fleet, but he couldn't let her know he was letting her win. He had to try. A couple more goes and he managed a hit. Once he destroyed the entire ship, Molly removed the piece from the board. The screen changed in front of Jack. He'd never owned the electronic version, but was sure he would have recognised this feature. A sequence of numbers appeared on the screen, unrelated to the game. An error code?

"Have you got any numbers on the screen in front of you?" said Jack.

"Are you trying to cheat, Daddy?"

"No, it's just, no, your turn."

Jack allowed the game to continue, and Molly soon triumphed. He spun the board around and her screen also displayed a series of numbers. This wasn't right. Someone had modified the game.

Why would Reggie have concealed the information in an old board game box when already hidden in the chimney? The game was part of it. He just didn't have a clue what the numbers meant.Jack jotted them on a scrap of paper and Molly finally admitted her readiness for bed. He resisted the urge to carry her onto the back of the lorry, but both he and Andrea tucked her in.

They gave it a of couple hours, Jack doing a circuit of the field every thirty-minutes to check for any unwelcome guests. When gentle snores satisfied them Molly was asleep, they retired to bed themselves. Exhausted from the stress of the last few days, Andrea dropped off asleep straight away, but Jack was wide awake.

He opened Google on the browser of his phone. Jack typed in the numbers he'd found on Battleships and didn't expect to uncover much, but he got a hit with each one. It was now obvious. Each one referred to a shipping vessel identification number. He clicked on a link to a ship tracker and retrieved the names of the vessels and their destinations. It was no surprise that one headed towards Sunderland, and it arrived tomorrow. A second string of numbers related to specific containers on the ship.

Jack had stumbled across killer information, but had no way of passing it on. He knew they monitored calls from, or to, his and DS Ramsay's phones. Jack could go to a local police station, but his story was ludicrous when he said it aloud, and he had no way of knowing how involved the police were in the organisation.

Kent was much nearer to Reggie's relatives and their enemies. It wasn't worth the risk.

As morning broke, the entire family was awake and active. Jack promised Molly that she could start the competition, both a treat and a distraction for her. He took out his one remaining pigeon, stroking its head with his forefinger and spreading its wings out to marvel at this feat of natural engineering. "Sorry, mate, but I won't be there to see you win the big race. Make sure you bring the prize home for me."

Jack placed the bird back in its basket and gave it a handful of feed. He'd fed the rest of the birds earlier, and they were ready to go.

As his watch hit 6am, he shouted "Go" and Molly pulled the lever.

A flurry of wings shattered the peaceful morning as the birds whooshed above her. Tiny white feathers floated to the ground, one landing in Molly's hair. Her orange locks matching the early morning sun. The birds turned right as a group, then left, getting their bearings until they decided which direction was North, which way was home. As they disappeared into the distance, heading home, Jack knew he had to do the same and face whatever that brought.

As far as pigeon racing days went, the weather was perfect. Cool, bright and hardly a breeze. There was, however, an enormous cloud on the horizon for Jack. As well as having no clue how his prize pigeon would do, he had no idea on whether he'd survive the day. He had a plan, albeit not much of one, and it relied on many things and many people falling into place. Not one of which he was confident.

An air of menace hung over the temporary pigeon lofts. The ousting of Bill Tindall was uncomfortable, though most club members recognised he had to go. He'd betrayed their legacy and years, decades, of tradition were in danger of disappearing. If this was to be their last race, it should have been a day of celebration, of remembering the traditions that had gone before them. But Jack's absence, and several expensive cars with cheap occupants at the end of the lane, suggested things could turn ugly.

"Try to ignore them, lads. They're just attempting to intimidate us," said Ted.

"They're making a canny job of it. I bet they're the bastards that torched the lofts."

"Imagine so." Ted tried to appear unfazed as he spread seed out on the roof of the loft.

"Shouldn't we have a word with them? Ha'way, there're loads of lads here, we could take them."

"Ignore them. They're not here for us."

Ted understood why the gang arrived en masse. It wasn't just intimidation. Jack was in serious bother and left without hinting when they were coming back. He guessed the heavies on the side road meant they hadn't located Jack, and he'd avoided harm, for now.

A BMW drove past the queue of four-wheel drives and pulled up beside the lofts. DS Sidra Ramsay climbed out and stretched. She noted the numbers of registration plates, but knew it did little good. Sidra didn't scare them. Far from it, they watched her every move with interest.

She approached Ted. "No Jack?"

Ted shrugged. "Doesn't look like it."

"I don't suppose you know where he is?"

"Nope." He took out binoculars and searched the sky for any incoming birds.

"Have you heard from him?" She was aware others were listening in and she'd get nothing from Ted.

"Afraid not." He grabbed his flask. "Cuppa?"

"I'm okay, but thanks for the offer. Mind if I look around?"

"Free country."

Sidra wandered over the scorched earth where the lofts once stood. A slight smell of burning lingered in the air. She looked along the river to the docks, where a container ship unloaded its cargo. Forklifts and men performed a ballet below; busy, but nothing compared to how they would be if Maurice Groom and his group had their way.

A commotion erupted in the lane. One of the pigeon lads had kicked the door of a Range Rover and shouted at the occupants. The driver, taking exception to this, heaved his seventeen-stone frame out of the four-wheel drive. Ted dragged his friend aside as Sidra limped in between them.

"Problem?" she said, flashing her warrant card.

"There will be," said the driver, an Eastern European tinge to his accent.

"Can I ask what you're doing here?"

"Just enjoying the view." He glared at Sidra, a smug grin on his face, and got back in the car and wound his window up.

Sidra decided not to pursue it and risk escalating the situation. Their presence was for the same reason as hers; Jack Ferris. He'd given her the biggest tip off of her career with Harold Beeston's house. An arms stash and three bodies in the garden; a haul that could make careers. But only if convictions followed, and as yet, no evidence linked the guns or the remains to anyone other than Harold Beeston.

Sidra had her suspicions, but she needed confirmation, with Jack key to that proof. Except he'd disappeared. Not at home, and he wasn't answering his phone. His friends and colleagues were brick walls, and she was unsure whether his disappearance was through guilt or fear, or something much worse. The thugs lining the lane reassured her, if they were here; they hadn't found Jack, there was little chance of him turning up here now.

Chaos ensued at the station, and the big boys arrived to take charge. Whilst nominally her investigation, she understood who wielded the power, and it wasn't her. Sidra put up a fight, but darker forces were at play. Her drive up to the lofts was as much about escaping the bedlam as it was about finding Jack.

"That cuppa still available?" she said to Ted.

"Hope you prefer it milky," he said as he poured her a cup.

They both stood in silence for a while, admiring the vista out over the harbour and to the North Sea. The background hum of the docks offering a soothing soundtrack.

"What happens next?" said Sidra.

"Good question."

"With the pigeons, I mean."

"We wait," said Ted.

"That's it?"

"Not much more we can do." He picked up a bag of seed. "We can entice them in with food, waving hankies and calling them in, but they're homing pigeons. They know where we are, and we accept they'll turn up when they turn up."

"Hoping your boy turns up first?"

"That's the way it works."

A whooping sound came from behind Sidra, the pigeon lads making the noise. The thugs down the road, alerted by the sudden disturbance, got out of their motors, readying themselves for trouble. Sidra stiffened.

"Looks like we've got ourselves some action," said Ted, pointing towards the horizon.

The volume levels increased as everybody was whooping and hollering, aiming to entice their bird home first. The gangsters leaned against their cars, hands resting near their inside pockets as if they were ready to draw weapons. They weren't used to pigeon racing and to the untrained eye; it was a peculiar sight. Grown men waving white hankies in the air whilst making high-pitched whoops to their feathered friends. Birdseed tins rattled and a groundswell of excitement grew amongst the men. It had been a tough couple of weeks for them, and their club was falling apart, but this is why they did it, the reason it was special. Race day and watching your birds come home.

"It's Jack's," said Ted.

"What is?"

"The bird in the lead."

"How can you tell?"

"We just know."

Sidra admired their sixth sense, a sixth sense that came from years of experience and knowledge. A sixth sense she wished she possessed because hers was telling her something else was at play, something she was missing.

The first pigeon landed almost right into Ted's palm, and he took it straight to the timing machine to get its arrival logged. Sirens below them distracted Sidra. Blue flashing lights flooded Jack's yard and surrounded one of his trucks. Had he been hiding under her eyes all along? Why hadn't they informed her of this development?

Sidra was tempted to race down the hill and get involved, but she had a good vantage point from where she was. If they'd excluded her up to now, there was little she could add to proceedings. The gangsters looked on with interest, but not surprise, laughing and joking amongst themselves.

"You want to hold him?" Ted was behind Sidra, offering the prize pigeon.

"God, no. They're flying rats."

"You'll hurt his feelings. Go on, I promise, once he's in your hands you'll be hooked, you'll recognise their majesty."

She took hold of the pigeon. "He won't fly off?"

"He's home now, he's not going anywhere."

Sidra held the bird in both hands, terrified she might break it. It cooed as she stroked its head. Maybe she should consider pigeon racing as a career rather than police work. She spotted a small piece of paper in the ring around the pigeon's ankle.

Ted nodded.

Sidra removed it whilst appearing to stroke the bird and slid it up her sleeve. Sidra handed the bird back to Ted and put her hand in her pocket, depositing the paper there.

She looked towards Jack's yard. "I suppose I should head down there and discover what the big drama is."

"Jack's a good bloke, DS Ramsay," said Ted. "Look after him."

Sidra nodded.

As she passed the gangsters, they laughed and shared a joke at her expense, in a language she didn't understand. Her life had been full of snide comments and insults. It was nothing new.

She pulled up just short of the gates, where she read the note. Sidra glanced at her watch and marched into the yard.

"Who's in charge?"

She was pointed towards DC Stoker. He greeted her with a smirk.

"DS Ramsay," said Stoker, "what brings you here?"

"What's going on?" said Sidra.

"We had a tipoff."

"From who."

"Confidential source."

"About what?"

"Potential contraband in one of these wagons." Stoker smiled at his mate. "We would have told you, but you left the office without saying where you'd gone."

"Have you found anything?"

"Yes, and no."

"Which is it?"

"We've found no goods, but we have uncovered parts from a modified pigeon transporter. It looks like our friend Mr Ferris might be smuggling more than pigeons into the country."

Sidra surveyed the scene. There were at least thirty armed men and women involved in the operation, almost everyone at their disposal. "Excellent work. Your informant must have been onto something."

Stoker smirked again. "He usually is."

"I need the entire yard searched from top to bottom. I don't care how long it takes."

"Sure thing."

"I need everything logged meticulously, and you to handle the whole search. Could make your career if you find something incriminating."

He nodded, still smiling. "Yes, Ma'am."

"It'll keep you busy for a while."

"Looks that way."

"As you'll be doing it on your own."

The smile went. "What?"

"I'll leave you a couple guys to keep the place secure, but you've done splendid work up to now. I'm sure you can cope with this."

"But—"

Sidra had already walked away and was gathering the rest of the armed police and giving them instructions. She glanced back at Stoker, who was making urgent phone calls, as she knew he would.

The thugs at the top of the hill were no longer observing

the yard and had their eyes on two containers being loaded onto trucks on the docks. Once the containers were on the trailers, they returned to their cars and left.

Ted sat in a deckchair, a pigeon in one hand, cuppa in the other, watching events unfold. He had faith in Jack, and he hoped his faith in DS Sidra Ramsay wasn't misplaced.

The armed team got back into their vehicles and withdrew with their lights flashing, leaving Stoker dialling frantically, praying someone would answer.

**

The black Range Rovers pulled into the landfill site and up to the warehouse at the back, where the shutters opened on their arrival. They were out of sight of the public tip, which was as busy as usual. The hustle and bustle distracting from the two eighteen-wheelers scheduled to arrive from the port.

Chapter Thirty-Seven

Sidra had to move fast. Jack's note identified the ship sat in the port and two containers that, if he was correct, could be the biggest drugs seizure ever in the North East of England. There were protocols to follow, and authorisation needed granting, but Sidra didn't have time. Once those containers had left the docks, it became much harder to intercept the shipment. Once they reached their destination, the gang would chop and distribute the drugs before she obtained a warrant.

Sidra screeched to a halt at the barrier outside the port and produced her warrant card for the security guard. He was unimpressed. Whether he was in on the conspiracy or merely incompetent, she wasn't sure, but he wasn't letting her onto the docks without good reason.

Three van loads of armed police pulling up behind her gave him that motivation. The guard lifted the barrier and let them through.

Sidra dodged the myriad of forklifts whizzing around the place and pulled up next to someone with a clipboard, assuming he was in charge. He was more forthcoming, but unhappy with the interruption.

"We're on a tight schedule here," he said. "What do you want?"

"Two containers listed here. Are they on this ship?" She showed him the two numbers on a scribbled note.

He raised his eyebrows and checked the clipboard. "They were."

"Were?"

"They've already been unloaded."

"Where are they now?" Sidra looked around for any random containers left sitting on the dockside.

"Gone. Like I said, we're on a tight schedule."

"Do you know where?"

"Once they've left here, it's nowt to do with me."

"Shit."

"I can tell you which trucks they were loaded onto."

"Brilliant." Sidra made a note of the registration plates and circled her hand in the air to show they were leaving. She put an order out for all vehicles to locate the trucks, but she had a fair idea of their destination. And it wasn't far away.

She planted her foot on the accelerator and hoped she could reach the landfill site before the lorries did. Sidra phoned her boss to receive authorisation but disguised her lack of disappointment when he didn't answer after two rings and she hung up. Sidra ignored at least three red lights, relieved the vans behind her held the same disregard for road safety. Then she came to a stop. As ever, there was a massive queue to the public tip, and it had encroached onto the main road. Cars spread right across the roundabout, preventing anybody from either entering or exiting it.

She got out of her car and clambered onto the bonnet,

wincing at her calf strain, to get a better view. Traffic on the slip road to the left, coming from the main landfill site, backed up way past the entrance and the two wagons queued, waiting to turn right. There was still a chance.

Any other time, she'd allow the delivery, gain a search warrant, and seize the goods on site to capture the recipients rather than just the delivery drivers. Unfortunately, she knew only too well what would happen when attempting to secure a warrant against Sunderland's number one businessman. Sidra had to act now and took out her radio. "Hard stop, everyone, hard stop. Take them now."

They cleared a path from the roundabout and half on the pavement, half off, they raced up alongside the wagons, stopping the first one just before they turned right.

At the sight of the guns, the drivers stepped from the cab without argument; their liberty was now at stake, and pleading ignorance was their only defence. They had to cooperate and opened the wagons. On first viewing, they were packed with pallets of machinery, machinery for a giant waste recycling unit. Panic set in for Sidra. What if this was a terrible mistake? She hid her concerns from her colleagues. Slow and methodical would win the day. She called the dog handlers to the front. If there were drugs, they'd discover them.

Maurice watched on from the office window, his knuckles white as they pressed into the windowsill. He called Patricia and pointed to the bag full of documents on his desk. "Destroy those."

"All of them?" Patricia still wasn't happy at being shouted at the other day and displayed petulance ever since.

"All of them." Maurice glanced out of the window again. "And the laptop and memory stick. Take a hammer to them. Smash them to kingdom come then dispose of the remains on the landfill." He ran to the door. "I have to go."

"Laptop, I can't see—"

"Just do as you're bloody told for once in your fucking career." He slammed the door behind him and sprinted down the stairs, making a call as he left. Maurice got no answer. He dashed to the warehouse and delivered the news. His Eastern European associates were less than thrilled, and it was clear where they thought the blame lay. "This was your responsibility, Mr Groom. No consignment, no payment. You understand what that means?"

"I'm painfully aware of what it means, but right now we need to escape and dispose of any evidence of our activities."

The back gates to the site opened, as did the doors to the second warehouse. Hundreds of eyes looked on in fear as the armed gangsters entered.

"Leave now. This is your one chance to disappear. Anybody still here in five minutes will be dead."

Not everybody understood English, yet they all understood the sentiment. The illegal immigrants made a run for freedom. Maurice and his associates didn't hang around either. Sidra heard the roar of the engines and the Range Rovers left. That wasn't her concern. She needed to find evidence in the back of this truck.

A dog barked and wagged its tail as it pointed its nose at the panels of the truck.

"Bingo."

Chapter Thirty-Eight

From the bus crash and death of the school's lollipop man, to the drug haul linked to the docks and the discovery of guns and dead bodies at a nearby house, it had been quite the fortnight for Hendon Dock's Primary School. It was a wonder anybody had time for anything else. But if Mr Fitzpatrick had one motto he lived by, it was that 'the show must go on'. The fact Mrs Ferris hadn't been to school for the last few days added to his concerns. But at least it gave him complete artistic control over the production of MaXbeth, and it promised to be the greatest performance this little school had ever staged.

The kids were excited, and the hall was full of parents and dignitaries, including none other than the chair of the board of governors, Maurice Groom. Maurice was there under sufferance. The drug bust wiped out every shilling of savings, and more. He'd borrowed against the businesses and they'd crumble once the banks came knocking. Worse still was the debt he owed to others. A debt that not only torpedoed his share in the dock's expansion, but one that put serious doubts about getting out of here alive.

Maurice couldn't help but notice the interesting characters lurking in the car park. Whether they were looking for him or Jack Ferris, he didn't know, but his play was nearly over. He had to attend the ridiculous school show to save face. Rumours had been circulating that the drugs were bound for his warehouse and several illegal immigrants apprehended wandering the streets of Sunderland claimed to be former captives on his land. Maurice hadn't commented in the press, but avoiding the annual school showpiece would have been an admission of guilt.

Reporter Nancy Whitworth was in the crowd. He could grab her and give an exclusive interview, putting his side across. Damage limitation. It would have to wait, as DS Sidra Ramsay was also in attendance. The one straight copper in Southwick Nick, and the one who scuppered his drug delivery.

Maurice had hoped the raid on Jack's yard would have been a distraction, kept the armed unit busy whilst the drugs sailed past them a few hundred yards away. And it worked until DS Ramsay's intervention. He glared at her; Sidra smiled back.

Mr Shakespeare sat at the opposite end of the row, not wanting to link himself to Maurice.

His benevolence was welcome when the school needed a new bus or updated equipment. If any of the rumours about him were true, and his involvement needed explaining to the Local Education Authority, his presence became a burden.

Mr Fitzpatrick gave out last-minute instructions, hoping the nervous energy of the kids transferred into star quality on the stage.

"Mrs Ferris?" Fitz was surprised to see Andrea appear backstage. "I didn't see you come in."

"We sneaked in the back way." She was with Jack and Molly. "There's been a change of plan."

A heated exchange followed where Andrea reminded Mr Fitzpatrick more than once regarding who was in charge.

"You're going to ruin all the hard work I've invested in so you can make your daughter star of the show?"

"Something like that."

"That's outrageous. I bet Sir John Gielgud or Joe McElderry were never forced to put up with this."

"I'll do you a deal."

"What sort of deal?"

"Are you capable of stepping in to do a script-in-hand performance?"

"Me?" Mr Fitzpatrick placed his hands on his heart.

"Yes."

"But the show is for the children."

"That's a yes then?"

"If Fitz is what the show needs, then Fitz is what the show shall get."

Andrea handed him a script and rushed Molly to where the other teachers and a few helpful parents were doing the costumes. "I need a hand. Can you make Molly six-foot five with shocking white hair?"

She left Molly in make-up and briefed the rest of the children with their duties. A couple were disappointed at losing their star roles, but she made it up to them by saying they could each choose a song to perform at the end.

Jack peeked out from behind the curtains. Everyone was in place. He was sorry for dumping this on DS Ramsay. He'd tried to help her with the tip offs, but with Maurice and his associates still not incarcerated, his life was in danger. Even if he passed over the evidence he held, it would be months before it got to court. With the police under the pay of Maurice Groom, it may never reach court.

Only one choice remained for Jack. Go big or go home.

The crowd went silent as the curtains opened, revealing a group of children huddled on the corner of the stage.

"I'm scared," said one.

"We must escape."

"We have to tell the police they have held us captive."

Two further children dressed as police officers walked on stage, twirling their truncheons to sniggers from the audience.

"Can you see anything?"

The second policeman looked at the crowd in the corner. "Nope, everything appears to be in order."

More giggles from the crowd, although none recognised this from either Macbeth or the X Factor.

Molly appeared from the opposite side of the stage. Given the time constraints, the team behind the scenes had done a magnificent job, albeit breaking every Health and Safety rule. She stood on top of a chair which itself was on top of a trolley wheeled in by two of the parents. A large coat hid the chair and trolley, and she sported a spectacular white wig. It was crude, but a few in the audience guessed who the character portrayed.

"Good work, lads," she said as she handed each of the police officers a brown envelope. More laughs from the audience. Maurice squirmed in his seat. He didn't like the way this was going.

Mr Fitzpatrick burst on from the wings in a smart suit and retro sixties glasses and delivering an exaggerated cockney accent. "Awight my old china? I need the docks for my smuggling operation and you're going to get them for me, cocker."

"You've found just the gentleman for the job," said Molly,

"if the price is agreeable."

"I'll give you a slice of the action," said Mr Fitzpatrick, "but get it wrong and I'll slice you up."

Fitz marched off, and another child stepped on stage. Padded out to look fat, he sported glasses, but they soaked his head to portray sweat. "We've got a problem?"

"What sort of problem?" said Molly.

"They won't sell and intend to expose your master plan."

"We'll kidnap his daughter, he'll soon change his mind." She ruffled the young lad's hair, then was wheeled off stage.

It confused the audience; they didn't know what they were watching. If it was a comedy, it wasn't funny, and if not, it was heavy for a primary school play. Maurice knew what it was and checked the exits. He couldn't stand and walk out, but he couldn't stay here and face the humiliation. Maurice sunk further into his chair.

Molly returned to the stage, this time as herself and carrying Arthur, her Action Man.

The boy in the padding returned. "Sit in the corner where I can keep an eye on you."

"Why am I here?"

"Because your dad wouldn't do as we told him."

A large television flickered to life at the back of the stage, and the chubby face of Derek Pearson filled the screen. "Because your dad wouldn't do as we told him."

There were gasps from the crowd. The video confused Maurice. How did Derek get filmed?

Molly ran off the stage and came back minutes later dressed as Maurice again. "What happened?"

"She escaped." The child dressed as Derek also dashed off the stage.

Mr Fitzpatrick returned. "You promised me you'd sort this."

The TV played again, showing the school office, and Maurice's face was the one on camera. "Don't worry, I'll get you that land, whatever it takes."

More gasps and a handful of boos. Maurice had seen enough. He faked an incoming phone call. "Sorry, I need to take this."

He skirted around the edge of the hall, DS Ramsay following from the other side. Maurice's mind was in overdrive. He'd spent his life in control, controlling the message and what everybody thought of him, but he couldn't spin this.

Nancy Whitworth took a photo of Maurice and that led to half the crowd breaking the embargo on camera phones at the school play. Everybody was filming now. Half filming his escape, half filming his performance on stage. Maurice stumbled through the double doors into the entrance hall and made a run for the main exit. Sidra was in hot pursuit.

As he burst through the exit, a sight he wasn't expecting confronted him. One of Jack's trucks, with the whole side of it emblazoned with the emails, incriminating him and many more. Emails that had been on the laptop and memory stick Nancy Whitworth had squirrelled out of his office. He had no time to waste and turned left towards the car park, where two men clad in black approached. DS Ramsay hadn't come alone. She'd brought reinforcements, evading arrest was futile. Except these men weren't interested in arrest, Maurice noticed the tattoos.

And the guns.

He made a sharp right as the first shot sounded and the bullet whizzed past him. As the second rang out, he crumbled to the floor in a heap.

"Stay down," said Sidra as she lay atop him, following a perfectly executed rugby tackle.

The gunmen continued to approach, but the lights of Jack's wagon blinded them as he drove it straight towards the danger, his horn blaring. More shots rang out, but they were no match for an eighteen-wheeler as it knocked the gunmen flying.

Maurice looked up from underneath Sidra to a crowd of onlookers, each one videoing his downfall.

Chapter Thirty-Nine

Molly sat in her favourite seat on the school bus and joined in the singing. "Charlie had a pigeon, a pigeon, a pigeon…"

She could have travelled into school with Andrea, but wanted some independence. Andrea and Jack smothered her since the kidnap and they realised they needed to give her space; even if it was a space where they still kept a close eye on her. She looked towards the docks where construction work had begun.

Maurice's arrest and subsequent conviction hadn't prevented the development. He was merely a pawn in the operation, and darker forces were at play. The Secretary of State approved the proposals as soon as they'd landed on his desk, using increased security as the major factor in his decision.

"Charlie had a pigeon, a pigeon he had…"

Maurice took his punishment without complaint, knowing silence and an early guilty plea were his best chance of survival. He gave nobody up, including Noel Cardwell, and the emails and videos weren't enough to incriminate anybody else. The London crime syndicate had stepped back into the shadows but continued to pull the strings.

The courts convicted members of the Eastern European gang of gun smuggling and the murder of the two immigrants. Yet they were barely out of the picture before a Turkish syndicate replaced them.

"He flew it all morning, he flew it all night…"

As part of the expansion plans, they agreed to find a new site for the pigeon lofts, with the expense covered by the developers.

"And when it came home, it was covered in…"

The bus driver glanced in the mirror at Molly and her friends with a big smile on his face. Mr Fitzpatrick loved the new role. There were few jobs where he got to sing every morning.

"Charlie had a pigeon, a pigeon, a pigeon…" he sang.

He'd even landed himself a few minor am-dram roles following the publicity he received following the school drama. Andrea allowed him full reign to produce the next school play, without interference from her, and the new headmaster, who replaced Mr Shakespeare after his sudden resignation, backed her decision.

Nancy Whitworth got her exclusive. Her part in exposing Maurice Groom won her an award and a role in a national, albeit free, newspaper. She now mentioned her award instead of her being highly commended at university.

Reggie's family had been back up north to visit Jack. Whilst they'd taken a keen interest in the dock's expansion, it was too hot even for them to handle, and they stepped aside. Reggie's undercover surveillance sent shock waves through the criminal underworld, and they happily let the rumour grow that they'd collated information about everyone.

The flip side of this was that Jack possessed a fair amount

of information on them if he chose to share it. Out of respect for Reggie, they'd agreed not to interfere in each other's lives. As a goodwill gesture, the family gave Jack the proceeds of the sale of Reggie's house. Most of which he put towards the fund to pay for the next ten years of pigeon club away trips.

Noel Cardwell disappeared from public life. His involvement in the docks deal forever hinted at but never proven. A solitary birthday card sent to Molly suggesting he may have learned something from the experience.

"Charlie had a pigeon, a pigeon he had…"

Molly was excited. She was now coming up to the favourite part of the bus journey. The part that could have sparked a totally different emotion following the crash.

"He flew it all morning, he flew it all night…" The whole bus, including Mr Fitzpatrick, sang along.

The bus headed down the hill.

"And when it came home, it was covered in…"

"Daddy!" Molly knocked on the window and waved.

Jack waved back with his left hand, his right brandishing his lollipop stick, and Sunderland's latest Road Crossing Operative couldn't be happier.

**

The End

Acknowledgements

Lisa, Monkman and Bill, your feedback has been invaluable, and your red pens welcome.

Iain and the rest of Holmeside Writers, thanks for all the encouragement and for putting up with me twisting on about editing for two years.

Sunderland Culture have been a massive help, not least with the Creative Development Bursary that helped make Burying Reggie as good as it could be. More important than the financial aspect is the constant positivity, support and encouragement, especially from Laura Brewis and Helen Green. It really is appreciated.

Thanks also to Freya North and Mike Gayle for the feedback, making me think differently about the book and giving me an insight into their world.

To my Twitter and Facebook friends, thanks for sharing, encouraging and keeping me in check whenever I came close to being an online book bore.

Most of all, thanks to my readers, who give me a nudge every now and then to remind me that they enjoy my work and want to see more of it. I hope Burying Reggie meets your expectations.

This novel was supported with funding from Arts Council England and the National Lottery Heritage Fund, through Sunderland Culture's Creative Development Fellowship.

Thank you for reading Burying Reggie. If you enjoyed it, please leave a review, I would really appreciate it.

You may wish to read my other novels.
You can follow my website and blog at www.alan-parkinson.com and follow me on Twitter @Leg_It. https://twitter.com/Leg_It

To stay up to date with all Alan Parkinson news and receive exclusive, free offers, sign up for my email list.
http://eepurl.com/dqk389

Leg It

How long would you wait for revenge?

Fifteen years since Peter Wood left school and disappeared, he returns.
Is he back to make peace or is he back for revenge?

Childhood in the eighties was fun for but nothing lasts forever.
Running away seemed like his only option; as did his return fifteen years later.
Will his old friends forgive him for going?
Will his enemies forgive him for coming back?
Will Pete win back the life he thought he had lost or will he Leg It?
A classic laugh out loud tale of love and friendship, revenge, gangsters and rubber pants.

Alan Parkinson's debut novel Leg It is set in Sunderland and mixes crime and humour in the style of Christopher Brookmyre and Colin Bateman.
Alternating between the lead character's schooldays and the modern day, it gradually reveals his reason for moving away and motivation coming back.
A fast-paced comic thriller that will bring back memories for anybody who went to school in the eighties and will strike a note for anyone who ever wanted to put right what happened in their teenage years.

Available on Kindle, in paperback and hardback.

https://www.amazon.co.uk/Leg-Alan-Parkinson-ebook/dp/B004IE9Z46/

Idle Threats

Liam hates his job working for Phonetix Mobile. Fighting for every second and battling with every customer, he is close to the edge. Bumper's business is going under. His debts are rising, his drinking is getting worse and his wife has had enough. Jodie is unemployed and is desperate for work to give her son the life he deserves. Her mobile phone on the other hand, appears to have no intention of working.

They are all brought together by an armed siege that could change their lives forever.

The long awaited follow up to Leg It, Alan Parkinson's debut novel. Idle Threats, set in Sunderland, is a fast-paced tale of guns, bombs, gangsters and sombreros.

Comic crime fiction in the style of Chris Brookmyre and Colin Bateman, Idle Threats will have you on the edge of your seat.

A must for anyone who has ever suffered either working in a call centre or spent hours on the phone to one.

Would you take it one step further and take a gun into a call centre to settle your grievances?

Available on Kindle, in paperback and hardback.

https://www.amazon.co.uk/Idle-Threats-Alan-Parkinson-ebook/dp/B013P6CCJC/

Life In The Balance

How far would you go to make amends?

Manuel Frost is obsessed with right and wrong. Each day he logs good and bad deeds that he witnesses into a ledger that nobody is allowed to see. Each night, if the books don't balance, he sets out to perform deeds of his own to even them up.
He interferes in events until they inevitably spiral out of control and he has to make the ultimate sacrifice to balance the books.

A comic contemporary novel in which socially awkward Manuel takes his obsession too far, often with hilarious results.
His relationships with his overbearing mother, his boss Chloe and his colleagues often leave him confused. The one thing he has that he can rely upon is his ledger. Except his attempts at keeping the books balanced don't go as planned and he is forced into a series of increasingly ridiculous situations.

Oliver and Tony are hapless ex-cellmates who barely tolerate each other. In debt to the local gangster they need a plan to escape the life they have created for themselves and try and repair the damage with their families.
But they hadn't factored Manuel into their plan.

Will Manuel listen to his mother or follow Chloe's advice? Or will the cat be the one to save him?

Offset all the misery in your life and read Life In The Balance.

Available on Kindle, in paperback and hardback.

https://www.amazon.co.uk/dp/B072N164LY/

Troll Life

Could you change the habits of a lifetime when everything you have ever known is at risk?

When an internet troll is exposed, he is forced to come off benefits and seek employment in a call centre he has been trolling.
Turning his life around is not easy, especially when his past begins to catch up with him and he has to confront the one person he fears most.
Himself.

Troll Life is a comic tale of hopes and fears, revenge and redemption.

With the humorous style of Christopher Brookmyre and Carl Hiaasen, Alan Parkinson's fourth novel explores the world of online trolling and the many frustrations of working in a call centre.
Office politics clash with one man's struggle to leave his past behind and become a productive member of society.

Available on Kindle, in paperback and hardback.

https://www.amazon.co.uk/gp/product/B07J55GM6F/

* * *

Printed in Great Britain
by Amazon